Wars & Wings

Enlighten Series, Book Three

||||||| || |||||||| |||||| || ||| |||
I0679793

USA Today Bestselling Author
Kristin D. Van Risseghem

Kasian Publishing
11923 NE Sumner St, STE 759356
Portland, OR 97220
www.KristinVanRisseghem.com

Cover design by Angela Fristoe, Covered Creatively
www.CoveredCreatively.com

Author photograph by Jessica Krueger Photography,
www.JessicaKruegerPhotography.com

Formatting by Jaye Cox
Formatting the Affordable Way

Edited by Rebecca Jaycox

Other works by
Kristin D. Van Risseghem:

Enlighten Series:

Swords & Stilettos, Book One
Daggers & Dresses, Book Two
Wars & Wings, Book Three

Novellas:

Fires & Fairies, Sidelle's Story
Arrows & Angels, Kieran's Story

Short Stories:

Poisons & Princes, Finn's Story
Ninjas & Nephilims, Shay's Story

Slayers & Protectors Series:

Dragon Magic, Prequel
Dragon Slayers, Book One
Dragon Wars, Book Two
Dragon Protectors, Book Three

Sign up to the Six Queens's Roundtable Newsletter
and get a FREE eBook.

Go to: www.KristinVanRisseghem.com

This final book of Zoe's adventure is dedicated to all my fans out there, who have supported me in my story telling. Thank you!!

1

Zoe

My head throbs in time with my beating heart. At least there's that bonus; I still have a heartbeat.

I must be alive if I can feel my body, or maybe this is what death is like.

Under my palms is a cottony material. I run hands along it, trying to find the outer the edge. My back is pressed on top of something soft. A bed? I scrunch my eyes tight, refusing to open them yet.

There is no sound. No furnace humming. No birds chirping. Only the thump, thump of my heart.

This must be heaven.

My thoughts carry me back to the last night I can remember.

Prom.

A white dress. Driving to the Mall of America. Dinner. Dancing in the arms of Shay, my boyfriend. Twirling across the gym floor with my best friend, Kieran. Someone cutting in.

Blackness enveloped me.

But not before I heard someone whispering in my ear, "Finally. You're mine."

Who was holding me?

Aiden.

I bolt straight up, and my eyes fly open.

I'm in a room without windows or doors. How is that possible? I stare down. I sit on a king sized bed. To my right is a small love seat and table. To my left is a toilet, sink, and a folded privacy screen. The walls are white, reminiscent of a hospital room. The flooring is gray cement. I deduce that this could be a basement. But where?

How did Aiden bring me to this room? I have no idea how long I've been out. Without the sun or moon to let me know the time of day, my only guess is that it's Sunday.

My cellphone!

I pat the sides of my hips and feel the smooth chiffon. Nothing. Remembering that my dress doesn't have pockets, I had to use the strap of my bra. Tacky, but it's a good thing I did. My fingers brush against the slim, metal devise. I clutch my phone and stare at the screen. It's

2

missing the date, but the time is flashing: 10:34 A.M. That's not possible.

I check the battery life, and it's holding at sixty percent. At least something is going my way.

I gaze at the bars of service. Nothing. This is bad.

I dial Shay's number. The call doesn't go through. I quickly write a text. The stupid phone says it can't be delivered. I must not be on Earth. Did my kidnapper take me to Hell? Or to an alternate dimension?

I am going to kill my neighbor as soon as I see the whites of his eyes. Or, I should say the black of his wings. My fingers curl into tight balls as more memories come crashing in.

The live band was ending the song *Ever the Same* by Rob Thomas. I was on the dance floor with Aiden but looking at Shay and Kieran, who were standing off to the side. I twirled in Aiden's arms as he dipped me low to the floor. My head tilted back, and I watched upside down as Shay leaned into Kieran and said something. Gold Light blasted from Kieran's angelic body. Shay moved with lightning speed but didn't reach me in time.

Black wings wrapped around me.

The guttural cry of Shay screaming *"NO!"* still rings in my ears.

I realize without a doubt that this is Aiden's doing. Stupid of me for trusting him. That lying, back-stabbing no good being with wings. He's no angel, that's for sure, with everything he's done: friending me, taking my nemesis to prom, and now adding kidnapping to his rap sheet. Oh, no. He's no angel at all. I can't bring myself to think of him as anything worse than that. He's not a Demon Knight or a Marquises Demon. I'd know if he were. Wouldn't I? He's in a category all by himself.

Yes, I would. My demon radar would have gone off at some point. I've spent time alone with him on many occasions, and nothing about him seemed out of place. He screams bad-boy and loner but demon? Kieran would have known if Aiden was an angel, though. And Sidelle would've known if he was a fairy. I guess I never bothered to ask either one of them, but they didn't let me know either.

Although, he could be a Nephilim; he does have wings, black ones to match his heart, if he even has one. I slam my fists against the bed.

Thankfully, I'm still in my prom dress, so at least Aiden hadn't undressed me when he locked me into this prison. I wiggle my toes, and my stiletto shoes are not strapped to me feet. A quick scan of the small room informs me that they are not with me. Drats. Remembering I left them in the gym, I recall that during the night I flung them off into the corner. Now, how am I going to make my great escape in bare feet?

First, I need to figure out where am I and then how to get out of this place that has no doors or windows. Sliding off the side of the bed, I stroll to the couch, but I stop right before I reach it. Like an invisible wall, I can't penetrate it to sit down. My hands run up and down trying to discover a weakness in the force, but none can be found. Why put furniture there if I can't use it?

I pad across the foot of the bed toward the make shift bathroom. My fingers reach out to grab the edge of the screen and wrap around it. I drag it a couple of inches to make sure it moves. Turning toward the sink, I flip the faucet to the hot position, and immediately warm water flows onto my hand and down the drain. But what I find most interesting is that there isn't any piping running into the floor. It's as if the liquid empties into nothing. But at least I have running water. Now to check the toilet. While it seems new, I don't dare want to get sick from unsanitary conditions or anything. I roll out a panel of toilet paper and press the flushing handle. All looks to be in working order, and again, there are no plumbing pipes.

I edge around the toilet to examine how far the space is around the area and it's not much. Another invisible wall meets my hand about a foot farther back.

Returning to the bed, I hop onto the mattress and jump up toward the ceiling. I can't reach it, so I plop back down and wait.

Wait for my friends to rescue me.

Wait for Aiden to come back to answer a few of my questions.

Wait for me to come up with a plan.

Wait.

My tummy growls. Great. There is no sense of having a bathroom if I don't eat or drink anything. I don't have my clutch either, because why would I if I'm dancing? Usually, I keep an energy bar or some other snack food in my purse everywhere I go.

I sigh.

There is nothing to occupy my mind with. I can't count ceiling tiles because there aren't any. I can't count wall cracks because they are smooth. I can't count patches on the lavender bed quilt because it's one large piece of material. The only items worth counting are the two-inch purple yarn ties holding the top and the bottom together; there are 120 of them.

I worry about how long I'll be kept here. I wonder if my friends are already out looking for me. I have a gut feeling I'll be here a long time.

It's hours later, and I'm bored out of my mind. This must be the worst way to die. I dismiss that thought because I refuse to acknowledge that this is my end. It's not. It can't be.

It has been prophesized that I save the world by uniting the Orders together to battle against evil. And Aiden, I have decided, is definitely evil. The next time I lay eyes on him, he's going to wish he were never born. Figure of speech since Nephilims are the only Enlightens who are born. I have yet to determine how I'm going to make him suffer if I'm in here, and he's out there doing who knows what.

But still.

I check my phone for the millionth time again; it's a little after six. I've been captive for maybe less than twenty-four hours. I must have dozed at some point because now I'm beyond famished. It's still too bright in the room, which reminds me that I never recalled seeing any lights or switches. I crawl off the bed and walk to the sink. Using my hand, I cup water into my mouth. At least I won't be dehydrated. I'll need all the strength I can muster if I'm going to kick Aiden's ass when he steps through the proverbial door.

I scream from everything that's been building up in my mind: frustration that I trusted him; anger for getting myself kidnapped by him; depression that I won't get out of here alive; worry that the world will no longer exist because I have failed in my mission, and Sammael escapes from his prison.

The non-lights dim, and a silver serving tray bearing an unwrapped turkey sandwich, a bag of FunOnions, a napkin, and a diet strawberry soda can appear on the bed. I note that no utensils are on the tray. At least he's being cautious and rightfully so. I'd use the spoon to stab him in his scrawny neck.

Leary to eat anything not commercially wrapped, afraid that Aiden might have tampered with it, I rip open the bag of chips. I inhale and savor the onion fragrance, forcing myself to eat slowly, chewing everything carefully and fully, not knowing when my next meal will be. Plus, now I have something to do.

Powering down my phone to conserve the battery, my thoughts return to Shay. I know he's going ballistic searching for me. He'll leave no stone unturned. He won't stop looking for me. I bet he'd travel into the depths of Hell for me. Oh wait, he was already there when the demons kidnapped him and tortured him for information about me.

Since Shay and I are soul mates, could he feel my discomfort? I couldn't detect him, but over the last few months, we've been through a lot and we've grown. Maybe a plan is forming. I'll have to think more on that.

I toss the empty bag of chips on the floor, and pick up half of the sandwich, wishing for plastic wrap so I could save part of it for later. Carefully lifting the top piece of bread, I smell for anything weird. Nothing. I set it back onto the tray.

My BFF, Kieran, also will move the heavens to find me. He waited centuries to discover the girl who would save the world. It's not in his character to stop.

And Sidelle went into her nemesis's territory to help me get back home. I know she'll, too, look into every alternate world known to her to rescue me from Aiden's clutches.

A smile stretches across my face, thinking of Sidelle and wondering what she would do in my place. She'd say some snarky comment about not letting this situation dampen any of my training. Of course, she'd probably use her glamour to get her out, and I don't have that option. Or do I?

Carefully reaching for the can of pop, I crack the top open and savor my first sip. Just because my sparring partner Cali isn't here with me, doesn't mean that I should stop conditioning myself. It will take my mind of my confinement. I move the tray off to the side of the bed.

I wish I had shoes and a change of clothes, but I make do. Raising my leg onto the bed, I stretch my calf muscles, hold it there for ten seconds and release. Switching legs, I repeat. I reach one arm into the air and grab the elbow with my other hand, letting the free arm dangle down my back. Rotating my head from ear to ear, until I hear a much-needed pop, then stand in front of the bed, making circle motions with my arms and my legs. After a few lunges I'm ready. In prayer position, I clear my mind and start the fighting dance. With graceful movements that flow like water, my arms and legs lengthen, stretch, and retract. The motions become a cross between yoga, ballet, and karate.

I'm not sure how long my routine lasts because I won't make myself turn on my phone to check the time. Sweat beads along my forehead, and the hindrance of my long skirt limits my movements, but I can't get myself to rip the bottom off. It is my prom dress, after all.

To cool down, I splash water on my face, and I wish I had a bar of soap to scrub my face clean of makeup. Grabbing one of the pillows, I tug off the cover and use it as a washcloth. Much better. I almost feel like a new girl. Almost.

I head back to bed and eat the sandwich and finish the can of pop. If Aiden wanted to kill me, I don't think he'd do it with poison. That's not his style. With nothing else to do, I lie across the bed, telling myself that every day, no matter what, I will do at least thirty minutes of exercise.

Eventually, my eyes close, and I dream of an aqua pair staring back.

2

Aiden

Saturday night, prom.

I couldn't have pulled it off without help from an inside source. During my recon and sorting through the wealth of information on whom would become my neighbor, I uncovered a hidden gem about one of Zoe's friends.

Quinn is your typical high school girl. She dates the star basketball player, does extremely well as one of the cheerleading captains, and is a Nephilim. Or at least she will become one. I could smell her mixed blood as soon as I drove onto the school grounds.

That first encounter with so many students milling about the parking lot, I couldn't pinpoint who it was. My only thought is that someone is undergoing the change.

And this is the main reason I enrolled into school.

I recall everything that I had to endure to bring me to this night. Prom night.

After many months of careful planning, meticulously going over every detail, timeline, and note taking of Zoe's daily whereabouts, I finally learned something interesting about her.

Why would an angel, a fairy, and a Nephilim guard her night and day?

It was easy to identify the angel, especially a good-hearted one like that golden guardian, Kieran.

Gag.

It took me a bit longer to figure out what exactly her friend, Sidelle, was. I never got close enough to her to smell frost or rain, telltale signs of being a fairy.

Puke.

But the clincher was targeting that no-goodie Nephilim who reeked of both angel and demon power. I know the smell of demons. Intimately.

The start of a plan took hold in my mind.

How could I get her alone to confirm my suspicions?

First, I had to devise the perfect ruse.

Maybe it was a blessing in disguise that my father told me to come to Minnesota. Because right now, I am living next door to the one I'd been searching for. All I had to do is gain her trust.

That being said, it was a bit more difficult than I thought

it would be. I had heard of the Minnesota Nice, and yes, Zoe was nice to me when we first met. Her mom had brought brownies with a dish of hospitality on the side.

My sister forced me to attend high school.

Barf.

But that allowed me to spend more time with her, so I guess in retrospect, it was a good idea. Not that I'll ever thank my sister.

I had dropped into Zoe's life at the perfect time. Prom season. I'd known from watching other Ordinaries that springtime was a rite of passage for most teenagers.

And of course, Zoe was no exception. She planned to attend the dance with that Nephilim boyfriend of hers. I had heard rumors of her going with other friends she hung around, which had prompted me to ask my arm candy, Morgan, to go. There was a deep hatred seated in her soul for Zoe, and a darkness that surrounded her spirit.

It wasn't hard to convince Morgan to go to the same restaurant as Zoe's friends. I only had to do a bit of digging to know where that would be, all the tiny details to throw her and her companions off my trail before I'd take her to my prison.

Morgan droned on and on about nothing. I ignored her throughout the entire dinner, going over the plan again. By the time we drove back to the school, I could say that I was almost giddy with excitement. And these days, it took a lot

13

to get me happy.

Of course, Morgan and I were late getting to the gym. She had other plans for me, and why not? It gave me time to delve into her soul and understand her. We both had needs. Hers happened to be more physical than mine. We could use each other for the time being. She had found an unlocked classroom and shoved me through.

I hadn't been with an Ordinary for many years. I knew how to play my part to get what I wanted. While Morgan kissed my neck with sloppy technique, I buried my hands into her long, black hair. Lifting her up to sit on a desk, I brushed my lips against hers. She welcomed me by parting her mouth. My body pressed up against hers while Morgan's hands roamed down my back. Moans escaped from her.

Focusing on my powers, I drove them into Morgan's mind to get a clear picture of her hatred for Zoe. I wanted to know the reason she was her sworn enemy, as she had told me once.

And there it was.

A long time ago, they were friends. Morgan was a shy newcomer to school. They looked to be around five or six years old. A blond boy, I knew to be Kieran by his unmistakable blue eyes, stood next to Zoe as he protected her from Morgan taking her lunchbox.

She still befriended Morgan by inviting her to birthday

parties, sleepovers, and sitting with her at the lunch table. Everywhere she went, Morgan followed. A couple of years passed, and the two became inseparable. Morgan loved the attention, being in the spotlight as Zoe's best friend. There was a power struggle between her and Kieran, both vying for her BFF title. Ultimately, Zoe chose him.

Hurt and betrayal flooded Morgan's childish mind. Zoe had never reciprocated Morgan's deeper friendship.

On their last recess when the girls had played together, something happened. A small bird flew directly into a window, stunning it. She, Morgan, and Cali surrounded the animal. Morgan poked it with a stick to see if it was still alive. It didn't move.

Cali started crying, but Zoe said, "No, it's not dead. It's playing with us." She looked around and told the girls to not say anything; she had special powers and watch what should could do.

She picked up the bird in her small hands. Light surrounded the wings with a faint purple glow. Suddenly, the bird's head twitched, and it came alive. It flew away as the girls gasped.

Morgan couldn't believe her eyes. Zoe had brought that bird to life with magic. She hadn't trusted her from then on. Morgan's mother had told her stories of people being able to do things that were not normal. She said those people were witches and were evil. They were abominations to the world.

"Freak!" Morgan screamed at her. "You're not natural. You shouldn't be able to do that."

"I'm not a freak," Zoe said. "I—

"You're a monster."

"No, I'm not. And you owe me an apology for calling me names. We're friends, and friends aren't mean to each other."

"I will not say I'm sorry when I don't mean it."

Morgan had turned her back on her former schoolmate. She would not apologize for voicing her opinion. That, coupled with the devastation that Zoe had picked Kieran over her, Morgan chose to break their friendship. A deep hatred swelled in the girl's heart, and ever since Zoe had been horrible to her.

Those scenes played out in a matter of seconds in my mind. Now, twelve years later, Morgan still expected an apology for treating her like a crap friend, but Zoe didn't understand why Morgan walked away. That's what had hurt Morgan the most.

"Hey, where are you?" Morgan's sing-songy voice asked. That pulled me out of her mind.

"No place, I'm here with you."

"Are you sure? Because you're half naked, and yet I'm standing here with all my clothes on." She waved a hand down her body.

"And you will stay that way." I re-buttoned my black shirt and adjusted the tie. "We have to go."

"What? Why?" Morgan started slipping her dress strap down her shoulder.

"Because I said so. Now come on. We need to get to the dance." Turning away from her, I marched toward the door. "Are you coming? Or am I going in there alone?"

"Fine, give me a sec." She took out a mirror, straightened her red flowing gown and hair, and slinked passed me. "Let's go."

We are now one of the last couples to enter the gymnasium since it's been an hour since the dance started. With a gust of wind, I blow open the doors. Everyone stops and stares as we saunter into the room, hand in hand. Morgan sashays across the room like she owns the place. Her two bookends, Ashel and Abby, flank us with their dates.

"What are you all staring at?" she yells. "I'm fashionably late. The party can start now."

I spot my victim and stroll to her side to ask if she will save a dance for me. Oh yes, I play my part well. She hesitates, confusion in her eyes when she looks at me and then Morgan.

"I can't believe you took Morgan to prom. Doesn't our friendship mean anything to you?"

I hold up one hand. "Whoa, hold on. I came to this

17

school late in the year and didn't have anyone to bring. She was available, so I asked her. I know you two don't get along, but—"

And now I know the real reason.

But she relents and will save a dance.

I see my chance. Kieran is dancing with his best friend, and I am able to cut in. We spin and weave around the dance floor. I dip Zoe low and her head tilts back. She can see her friends standing against the wall.

I lean into her ear and whisper, "Finally, you're mine."

The Nephilim launches himself off the wall when I glare at him.

Light fills the gym by the angel.

But both are too late in coming to Zoe's rescue.

3

Zoe

Sometime during my slumber, the non-lights turned off, blanketing me in total darkness. It's a good thing I'm not scared of the dark. Well, okay, maybe I am a wee bit, but who could blame me? I'm being held captive in a white-walled prison for who knows how long and where. I have no clue what Aiden wants from me, and most importantly, I don't know how things appear and disappear from the room.

I had left the serving tray on the foot of the bed and now when I stretch out my leg, I feel nothing. The tray is gone.

Being surrounded by darkness is one thing, but having the room devoid of sound does something to me. I wake in a panic, my legs tangled in my dress. Feeling like I'm being watched, I sit up, but of course I can't glimpse my hand in front of my eyes.

"Who's there?" I ask. It's the first time I have spoken out loud since Aiden took me.

There's no response, and I no longer feel eyes on me.

I lie back down, but sleep does not come.

Instead, Shay's warm hand caresses mine and comforts me. Even though it really is my own hand, I imagine it belongs to him. I clear my mind, thinking only of my boyfriend. His aqua eyes. The way his body molds and fits exactly next to mine. The way he always says his name, "Name's Shay." His musky lavender scent, with a hint of something sweet like a strawberry, envelops my senses.

My mind runs through every conversation we had. The first time I laid eyes on him in the warehouse. Our first date at Cali's house. Our real first date when he took me flying. My protection detail nights with him snuggled against me. The night we found out what the tingling meant when we touch—it means we're soul mates.

Shay is my world. I thought I'd lost him, but we found our way back to each other. It was me who pulled him from his coma-like state when we finally rescued him from his demon captors. I had accidently walked into his dreams. We both stood there as if it was real, but I knew deep down it wasn't. He, of course, thought he was dead and was seeing me in Heaven.

I hope that he's exhausted enough to be asleep, so we

can connect in our dreams again. Hope sparks in my chest, but doubt creeps into my mind. This is only the second time I've tried Dream Walking. Plus, the first time, I was physically touching Shay's chest.

My body relaxes, and my mind's about there when a cold shimmer caresses my body. I smile at myself. I did it. I'm tossed onto a beach, our beach, and sit and stare at the ocean. I wait, but Shay must not be sleeping; he never shows.

Pulling my thoughts back to the white room, the landscape dissolves.

I pat my stomach, feeling content as normal dreams take me away.

Sometime later, that tingling feeling runs through my body again. The non-lights turn on, and my foot touches something. My eyes fly open, and there sits the serving tray with a bagel and cream cheese and an extra-large chai tea latte.

Disappointment floods me. Drats. I thought I had made a breakthrough, and this could be my way out. Instead, it means that I can feel the magic or whatever causes the tray to appear and disappear. During my time of zen, was I one with the room? I'd have to conduct some experiments on that concept.

Pealing back the foil top, I use the bagel and dig into the cream cheese. No utensils again. But there is a white washcloth and hand towel draped along the handle of the tray. I look toward the sink, and the pillowcase I used to remove my makeup is gone.

I reach for the steaming cup of chai and take a deep breath of the spicy cinnamon flavor, hoping that this will be as good as the one I usually get from the local shop, Coffee Grind. It's not.

After the light breakfast, I force myself to do my workout, and then I will treat myself with the meditation exercise.

Again, I relax my body and mind and think only of Shay. The way he smiles. His blond hair. The impressive six-pack he tries to hide under T-shirts. The black attire he always wears. His 1957 Lincoln convertible, Angel. I know it must be close to noon or sometime in the afternoon on Monday. It's been two days since I've vanished. There is a slight pull from the center of my body. I can feel my angel Light scanning, searching for him. My mind's eye and Light sync together, and bam.

I'm thrust into a dream-like state. Shay stands on a shoreline, looking out across the horizon. He doesn't see me. He must not feel me either since he doesn't turn around.

I call out to him. "Shay?" Tears stream down my face upon seeing him.

He spins when he spots me. His face is ashen. The bright

aqua eyes I know are dull and lifeless. His shoulders slump, probably from exhaustion. "Zoe?" he asks. "Is that really you?"

I sprint across the sand, and we collide as he embraces me. He pats my body down as if to make sure it's me and not his imagination, even though it is. I'm still wearing my white prom dress, and he's in fresh black fatigues.

"We've been looking for you everywhere," Shay says. "Where are you being held?"

"I don't know where I am," I say. "I don't even know if Aiden really has taken me because no one has come in or out. I'm locked in some sort of magic room."

"What do you mean by magic room?"

"I can feel when something is going to happen to the room." I watch his face blanch. "No, it's nothing bad. So far it's been a serving tray that comes and goes with food on it."

"So, he's at least feeding you?"

"Yes."

"Oh, God, Zoe. If I could take your place, I would. You know that, right?"

"Yes, I know Shay, but I wouldn't want you to. You've been keeping me company until you can figure out a way to rescue me. I hoped that Dream Walking would work, and we could use it to communicate with each other."

"Smart thinking. That's my girl." He runs a finger across

my cheek. "Don't cry. We'll find you."

"I don't know what he wants with me. I know he's there; he won't say anything."

"Now that I know you're at least not physically hurt, we'll look into all the reference books about magic rooms. I might have to ask my dad or the Council if we don't find anything in the tomes. Hang in there, and don't give up."

"I won't. It's only been a couple of days. I can wait a few more."

"Actually, Zoe, it's been ten."

"Ten what? Days?" I'm shocked.

He nods.

"How is that even possible?" I ask. "I've had two meals in that room."

"I don't know, but time must move differently there. It may mean that you're in the Void or Fairyland." Shay tugs me forward and kisses my forehead. "That narrows it down. I'll let Sidelle know, and Kieran and I will read through the scrolls about the Void, who can create them, and where."

"Okay." I wrap my arms around his waist and hang on for dear life. A tug starts in the center of my body that I take as a sign that my time with Shay is about to end. Quickly, I stand on my tiptoes and find his mouth. I give him a searing kiss, one that hopefully says everything I need to tell him and that he understands. "I love you, Shay."

"I know, Zoe, I love you, too." He kisses me again. "I'll never stop looking for you. I promise. Be strong."

"I don't want to leave, but I think I have to. I'll try to do this again, but since I won't know how much time passes, I'll give it another shot in what I think is tomorrow night."

Our mouths meet for one last kiss, and my body fades from the beach.

4

Shay

Saturday, prom night; two hours after Zoe's disappearance.

All I remember is yelling "No!" toward my girlfriend and her dancing partner.

My body moved on autopilot until Kieran could get me to his house and regroup.

Now, I sit on the couch next to Sidelle as Kieran proceeds to recap the evening for us, as he knows it.

"Let me tell you what happened as I saw it," Kieran says. "So Sidelle and Vash understand. Zoe and I were dancing. Aiden came up to us and cut in. I relented and stood by Shay to watch. Shay told me that he thought the person Zoe was dancing with, was the same who kidnapped him. His outer appearance changed, but the eyes remained the same. The same color as his own. I was baffled by that because we've all known Aiden for a couple of weeks. He moved in with his sister and they bought the house next door to the Jabrils."

Neighbor?

That threw me to see red. My wings appeared at the dance, scaring attendees and teachers. I remembered seeing a bright flash of golden rays, and assumed that Kieran also couldn't hold in his anger. He released his angel Light.

I reign in my anger from those thoughts and tell everyone in the room that Aiden had stood taller, had broader shoulders, but I never saw his full face. Only the eyes. Now reflecting on that, I think it was on purpose that Aiden only let me see some of his features.

I remember we dashed toward the couple, trying to snatch Zoe away from Aiden. But we were too late. Partners who had been dancing in the area stopped and screamed upon seeing Aiden's black wings and witnessing two people disappear from the gym.

The room turned chaotic in a matter of seconds. Kieran had a better grip on his Light than me. I had let my silver Light escape, which projected around the center of the room, like a disco ball.

Vash and Sidelle sprinted to my side, trying to calm me and understand the situation. Kieran, of course, took charge and Mind Wiped everyone and directed Sidelle to take me back to Kieran's house.

I barely listen to Kieran's recap as all I want to do is go search for Zoe. My hands fist on my lap as flashes of Aiden's cruelty enter my mind.

He had chained me to the wall and had kept me prisoner. Aiden knew exactly what I was and used enhanced metal that was dipped in the River Stixx. He tortured me for information I didn't know at the time, nor did I want to confirm anything he asked. Aiden used a black sword. The sheath was made of obsidian from the deepest places of Hell, and it carried a reddish hue. Using the blade, he had branded me with an X across my chest as his parting gift. I had only seen his eyes as he disappeared. But I knew them, as they were the same color as my own. And in all my years, never once had I run into another being with aqua irises.

"I asked you, Shay, if who chained you wherever you were being held was Aiden?" Kieran asks, and it occurs to me he must've been speaking to me for a while. "Are you sure it's the same person?"

I'm too numb to say anything. It's not until Sidelle taps me in the shoulder that I come out of my daze.

"What?" I shout.

"Is it Aiden or not?" Sidelle asks. "We'll find her, Shay. She's strong, and we need you to keep your head if we're going to rescue her."

I nod and inhale. "I'm pretty sure it's the same guy. He never showed me his face when I was in Hell, but no one else in the world has aqua eyes like mine. At least that I know of. It has to be him."

"That changes things a bit, doesn't it, Kieran?" Sidelle asks.

"Why should it?" I ask.

"He's Zoe's neighbor, he attends school with us, and they have hung out together," Kieran says.

"It doesn't matter if he's been friendly to her." I stand, and my wings appear. "He's an evil S.O.B. and if he's kidnapped her, I'll kill him." My legs carry me to the window. Calming breaths take my anger down just a notch.

"Shay, take it easy. We all want her back. What do you think he is?"

"He's not a Nephilim, that I know," Kieran says.

As soon as Kieran's voice rings out, my rage builds again. If I don't get out of here soon, something is going to break. I find myself leaning against the mantle. The wood shatters.

"Well, he's definitely not a tree, Shay," Sidelle chimes in. "And I don't think he's a fairy, either, but I'll ask Finn, too."

I toss the wood fragments on the floor and shrug an apology to Kieran. Sidelle waives her hand as green glamour shoots from her palm and fixes the fireplace.

"He didn't feel like he has any Light, but he could mask it if he's an Archangel," Kieran says. "I'll confer with Michael. I guess the first thing we need to figure out is who Aiden is, and why he took her."

The room is heavy with silence, each of us deep in our thoughts and prayers. I know they are trying to help me, but I feel like I've failed her. I swore to protect her. We all did. Zoe's my responsibility. She's my girlfriend, for crying out loud. If her boyfriend can't protect her, who can?

"Vash, you've been quiet," Kieran says. "What do you think?"

"Let me get this right. The person, or being—and I say that because we don't know what Aiden is—has been impersonating a human and lives next door to Zoe. He appears, normal. Doesn't he live with his sister?"

"That's what he says, but let's find out about the woman, too," Kieran suggests.

"He enrolled into school, but I haven't had a chance to chat with him," Vash continues. "Shay, you say he has similar physical features as the same being who held you prisoner, and only based on the color of his eyes. I do agree that you have a very unique color, but we need to know who can hide abilities. It doesn't add up." He shakes his head. "Kieran, you've seen him the most between the rest of us. What does he look like to you?"

"Physically?"

"Yes. Shay said that he's taller and has a different body structure. Something is off about all of this."

"If I recall, he's shorter than me ... so a bit under six feet. I never studied his eye color, but they could be greenish-blue. And his hair is brown, almost like Zoe's and —"

"No, that's not right, Kieran," Sidelle interrupts. "He has black hair like mine and dark green eyes that sparkle in the light—"

"See?" Vash says. "Even our descriptions of him have inconsistencies. We must know if angels can mask what they are. I know he's not a wolf, otherwise I would have smelled him as soon as I entered the gym."

"Zoe kept telling us that she thought Aiden looked a lot like Shay. That they could be brothers. But I never listened. It didn't dawn on me that he could change his appearance or at least to what we each see about him. Now I just feel dumb that I didn't believe her or had her explain it better."

"All right, let's talk with our Orders and see what we can find about Aiden and his sister and everything there is about masking." Kieran stands. "I've never heard of any angel able to do anything like that. Does that sound okay, Shay?"

I don't say anything, so Kieran pivots in my direction. His eyes portray all the sorrow an angel can muster. I know he's as devastated as I feel. He and Zoe have grown up together, they live a couple houses from each other, and he's her best friend. I've known her all her life, too, but we're soul mates. We have a special connection.

Sidelle and Vash stand to leave.

Crap. How could I have forgotten?

"I have one more thing to add to the list of tasks. Last night, Zoe Mind Walked into my dream. I thought maybe she could, but she's only ever done that once before when I was in the coma. She said that she didn't know where she was being held. The room has no windows or doors and it's magical. Only non-weapons can be conjured, and he's feeding her meals. She also said that Aiden hadn't appeared to her yet, so she can't confirm if it's him or not. She's physically fine and has been doing daily exercises to keep her mind off where she is. Now, we need to know everything about magical rooms, who can create them, if they leave a signature or anything, and where they can be created."

"All right, everyone add that in your discussions with your supervisors," Kieran agrees. "And pack members for you, Vash. Let's try to get together in a couple of days. I don't want to go too many nights without any new information. We're all anxious for Zoe's return, and I know it's going to be difficult to stay calm without an actual plan in place. I'll also let the Reperio Team know of this, so they can create a plan."

We agree to meet later in the week, unless someone

finds a lead. Sidelle and Vash leave to start their inquiries. Kieran vanishes from the den, and I shuffle to my bedroom. I know I won't be able to sit here and do nothing.

After I open the door to my room, I dig around for a duffle bag and toss in a couple changes of clothes, all the knives and daggers I can find, and head to the kitchen for energy bars. My last stop is to the weapons room.

I press my palm to the reader. It *beeps* and the door slides open. I throw the bag onto a table and flip the hidden shelves. I grab a couple of .45's and several magazines and toss them in. Daggers in various lengths are fitted into my boots, my inner jacket and pants pockets, and into special armbands. Deciding to take more throwing knives, I clear off the shelf, and everything goes into the bag.

After one last glance around the room and at myself, I realize I'm well stocked. Zipping the duffle closed, I stalk out of the room and start my mission to find Zoe.

5

Zoe

Tuesday, ten days after prom.

It was glorious to see Shay again, even if it was only in our dreams. I knew he would be out looking for me, and at least we have some clues as to where I'm being held. Mind you, it isn't much, but I'll take it. For now. I let the memories of Shay seep into my soul and relax me enough to sleep.

In the morning, I'm calm enough to hold onto a few positive vibes, but how can I continue if I don't have a plan to get myself out of here? Aiden hasn't even come visit me, so I can't really confirm it's him who took me prisoner or if it's someone else. And if it's someone else, why? The room feels like it's closing in, and I'm about to die of boredom. I fear that soon I won't be sane anymore. And the not knowing what my friends and family are planning is driving me crazy. They have got to be worried sick about my disappearance.

Oh, God. My parents. They must be frantic. I wonder if Kieran told them what happened and who took me. They shouldn't have to go through anything like a child being kidnapped. What does my little sister think? Someone needs to be there for her.

The purple quilt wrinkles as I clench my hands.

I will be strong and not give into the madness. It's time for my daily exercise routine anyway. Stretching becomes my only escape from the mind numbing activity of doing nothing. I've taken to adding to my regiment by jumping on the bed, recalling my mom always yelled at me not to do that. I chuckle. Stripping the bed of the quilt, I lean the mattress against the invisible wall and use the box spring as a step. My legs rotate the up and down, and soon my calf muscles are sore. Tomorrow, I know they'll be hurting, but my body pushes on.

Ninety-eight ... ninety-nine ... 100.

And done. So now what?

To make more space in what I guess is about a twenty by twenty room, I lean the box spring against the mattress. I decide it needs to be on the opposite wall, so I know where the room ends. Taking two of the pillows, I lean those up against the walls without the bed.

The space is big enough to run in a large circle. I sprint laps until I'm so exhausted that bile rises into my mouth. Barely shuffling to the sink where a fresh, white towel hangs, I grab it to wipe my sweaty face and neck. Cupping my hand, I drink the cool water from the faucet.

I turn my head back to my makeshift exercise zone and then get a brilliant idea. Another workout will be added to my day. And now I have something to interchange the schedule with.

The two pillows leaning against the walls call to me.

Lumbering to the mattress, I hang the cases between the bed and box spring. I pound my fists into the pillow, testing its buoyancy. It's soft enough I won't injure myself. I kick the mattress with my left foot. So far, so good. The skirt of my dress hinders some of my ability, but I make due.

I still cannot bear to rip it off. Maybe someday in the future I will but not today. It is getting a bit frayed on the seams since I've been wearing it non-stop. There is no privacy in the room, say for the screen around the toilet, but since I have nothing to change into, I've been sleeping in it, too. I've been feeling eyes on me more and more, and if Aiden is spying on me, he will not see me naked. Ever.

Focusing my mind back to the task at hand, I knee the mattress. Punch. Jab. Kick. I repeat, faster and faster until I'm breathless.

Tomorrow, I decide I'll take it easy and meditate and possibly do some yoga poses. Not everything about fighting is physical. My mental health is just as important.

A few minutes after I slow my breathing, my stomach rumbles. A cold pressure wraps around my skin. The silver tray appears, balancing on the sink. I have no idea how much time has passed since the morning food, but if I were holding someone prisoner, I would have the tray appear in unequal intervals.

God, now I'm thinking like a criminal.

I toss the mattress back onto the floor and flop down and eat. Remembering about my cell phone and what Shay said about it being ten days later, I push the button to turn it on. The lights power up and flash 6:33 P.M., but the date is still blank.

Of course, I believe Shay. Eleven days have now passed. No wonder my dress is fraying. Almost two weeks and not a word from Aiden.

Glancing back at the screen, I check the battery. It's red.

I need a charger. I need to get out of here. I need to see those black wings.

My fingers run over the smooth, silken fabric, recalling Shay's warm arms wrapped around me in a protective shield. Seeing all my school friends' faces of delight as they sing, dance, and laugh together. At least I'll have some good memories of that night.

I sigh and with both hands, I reach to rip the material of the skirt. Hesitation causes me to stop. I can't do it. It's not my wedding dress, but it is special to me. The smelly dress reminds me that I do need to change my clothes or at least try to get rid of the stench.

A cool breeze floats across my face. My body shivers. I turn my head and find a new purple tank top, black yoga pants, and undergarments. This can't be possible. I swear I was thinking of this top I saw at Target the other day. Week? And here it is, laying beneath my palm.

I try thinking of something else to see if it appears. Focusing my mind and relaxing my body, I imagine a cell phone charger. I picture the black one at home, plugged into the wall near my white desk. The plastic case surrounded by metal prongs. The slim wires wrapped around more metal ends. But nothing appears.

Still in meditation mode, I picture my Kindle. At least maybe I could read to pass the time away. The tablet doesn't appear.

Okay. New strategy.

I blow my hair out of my face and focus on my angel Light. It's inside of me somewhere. Normally, I've only called for it when I was scared. Why hadn't I tried this earlier? Well, it's not every day someone finds out that they are an angel. It's not the first thing that crosses my mind. I'm still a newbie and haven't quite gotten used to having powers, let alone, mastering the ones I have.

Searching deep in my mind's eye, I look for that purple spark. Last time I needed my powers, I found it near my heart. It's not there. Something is different, though. A haze fills my mind's view and within the cloudy substance, billions of sparks are floating around. The Light is not in one place anymore; it's everywhere. It encompasses every cell in my body.

Maybe this room won't allow technology in. I think of the latest paperback book I was reading. Picturing the robotic leg of a girl, wearing a bright red shoe placed within a lighted circle as a purple shadow fades into the black. I think of the large, curly "C".

My palms are face up. My Light inside me is zipping around my body. I feel a slight pressure on my hands. Opening my eyes, I see the book: *Cinder*.

6
Aiden

Saturday, prom night; three hours after Zoe's disappearance.

I materialize and stand in front of Kieran's house. It makes it convenient that he lives down the street from Zoe and me. That saved me from tracking down where the protectors were holed up. And if anyone asks me why I'm out here, I could tell the passerby that I'm walking home.

I chuckle at my own cleverness.

But unfortunately, Kieran's property is warded against beings like himself. Try as I might, I will not be able to enter their residence or even step on the lawn. I'll need to find another way to spy on them.

School is the best option since wards are not permitted in public areas. Thank Hells for that, too. So far I thought I had done well about hiding who I really am. The guardians will run around the world trying to figure me out, and maybe by then, Zoe will have her wings.

I have to make sure that they are running in the wrong directions. This will not be a solo mission. I must ensure that enough time is wasted to allow Zoe to reach eighteen.

I watch as the front door opens. Immediately, I make myself disappear. The wolf and the fairy drive away. Since I can't get inside the angel's house, maybe I could get into the green-winged one or the dog's house.

Since the demons breached the Spiritus Packs' land, they have doubled the patrols and heightened security. That might pose a problem for me.

So that left me following the fairy. She drives around a few blocks and parks her car in front of a ranch-style house. As soon as she gets out of the vehicle, she inspects the neighborhood, but I know she can't see me.

Slowly traveling around the house, she spies on her neighbors once again. In the dark sky, no stars or moon shows to light her path. She waltzes like a fairy on a mission. I guess that she is on her way to Fairyland.

I have never witnessed someone using a porta, but some of the Marquises demons used one on their attack on Winter. Of course, they had help to get the portas opened. I was late to that party. I caught the tail end of the battle. The snow-covered land was dotted blue from the fallen bodies from Winter Fairies and blackened by demon blood.

Many Knights were still frozen to the ground and unable to get back to Hell to regenerate.

That could be a problem in the upcoming war if the land hasn't released his front-line fighters yet. A break for them? I don't even want to think about that.

At least the Marqs' corpses were no longer there. Only black stains painted Winter's land.

Their queen had already directed the transportation of her dead subjects. Workers gathered their fallen near the ice path leading to the front of the castle. I watched, invisible, as the queen spoke a language I didn't know. It almost seemed like a blessing of sorts. I had heard about the ruthless Winter Queen, but at this moment, she looked like she had actually cared for them.

With her hand raised high, the wind picked up as a blizzard rained over the bodies. Snow fell and as soon as a dusting covered the bodies, they disappeared. Crystals floated around the Ice Queen as she absorbed their glamour. Then she glided along the high path to her fortress.

A twinkling light broke me from my memories of that place. I shivered. It's too cold there for my liking. And here I had thought Minnesota was freezing. I had yet to know how cold since it's only the start of summer now. I hope this mission won't keep me into their winter months.

Sidelle walks to a little garden, and there in the center

stands an arbor made of driftwood. She glances around one last time and then waves her arms in an arch. The center of the arbor shimmers and through it, I see green lands, colorful trees, and the sun shining.

She steps through the archway. I watch her retreating form grow smaller as she flies through the field. The porta grows dark and closes. The night is back with a full moon and dozens of stars in the sky.

It seems that the guardians have all called it a night. Maybe it's time to nudge them off their path?

I reappear in Hell.

Home.

Well, it's actually my second home. But I try not to dwell on that. I shake my head, clearing my thoughts away. Now, I need my wits.

Entering the throne room, I stride toward the stone throne and gracefully sit on the seat, summoning my friends.

"Minions, come to me." My voice echoes through the great hall. "I have a special assignment for those of you up to the task."

Within a few seconds, a mix of Knights, a couple of Nephilim, and a handful of Marquises demons appear. I wasn't sure if I would be strong enough to hold the Veil open to allow this many through. My father's minions must see the writing on the wall and want to please the current lord.

"I will open the Veil in various locations. You are to disperse onto earth and create havoc in every place you land. Knights, I task you with increasing the murder rates, burglaries, and bar brawls in all the major cities around the world. You'll start civil wars in as many countries you can." I stand. "Marqs, you do what you were created for. I want to open the newspapers and read of torrential flooding, typhoons, tornadoes, and drought. And when you think that's enough, know that it isn't. I want to hear that hurricanes are at a record high, volcanoes are erupting even from ones that had lain dormant, and you are to decimate the lands with fire. Acres must burn from city to city. I want the angels so busy these next few weeks that once they address one issue, another arises."

"Burn it down!" the Knights chant. "Burn everything down." The room erupts into excited chaos. "This night is ours." A frenzy overtakes the Knights, and a fight breaks out near my feet.

"Enough." I hold up a hand. "Save that for the humans. Now, go. Ready yourselves. Bring enough weapons to damage the souls of the Ordinaries. Stomp on their lives. Squish their humanity. And above all, extinguish their hopes and dreams."

A shimmer passed over my body when I lied in bed that night. It was Zoe's voice telling me she was sorry. I didn't know what she was apologizing for, not that I care. She doesn't have anything to feel bad about.

I had finally found her.

I hated, absolutely hated, the idea of going to Minnesota. The land with freezing tundra, mosquitoes the size of small birds, and only five months of being warm outside. That's not even half of the year. I liked it hot, where the blistering heat scorches the land every day of the year. I only heard of how cold it could get in the winters, and was not looking forward to experiencing them. Not one bit. Parkas were not in my wardrobe. They covered too much of my perfect body.

I had a good life where I'd been staying. So what if people didn't like me and call me their friend? Who needed them when I had minions to boss around? I could be myself when I hung out with them and not have to hide who I really was. I could be 'normal'. The only thing I could think of that was missing in my so-called life, besides being screamed at all the time, was the constant ache of someone I'd lost.

For eons, something was amiss. A dull pain that nothing seemed to quench bothered me, and no amount of bad deeds seemed to fix the problem. I didn't even know what the issue was or who was lost. How could I find something or someone I never knew about?

But overall, I had been content. I flew under my father's radar, even though I knew my future was in the family business. Until Dad said otherwise. Nope, the business could run without me. I was not about to set my neck on the line, not when I've had to protect myself from the rest of the family.

I was forced to come to the state of Minnesota, where they're known for their renowned medical and research facilities. The world-famous Mayo Clinic was there. My 'sister' applied for a position in a private hospital and she accepted. Why not use a microscopic bit of magic to get in and learn the lingo in a matter of seconds?

I didn't want to leave. I rebelled a bit. Okay, a lot. It had started out with not coming home for a few days at a time, or not checking in. As a grown adult, I shouldn't have a curfew. I started to talk back, caused some fights, and resorted to plain old showing off my abilities. Immature? Yes.

Finally, Dad had to intervene and set me straight. He told me to quite acting childish. I hated high school the first time around and even the second. I appeared older that sometimes it was hard to pass off as a young twenty-something guy.

One night I had the most bizarre dream. I kept getting flashing images of a girl's face. I didn't know her but felt she was important. She had long, brown hair and dark green eyes. As the dream continued, I noticed she was of medium height, shorter than me. She came to under my chin, which would probably place her around five-foot-seven. I was happy about that because it meant that at some point, she would be standing next to me. I saw a yellow house, her running around a track, purple wings, and a sword—but somehow different from my own.

There really was no storyline to the dream, only images and somehow, somehow my gut told me that I would meet her soon. After I told this story to my 'sister,' she pushed me to go find her. It was she who nagged Dad until he had mandated that I go.

So now here I am, in the glorious, great state of Minnesota with Zoe as my prisoner.

I watch her in the vocivus room. Is it horrible that I didn't create any windows for her? No, she can't know where she is. Not yet. I need to know for sure, and that's still a couple of weeks off.

I observed her those first couple of hours, second guessing myself. No magic hums against the walls. Maybe I got it wrong? Maybe those three protectors have it wrong, too. Or maybe she's better at masking who she really is than I thought.

Zoe goes about her 'days' sleeping, eating, and exercising. As time passes she talks to herself. Mumbling, really, because I can't make out any of the words.

I take notes of her routines that remind me of dancing. She's fluid like flames that undulate to her own rhythm in the wind. The way her arms extend out; the swift kicks she projects. I imagine what a deadly force she could be with some training. Someone obviously started teaching her stances, punches, and kicks.

I chuckle to myself, knowing I interrupted her teacher.

I decide that Zoe's doing well for being a captive, and I'll check on her again later.

I'm off to see what those guardians are planning, but first I must check in with my recruit.

7

Zoe

Wednesday, eleven days after prom.

I did it! I can conjure.

Immediately, my mind goes back to the room of requirement in the Harry Potter books. I guess this is sort of like that. My needs must be strong enough for my Light to conjure it. Just another thing I learned I could do. I always thought my Light was a defensive mechanism since it was only ever used in battles.

Protective Shields and Ribbons are the only objects I've created thus far. Now, I can add Conjuring to that short list.

I'm on a roll, and it's like the floodgates have opened. More tank tops, T-shirts, shorts, and pants appear. But it's more than clothes. Bars of soap, fresh towels, and a hairbrush lay near the sink.

That small couch and table mock me through the invisible wall. I stand and press my palm against it. Purple light shoots from my fingers. Radiance ripples from my hand outward like a drip of water that creates a wave. Humming fills my ears. The barrier shatters, and I step to the furniture.

A satisfied smile spreads across my lips.

Aiden can keep me here, but I think I figured out how I'm going to get out.

I hurry back to where the bed is, so he doesn't know I broke the wall. Maybe he won't notice or can't tell.

Moving the bathroom screen—okay, I use my Light—I make the screen larger to allow more privacy. Quickly, I undress, take a record shower, and jump into my new clothes.

As I step out from behind the screen, a shadow moves and startles me. A loud gasp escapes my lips.

Aiden leans against the far wall, arms crossed in front of his broad chest. Of course, he is dressed in all black, and his wings are hidden.

Clap, clap, clap. "Bravo," he says. "I was wondering how long it would take you to figure out how to use this room." He peeks at his cell phone. "It only took you under two weeks. I thought it would be much sooner than that, knowing what your worthless protectors think of you."

"You," I scream my best battle cry as my body launches

toward him. "Why did you take me?" My hands close around his neck.

"You don't know yet?" He disappears, but his voice is still audible. "You'll figure it out, eventually. So, until then, mums the word from me." He reappears on the other side of the room and scans me from head to toe. "A change of fresh clothes does the body good, wouldn't you say?"

"Why are you here?" I clench my fists, forcing myself to not show all my cards. "I mean, why didn't you come sooner. Why exactly now?" I run at him again, but he easily steps aside, making me miss my mark once more.

"I saw you break the wall." This time he makes his body barely transparent, resembling a ghost. He nods to the couch. "I knew it was time to make my presence known."

"Great, thanks." My tone sounds flat. I know he'll keep dodging my every move. "How long do you plan to keep me?"

He smirks. "I figured by now you'd learned that you can't escape this room, and we'll be spending many nights together from now on." Aiden waves his hand, and a large mirror appears on the far wall, sectioned off by a clear partition. "Now, you can see your friends. It's like watching live TV. There is no way you can communicate with them and let them know where you are. I've been watching them run around the world searching for you, and now you can, too." He taps his head. "But I'm smarter than that and them. They won't find you until I want them to. And I know you've tried to conjure a power cord. No mortal technology will work here."

I'm about to wipe that smug smile off his lip, when a new idea springs forth in my mind. Fight fire with fire, or in this case—Light.

Dipping back into the recesses of my mind, my Light hums within my bloodstream, zapping every nerve. It's ready to be called forth.

Purple light bolts out from my palms with such force, I stumble backwards. But I regain my composure and steady my aim at Aiden's hated face. He easily sends red Light to meet mine, making me think of dueling wands. But this isn't a movie; it's real life and I could die.

The Light dances back and forth like an imaginary tug-of-war rope, each giving and taking. Even though he's probably been a ... whatever he is for a lot longer than me, I'm holding my own. My hands and arms shake. I won't be able to hold this up for much longer.

"You don't have the stamina, Zoe." He looks like he could keep going forever. Well, I'm not going to let him win this one.

With renewed determination, I dig deeper and latch onto my anger with him: him kidnapping me, his betrayal of my friendship, and whatever else I possibly could be mad at him for. I package all of that into a ball and force it into my Light.

He staggers back but regains his stance. His mouth drops open, and then slams shut. Narrowing his eyes at me, his Light pushes me against the wall.

Sweat beads on my forehead. On shaking legs, I collapse onto the cold floor. My head hangs in defeat.

"Nice try, Zoe." Aiden straightens his shirt. "Better luck next time."

"Wait," I barely mumble, but I know he hears it. He glares at me, waiting. "What. Are. You?"

Aiden inhales and smirks again. "You'll have to wait to find out."

He disappears from the room, leaving me alone again. But now I have a special TV to watch. Seeing where my friends are and what they are doing to rescue me. Aiden just found a new kind of torture for me to endure.

The entire room hums with Light bouncing off the walls. The screen flickers on, showing Kieran's house.

8
Zoe

Kieran's body appears on the screen. He's just left Shay in the den. Both look so ragged, with dark circles under their eyes. Kieran's emotions are all over the place. His Light changes from red to green to yellow. I know he loves me. He ambles back into the den, but Shay is gone.

Angels! Where did Shay go?

I watch Kieran run to the weapons room. The door is wide open. He quickly glances at the racks and shelves, some guns and knives are missing.

Why didn't Shay ask Kieran to go with?

Kieran's wings appear.

He glances at the clock on the mantle. It's after two in the morning. He takes out his cell phone and texts someone. The TV screen zooms in closer. He's texting

Sidelle and Vash.

Kieran: Shay's gone. Anyone know where he went?

Kieran waits for a response.

Kieran: Going to see Michael now so will be offline for a while. Not sure when I'll be back. Hopefully, it will be some good news or a solid lead.

A few seconds pass, and his phone vibrates with incoming messages.

Sidelle: Nada
Vash: Nope

Kieran leaves the den and heads outside toward Pascar, the angelic fountain statue. She's the telecommunicator that was commissioned when the property was purchased to run as the safe house for all good Enlightens. Pascar has the direct line to the Council.

He scoops a handful of water and runs it over her feet. "Please inform the Council of Angels I need an audience with them," he says.

This is the first time he's spoken. The sound startles me.

Pascar's stone wings move and her eyes lower.

"I need to know where they currently are gathering, and let Michael know I'm on my way to meet with him."

She nods and goes back to her original form, her eyes turned upward along with her arms, reaching high into the sky.

Kieran's wings extend, and he pushes himself off the ground to take flight. He soars through the clouds, letting the moonlight bathe around him while the stars twinkle. He heads toward the Northern Star and passes through something.

With my Angel Light, I can see him fly through a veil.

He's greeted with a forty-story high rise building set in the middle of a small city. No other structure is higher than three stories. Most of the city is made of up houses, shops, and trading markets. It seems that today, even though it's the middle of the night to humans, the city is bustling. Surrounding the buildings are parks with winding pathways, ponds that overlook into the Ordinaries' world, and wonderful scenic displays.

He floats past all the pretty gardens.

The glass double doors of the Angel Tower disappear as he nears. The floors are built around a center atrium that goes all the way to the top. Kieran flies in the center to the top floor.

He sits in a leather modal-style chair. The waiting area is decorated in shades of black and white. A large black and white rug lay on the floor, covering two-toned white flooring. A small, white coffee table displays *Angel News* and a few other popular tabloid magazines humans enjoy. The room colors contrast his gold wings and tan pants.

"Kieran, come in, please," a voice booms.

I watch as Kieran disappears and then materializes into an office. Someone stands before an ornate white desk. His back is to us while he leans his palm on a floor to ceiling window that surveys the entire city. He's wearing a black suit. He turns to face us.

"I thought I would try out why humans call this a monkey suit." The older angel tugs at the collar. "I've only had this thing on for a couple of hours." His shoulders squirm. "I can see why they don't like wearing them. They're too constrictive to do anything. How do people dance in these things? That's where they usually wear these to, correct?"

It's funny to see an angel in a tuxedo. I snicker and keep watching.

"Yes, Michael," Kieran says.

So that's what the Archangel Michael really looks like? I would have thought him to be older, since he's one of the original angels. But this being who stands in front of Kieran only looks to be in his early forties. He's handsome in the suit. But aren't most angels?

"I know you're not here to listen to me talk about clothes, so don't let me stop you from catching me up to speed."

"As you are aware, Zoe was taken at prom." Kieran sits on a stool, letting his wings hang freely. "She has since contacted Shay and said that she doesn't know who for sure has her or where she is, but she is being fed."

"I see." Michael strolls to his desk and pulls out the chair, sitting. "But she was dancing with her neighbor, Aiden. Is that correct?"

"Yes. We believe that Aiden is disguising who he is."

"And why do you say that?"

"Shay thinks it was Aiden who tortured him when he was taken by the Marqs at Disneyworld."

What? Shay never told me that.

"He only saw the eyes of his captor, but they were aqua like his own," Kieran continues. "So when he saw Zoe dancing with someone who also has aqua eyes, he thought it couldn't be a coincidence." Michael nods but doesn't say anything. "There are some discrepancies with Aiden's outer appearance, too. We all see different variations of him, from his height, to his hair, to his eye color. I've always seen him like me. Sidelle said that she sees him like a fairy. Vash thinks that Aiden can mask himself."

What exactly is Aiden that he can do that?

"That young man, Vash, is going to be a great leader to the Spiritus Pack," Michael says. "They are lucky to have him. Unfortunate that his father had to pass so soon though." He leans back in the chair. "I've heard of some angels who are blessed with the gift of change, it's called Mutatio, but I've never met any of them who could. We all can change the way we look to the Ordinaries, but to change it individually to angels and fairies would be a real special case."

"No one has ever seen his Mark. I've never been that close to him to sense it or use my Light on him. Although Zoe swears he has a tattoo on his arm. She saw it in gym class."

"Hmm. Let me think and confer with the Council to see if they know of any angel who has enhanced Mutatio abilities." He writes a few notes onto a pad of paper. "Tell me more about what Zoe said."

"She said that she's being held in some magical room. She figured out how to conjure—"

Kieran's always had faith in me. More than I've had in myself these past few days.

"She did? That's great. It takes a lot of training to do that."

"Yes, but that's about all. Her training started a couple of weeks before she was kidnapped. Granted, she's progressing fast; it's not enough. We need to be warrior ready, and she's not there yet."

"She'll be ready."

Michael's faith in me warms my heart.

"How? If we can't find her to train?"

"Has she noticed anything about time in the room?"

"Shay said that time was moving differently. What

seemed like a day for her was really ten days."

"Sounds like a vocivus room."

"What's that?"

"It's like a locked box, in this case a place, that some Angels can create to store items to keep safe or from prying eyes. It's in a special place in the Void. Commonly, there are three Levels, but there is a fourth. Only the one who creates the vocivus room knows where it is and how to enter. There might be ways to track them because like all things, they leave a signature. It's a matter of finding that signature and homing in on it. We should team up with Bellator Software Services and see if they can write code to find a specific Light from a specific angel." Michael waves his hand over the sheet of paper, and more writing appears as a list of items to do. "We'll need a sample, so one of you will have to get inside Aiden's house and take some items. Be careful because if he is the one who has kidnapped Zoe, his home may be warded."

"So, we're assuming that Aiden is an angel until we find something to say otherwise?"

"Yes. What about Aiden's sister?"

"What about her?"

Yeah, what about her? She's a normal human. Or is she? What was their story? Oh, yeah, she took a job at the Mayo Clinic as a nurse. Is that a sham, too?

"We need to find out about her, and if she's an angel or

something else."

"I'll get the Reperio Team on it."

"One last thing." Kieran stands. "The Council has not agreed to my request to see them. I was planning to go them after this, but ..."

"I'll replay everything you've told me, and if I get any solid information about Mutatio, vocivus rooms, or anything else that may interest you, I'll let you know via Pascar."

"Thank you." He turns to leave.

Michael shakes his head as he adds to his list of tasks.

9

Aiden

Sunday, one day after prom.

"You're doing well, Quinn," I say as I step down into her basement. "Your parents let me in. You're training is coming along nicely." I pat her shoulder.

Quinn still doesn't have any idea who she is. I haven't broken that news to her, yet. She does know that she's different now, though. Most of her training has come easy for her, as it should be. As a Nephilim, she'll have enhanced human traits: speed, hearing, and most of all, she'll be able to battle against the Archangels.

"Thanks, Aiden. You've been an excellent teacher." She beams.

"Did you have fun at prom last night?"

"Oh, yeah. Caden and I didn't have any problems. We

were ahead of the mass pile up in the parking lot. I sure hope that Zoe is found, though. It worries me that she's been kidnapped. In a small town like this where everyone knows everyone's business, it's devastating." Quinn takes a swig of water. "I had no idea what had happened until I saw it on the news this morning. We were talking to Vash and Cali about maybe going to grab a late-night snack after the dance."

"I hope Zoe's found and is okay, too."

Quinn is easy to manipulate since she's so new at being a Nephilim. She hasn't come into her full, enhanced senses yet. Her change was only completed a few weeks ago. It landed her in the hospital since her parents didn't know what was wrong.

The doctors had kept her a week at the Mayo Clinic, running test after test, but unable to diagnose her with anything. Of course, they wouldn't find anything. There's nothing wrong with her, medically speaking.

On my first day of high school again, when I had strutted into PolySci class and noticed the petite blond girl, who stood barely above five feet tall, I knew. Her body gave off a slight glow. It surprised me that the guardian angel hadn't noticed her. Maybe he did, but he wasn't hovering about. His focus remained on Zoe. Always her.

Finders keepers.

Quinn and I sat together at lunch, and that was the start

of our beautiful friendship. I even obtained approval from Zoe. But first, I had to win over Caden and get him to break up with her. Yes, I could have stolen Quinn from right under his nose. I didn't need that complication. There are other ways to get what I needed from her.

Monday, two days after prom.

I pop back into the earth's realm and set out to find Quinn. With my senses now honed on her, I find she's at cheer practice. Her teammates are doing a new routine; one I haven't seen performed yet.

Yes, I'm one of those attentive boyfriends. Experience has brought me the knowledge that females like that sort of thing. Leaning against a bleacher, I wait for her to be done.

The basketball team has ended their practice as many of the players shuffle by me, heading to the lockers.

"Hey, man." Someone taps me on the shoulder. I turn and find Caden standing next to me. "You waiting for Quinn?" he asks.

"Yes."

"I'm glad that I could still take her to prom, even though you guys are together now. We had fun, just as friends. We've known each other all our lives. So we're cool, right?"

"Yeah, man. We're cool." I nod.

"Good." He claps me on the back and saunters away.

Caden's a decent kid. He was good to Quinn, but now that he's out of the picture, I'm able to spend what free time I have to shape and mold her into a weapon I can control. Between my time spying on Zoe, finding out what her guardians are doing, plus running Hell, and preparing for my father's release, I'm stretched thin.

I need Quinn to take some of the responsibilities off my plate. But the execution of this plan needs to be precise and cannot be rushed.

"Hey, babe," Quinn says as she saddles up to me and plants a kiss on my cheek. "You been waiting long?"

"No, not at all."

"What did Caden want?"

"Nothing important."

"I'm glad he's okay with you and me dating. I couldn't bear to back out on my obligation to go to prom with him. And I'm glad that you were okay with it, too. We both had dates to the dance before you and I got together. I think it says a lot about who we are that we don't back out on our words."

I wrap my arm around her waist and shepherd her out the gymnasium's door, steering her toward the locker room. "I'll wait out here for you while you change."

"Okay. I'll be quick." She brushes another kiss against

my lips.

Fifteen minutes goes by and Quinn emerges, hair still damp and in a fresh change of clothes.

"What's the plan for tonight?" she asks.

"It's a surprise."

"Oh, I love surprises."

"I know you do, and this is big."

I debated how I was going to secure Quinn's trust. I can't very well tell her what I am. She'd run for the hills, and all my hard work in influencing her would be for nothing. And I need her to execute my plan.

She is the perfect warrior and ruse.

We've been dating for over a month, and I know she's under my spell. The situation is delicate, and she'll be able to break it if it's not done correctly. She never received a Heaven's Mark on her wrist, so maybe I did get her in time.

I open the door for her as she folds into the Spyder. My car is red, fast, and daring. Just like me. Heavy metal blasts from the custom stereo, and she bops her head to the beat. The limited edition GT cruises along the streets of St. Joseph and speeds onto the freeway, heading for a remote field on the outskirts of the city's limit.

We travel hand-in-hand into the newly planted rows of early summer corn. Tiny stalks shoot a couple of inches into the air. Birds begin to quiet down for the night as the bugs come out to play.

"What are we doing out here?" Quinn asks.

"Babe, I have to tell you something." I squeeze her hand. "You know I care for you, right?"

"Of course, I do. I feel the same way about you. We haven't known each other very long, but I feel a connection between us."

I see excitement in her eyes. She thinks I'm going to ask something big. It's way too early for a marriage proposal. Silly human. Maybe she thinks that I'm going to ask her to be exclusive with me. I guess that's a possibility. Oh, hells. Does she think I'm going to tell her that I love her?

"Remember when I came to visit you at the Mayo and said that you were special?" I ask.

"Yes?"

Dusk is upon us. The sky is colored with reds turning to blues and purples. A full moon is rising on the horizon. Stars have yet to make an appearance.

"It's more than the common saying," I continue. "You are more than special. You're a..." I can't bring myself to say it. My eyes scan hers. They aren't afraid, but there is a hint of reservation on her part. She doesn't know where I'm going with this. "You're like me."

"What do you mean, like you?"

"I have enhanced abilities. Haven't you wondered why you are suddenly stronger at cheerleading ever since you were sick? Your body isn't sore anymore after practice, and your energy level never seems to run out."

"Yeah, I kinda have noticed that, but I just thought it's because I'm fit. I've been on the cheer squad since middle school."

"It's more than that. Your sight is now twenty-five, right?"

"How did you know that?"

"It's because mine is, too." I don't need to let her know that mine are even better than that.

"What are we?" Her pupils widen. "It's something bad, isn't it? I just know it. My body is telling me I'm not normal."

"Maybe you should sit for this."

"No, just rip the Band-Aid off and tell me."

I hesitate. "You're a Nephilim."

"I'm a what now?" She leans in like she didn't hear me. "Say again? Because I thought you said that I'm a Nephilim."

"I did. Do you know what that is?"

"A half-angel and half-human. I read YA fantasy books. I know what they are."

Surprisingly, she's taking this better than I expected. I thought she was going to be hysterical, and I was going to explain the whole Nephilim thing to her. Maybe she's in shock.

"It's going to be okay," I assure her. "I'm here and will

help you through it. I'm a lot further along than you, and I know exactly what you're going through. You won't be alone in this. We're in it together."

10

Shay

Prom night, three hours after Zoe has disappeared.

I leave Kieran's house with absolutely no destination in mind. All I know is that I need to get out and do something. I'm sure it's Aiden who has Zoe locked up some place unique. He's a first-class demon A-hole, and if he lays a finger on her, I'm going to end his existence.

I'll get my revenge on the torture he handed to me, but even more so for everything he's doing to Zoe.

Heaving my duffle bag into the trunk, I slam it shut, patting the hood as my way of apologizing to Angel, my car. I reopen the trunk to take inventory under the secret compartment. Inspiration had hit me after Zoe made me watch a few episodes of *Supernatural*. The two main characters drive a 1967 Chevy Impala, where the trunk's floor opens to reveal a whole battery of weapons they need to kill demons. Hammers, spikes, spears, and shotguns line the space.

Right now, I feel a bit like them. The brothers in the show at least have each other.

I close the trunk and sit in the driver's seat. Stomping my foot on the peddle, I peel out of the driveway. Google Maps launches on my cell. My finger presses the screen and it zooms outward. Now, I can see the Midwest region. Nothing speaks to me. I expand until the whole United States comes on the monitor. My breathing slows, and I briefly close my eyes. I shouldn't be searching on my phone and driving when I'm in this crazed state of mind.

I slow her down and park. The clock says it's after one in the morning. Hardly any cars are around in the small town of St. Joseph.

Taking a better look at the map, I start scrutinizing cities on the west coast: Seattle, Portland, Sacramento, and Los Angeles. I glance out my window, mulling things over in my mind. I return to the map: San Diego, Phoenix, Las Vegas, and Salt Lake City.

Las Vegas, Sin City.

That's it. It's the stomping grounds for the Knights. They flocked back there in the sixties when all the mafia bosses arrived. Gambling, drugs, and a whole ton of money made people do bad things. The Knights blended in so well. It's how the city got its nickname.

I can patrol the town until someone tells me something about where Zoe is being held. Taking the car out of park, I head for Las Vegas. If I drive the rest of the night, I'll be there in about twenty-four hours from now.

Time to get the heck out of here. At least now I have a plan. Maybe I should text Kieran where I'm going. Naw. He's meeting with Michael and the Council. Vash? I might need him if a couple of Marq decides to gang up on me.

Using voice on command, I ask the phone to create a text to the alpha.

Me: U up for a road trip?

I turn the car onto I-94 and head toward the Twin Cities. Party songs blare from the speakers from the Bose stereo. My thoughts go to the passenger seat when Zoe had sat there on our first date. That seemed like forever ago. My fisted hands smash against the steering wheel. The radio dims, letting me know that there is an incoming text on my phone.

Vash: Where and when?
Me: Now. In route to your house. Going to LV
Vash: That wise?
Me: Yes, I'll explain more in 20
Vash: Fine. Kieran?
Me: No. Angel biz

Fifteen minutes later, I wind my way down a street that leads to a dead end and stops in front of a massive wrought iron gate. To the left is a guard shack, but it's dark. Rolling down my window, I pull up to the speaker box and say my name. The gate opens. I continue down the road along the expansive property, following a street lined by gnarly, old oak trees and hills. Off in the distance, I could make out a lake, and every so often a house appears. When the last bend comes into view, the trees part, and there, before my eyes, sits a three-story mansion. Five white pillars line the front of the house, reminding me of the southern plantations in Georgia or the Carolinas. I pull next to a booth by the front door.

I'd never been to his house before, but Zoe had been, and she told me all about it.

Glimpsing the time, I feel bad for disturbing Vash's house so late. He could have told me no. I step up and ring the doorbell and wait. Lights flicker on and off, and I hear footsteps approach. The door swings open, and a tired-looking Vash appears.

"Sorry, man," I say. "Were you asleep when I texted?"

"Yes, but don't worry about it," Vash replies. "Come on it. I'm still packing a few things." He leads me into the foyer.

Two grand staircases curve up the sides to the second and third floor. In the center of the marbled hall stands the largest water fountain I've ever laid eyes, on that's inside someone's home. My eyes take it all in.

"I know," Vash continues. "It's a bit over the top. But it came in handy a few years ago when tornadoes ripped through the land and decimated most of the other pack houses on the property. Most of the members moved in here. I'll be back in a few minutes. Need to toss more items into a bag, wake my brother to tell him that he's in charge while I'm gone, and kiss Cali bye."

"Sure. Take your time."

"I won't take long." Vash turns and starts climbing the staircase, but stops. "Oh, and why don't we take a plane? It'll take two hours instead of twenty-four. I know you're anxious to get a move on."

"I've loaded my car with weapons—"

"Don't worry about security. We'll take the company jet. I'll call ahead and have them restock the belly with everything. Plus, whatever's in your trunk, we'll add when we get to the hanger."

I watch Vash's retreating form as it disappears on the third floor. He has his own jet. Two hours is better than twenty-four. The sooner we get to Vegas, the faster we'll have a lead on Zoe's whereabouts.

I don't ask about why Vash is doing this with me. I don't ask about his good-bye with his mate. I definitely don't ask about Jackson's leadership qualities. The ten-minute drive is not even broken with music.

We arrive at Flying Cloud airfield, and I see the jet already making its way onto the tarmac. No lights are on in the main building, but there are people milling around the hangers.

"Drive up to the security gate that leads onto the runway," Vash directs. "We can unload our bags and weapons directly onto the plane."

In front of us is a steal gate with an I.D. box. I roll down the window, ready for the code that Vash provides. The gate swings wide, and I proceed to the awaiting jet. The cargo bay has been lowered. We step out of my car. I march up the ramp, so I can inspect what's already been loaded. Vash has managed to fill the belly with every weapon that's legal to carry and some that are not. It's impressive.

"Leave your keys in the car," Vash says. "Someone will drive it to the parking lot. And don't worry about anything being stolen. I'm one of their top clients, and they wouldn't want to lose Bellator Industries. It'll be here and everything in it as you left." He grabs his bag from the back seat. "They'll wash her, too."

I toss my bag over my shoulder and step up the stairs into the plane. I've never been in a private one. The space is luxurious. Soft, tan leather high back chairs greet me on my left. A couch of matching material is on the right side, with a small conference table dividing the kitchen area.

There are no overhead compartments so for once, I can stand tall and spread my arms almost across the full width. In the rear is one bathroom and where the other would be on a normal plane, is a closet. That's where our bags are kept.

An older woman stands at the ready for orders.

"Thank you, Ellison, for working tonight," Vash says. "I know it was a short notice for you."

"It's not a problem, Mr. Bellator." She smiles. "Anything you need right away?"

"Not for me, thank you." Vash turns to me. "Do you want a drink or food?"

"No, I'm good for now," I say. "Thank you."

Ellison walks to the kitchen and takes out a folder, checking items as she opens and closes doors.

The door to the plane airlocks tight, and the captain comes over the loudspeaker.

"Good morning, Mr. Bellator. Everything is ready. We are set to go on your orders. Destination is Las Vegas Nevada, sir."

Vash stalks to a high-tech control panel and presses a button. "Let's take off when you're ready. Thank you, Captain Rego."

I sit in one of the recliners as Vash takes the couch. He sprawls across it. His body fills the length as his feet dangle off the end. He lays an arm over his eyes. I haven't known

Vash very long, and notice he's a man of few words. But when he does speak, they usually are of great insight and value. Maybe it's because he's been groomed to be his pack's leader, and now at such a young age, he is. Zoe had said that when she came to his house, he was carefree and fun. Now, all I see is a dark seriousness to him. Gone is his youth. Stolen from him.

The plane taxis down the runway and lifts into the sky. Soft instrumental music is playing through the speakers. It's peaceful and soothing.

"Don't you want to know why we're going to Vegas?" I explore the compartment for Ellison and find her past the bathroom and closet, sitting in a chair and reading on a device.

"Everything you say will remain confidential. Ellison won't repeat anything she hears. She's been our lead flight attendant for many years." He doesn't move from the couch. "I figured you'd tell me when you're ready. It's a short flight, so you can either tell me your plans now, or we can come up with something when we get there."

"It's the demon capital of the world."

"I know." Vash rolls onto his side and peers into my eyes.

"So, I figured that we could shake down a few bars and clubs and see who falls out and can tell us anything about where Zoe is being kept, who has her, and why."

"While I think on the surface that is a good plan, what's to encourage anyone from helping us?"

"That's where you come in." I swivel in the chair, breaking eye contact.

"I'm the muscle or the money?"

"Possibly both, but that's only as a last resort. The demons who congregate on the strip are there for various reasons and don't mess with the Ordinaries, so the Nephilim and angels leave them alone. As long as they continue to not harm the humans, we let them be. But some may have to be persuaded. I do know of a couple of Knights who may help, if the price is right."

"Don't worry about the money. I'll cover it."

"Sometimes, they seek other forms of payment."

"I guess we'll have to see what they want."

"Someone, somewhere has to know something." I recline to see how far it goes. It almost lies flat.

"Try to get some rest. However long this trip is, we'll need our strength." Vash flips onto his side and is out cold.

This is the perfect time to reflect on Aiden's eye color and what it could me, especially for me. There has to be a reason why he showed me only them. It's not that I've traveled the world and know every human, demon, or angel in it, but the aqua eyes are so unique.

I know where Nephilim come from: angel and human. Could he be the part of me that comes from the angel? Even if he's a demon, aren't fallen angels still created from Him?

Shaking those awful thoughts, maybe I should get some sleep while we're in the air. I'll need my wits once we land. If too many demons decide not to give me any information freely, I need a Plan B.

11

Zoe

Thursday, twelve days after prom.

After I've slept a couple of hours, curiosity captures my attention. I can't stand not knowing what my friends are doing. The mirror hangs on the far side of the room, begging to be looked at. It dark and shows nothing on the flat surface. Now to figure out how the blasted thing works. Of course, Aiden didn't provide instructions or anything. The room's Light has vanished from our dual.

Today's agenda will be to figure out the mirror, exercise, and consider all options on what Aiden is and what's his dealio.

I sit cross-legged on the bed, focusing my thoughts on Shay—his blond hair, aqua eyes, the way he always smirks at me like he knows some sort of secret. Each one is very near to my heart. I love them so much, even though Shay and Sidelle only recently came into my life.

Where are they, and have they found anything?

Maybe after Shay tells Sidelle and Kieran about our Dream Walking, Sidelle will go see her father in Fairyland. Time moves differently in that realm like it does here in this room, and I hope when she goes home a bunch of time isn't lost.

I picture the lush green grass, the tall trees, and the double-oak doors that lead into the massive throne room where I met King Oberon and the bright splashes of color throughout the kingdom and Aestas Castle. But nothing of Sidelle or her home appears in the mirror.

I think of Kieran. How he has always been there like he's a part of me. The three-story, white house down the street he calls home. It's really a safe house for all good Enlightens: Angels, Fairies, Werewolves, and Nephilim.

Still, no picture is shown to me.

Frustration surges through my body, and I'm about to give up and blow up the building anger when a sparkle catches my eyes. I squint to see if my mind is playing tricks on me. The surface ripples. I want this to work so badly my body shakes, and it's all I can do to hold back the power that's coursing through my hands, waiting to be released. But that much Light is bound to shatter the glass. I pull it back to the faintest glow, package it up into a ball, and float it to the screen. Coaxing it to do something. Some sort of magic performs every function in this room. Why wouldn't the mirror be that way, too?

As soon as the Light makes contact, the screen switches on like a TV that has locked in on a signal. The purple ball blinks in the right corner.

My yellow house appears. It's dark outside. A squad car sits beside the curb, a shadow in the driver's seat. All the lights in the cul-de-sac are off. The view turns back to my front door, and it morphs into the living room. My parents are sitting on the couch, watching the evening news. My father has his arm wrapped around my mom's shoulders. A box of tissues lays on her lap. Mom's eyes are puffy and red. I know she's been crying. Sadness washes over me, and I wish I could comfort her, tell her that I'm okay, and let her know I'll be home soon.

Even if that's a lie.

Neither of them speak, but I know what they would say. They'd tell me I'm loved, they are looking for me, and they'll never stop searching.

The news shows a major vehicle accident at the high school.

I briefly wonder when that occurred.

The reporter goes on to talk about something else about the same accident and the next picture on the screen is of the dance and one of the hospital. No sound projects from the mirror. It's like I'm watching a black and white silent movie but this is real. I just don't know what date it is.

What I can piece together is that after my abduction from prom, in the haste, multiple students hit each other while leaving the parking lot. A couple of kids are still in the hospital, recovering.

There was a bit of confusion with the prom attendees not showing up, coming late, or leaving the dance early, so an accurate head count wasn't confirmed until that following Monday. I am the only person still unaccounted for.

Of its own doing, the picture leaves the TV and moves up the stairs to the first bedroom on the left, my little sister's room. I feel like I'm watching the events like a ghost. Could I manipulate what I see?

The lights are turned off, but I can see a lump on the bed, slightly shaking. She should be asleep by now.

"Zoe, when are you coming home?" she whispers.

Can she see me?

"Stella?" I ask.

How can there be sound now? Another question to be answered later.

"I miss you." She sniffles and doesn't acknowledge her name. "No one tells me anything about where you are, why you left, or when you're coming back."

My heart breaks for her. My parents can't tell her

anything if they don't know what's going on. Kieran must not have said anything to them or her. He can't tell them the truth anyway. But just being with my family, giving them hope and support has to be enough. For now.

"Whoever has you, I hope they release you soon." She sighs. "It's almost finals week and you'll be missing them. I know you hate taking tests, but this is your last time being a junior. Your friends have come over to the house every day since you've been gone. Everyone is out looking for you. Please don't give up. Kieran has been here checking in on us. We're lucky to have him. His presence is soothing. Oh, and your boyfriend has been here a couple of times. He's still very cute. Well, so is Kieran, too, but I think you know that already. Anyway. Sidelle and Cali brought all your things from your locker home. I don't want to think that they have given up, that you won't be back to school.

"A couple days ago there was a prayer group for you. The whole town is rallying and coming together. Coffee Grind served your favorite drink to everyone. So we all drank a chai tea latte. Okay, I think that's all I have to tell you today. Oh, and I love you and hope you're safe. Good night, Zoe." She turns over and closes her eyes.

"Stella!" I scream at the screen as her form fades away. "I'm here, I'm okay." Fat tears roll down my face.

The mirror goes back to my reflection.

The Light stays a solid color and doesn't turn back on. I

know what I saw was days after prom. And now it's almost the end of the school year. My mind hurts thinking of all their pain, sorrow and questions about me that I'm sure my friends and town folks are asking.

12
Aiden

I hadn't believed in fate. But when I saw the girl from my bizarre dream after I pulled into that cul-de-sac in St. Joseph, Minnesota, I became a believer. She wore black leggings, an overly large purple hoodie, and purple shoes. She hadn't noticed me when I stepped out of one of the smaller moving trucks.

Before I could go over to introduce himself, my sister Sarah—that's what she wanted to be called—wanted me to help do a few things for her, and then I was free to do whatever. I bolted through the house and told her which room I wanted. I picked the upstairs bedroom on the far left for some reason. It was the one directly across from hers; the walls were a light purple. I guessed it was her favorite color. It's what sealed my decision.

When I was done, I marched out the front door and strolled on the sidewalk to her house. My new neighbors had a white picket fence surrounding the two-story yellow house, the exact one from my dream. I approached her, cautiously. She must not have heard me, so I cleared my throat to get her attention. She asked if I needed anything.

I loved the sound of her voice. That was the only thing missing in the dream: sound.

I told Sarah I wanted to stop over to the neighbor's house and introduce myself.

The sun was in the high school girl's eyes, but I could feel them checking me out from head to toe. I noticed her eyes widened when they locked with mine. I told her my name.

I was shocked again when she arrived and knocked on my bedroom door later that afternoon. Totally catching me off guard, I was nervous around her for some reason and hadn't expected her to offer to help me unpack. Maybe that's a Minnesota thing. In retrospect, I shouldn't have laughed at her. What was I thinking? Yes, it was cute how she got defensive about things, but for me to laugh at her when I hadn't even known her was unacceptable on my part.

I thought she had wanted to tell me something, but she held back. I wondered about that, her slight hesitations in her responses. What was she not telling me? I was glad I got to chat with her more that evening. She sure was spunky. I liked that about her. Her personality had not come through the dream, either.

On hells.

I wasn't expecting her to be so ... so. I couldn't even place the words to describe her. She reminded me of someone. An angel, maybe? I knew that I had to get to know her. A sickening feeling caused my wings to droop. If I had a heart left, it, too, would probably sink. She was going to be the death of me.

My real death.

Monday, nine days after prom.

Now, I'm having second thoughts on my whole plan with Quinn. No, I must continue.

A few days after I broke the news to her that she's a Nephilim, I invited her to my house after dinner, giving me enough time to make sure that Kieran and Shay were occupied with Knights and Marqs.

"The first lesson today is trying to get your wings to appear." I draw the shades. "It can be tricky since you don't know how to use them."

"I didn't even know I had wings until the other day."

"They've always been a part of you since birth." We sit

on the floor in my bedroom. I thought about the larger space in the living room, but I might have to answer a question about my sister. She loves the fact that she gets to boss me around while we're on Earth. I only let her since she's supposed to be my older sibling. Otherwise when we're at home, she'd think twice giving me an order. Quinn doesn't need to know anything about who I really am. "Relax your mind. Clear it of everything from school, your home life, and me even. Listen to my voice and focus on it and only my tone. Relax. Let it seep into your soul. Loosen your shoulders, down to the tips of your fingers. Think of your chest relaxing, and move that feeling down to your hips and into each of your legs. And finally stopping at your toes."

She breathes in and out. Our hands are joined as we sit cross-legged.

"Close your eyes. Control your breathing and match mine. Breathe in." I inhale and hold it a few seconds. "Breathe out." I exhale to the count of four. "In, two, three, four. Out, two, three, four. Yes, that's it."

I watch Quinn's body unwind almost to the point of a sleep stasis. Her face softens, and her head gradually tilts down to her chest.

"Breathe in and out." My voice just clears a whisper. "Now, think about wings growing out from your back, near your shoulder blades. Visualize the feathers. Sense them as a limb like your arms and legs. Believe that you have them." I inhale and exhale again. "Picture them clearly in your mind. Extend them out of your back."

The room begins to glow, a soft tone between orange and yellow. It reminds me of a slow burning fire, ready at any moment to warm and burst into billowing flames.

"Open your eyes, Quinn." Each eyelid lifts and meets mine. "Look behind you."

She turns her head to view her back. She stiffens. "Oh. My. God." I flinch at the word but quickly get my body under control. "They're beautiful," she says. "How do I move them?"

"Think about where you want each one to go, and they'll obey the command."

Gradually, the right one curls in and swings forward enough for her fingers to run across the feathers. The left one extends out and wraps us like a cocoon. Bright, glowing wings shine throughout my room as if it were daylight.

Nephilim wings are much smaller than mine since they have only half angelic powers.

I keep my wings tucked tightly behind my back. Quinn hasn't noticed them yet.

Her fingers lightly pinch the long, flight feathers. She says nothing, but awe is written across her face. She plucks a down feather from the coverts' wing area. She recoils and gasps. She's so enamored with her own wings that she still doesn't notice my black ones when I extend them out past hers. I watch as she looks around the room to figure out what blocks the light.

Her mouth forms an "O" as her eyes widen again. "Aiden." She reaches to touch mime. "Yours are so breathtaking. I don't even have the words to describe them." Her eyes flicker to her own wings and back to mine. "They're different. Why if you're a Nephililm, too?"

I blink. I wasn't prepared for that question. My mind scrambles to give her a response. I fumble. "Everyone has different wings; it's like a fingerprint."

"Oh." She doesn't say anything more and accepts my answer, going back to inspecting her own wings again.

13

Zoe

Saturday, twenty-eight days after prom.

With sorrow filling my mind, I don't feel up to doing my workout, but I must if I'm to stay fit.

Almost a month, that's how long I've been gone.

Moving the bed, I do four sets of leg lifts and six sets of windmills with my arms, repeating both two more times. After that I run around the room until my legs quiver and threaten to stop working.

I let my legs rest and go about punching the mattress. Somewhere between the hits my sorrow turns to anger as I deliver each blow harder. A slight pain throbs in my hands, but I ignore it. I need to get back to my family and friends. My arms, legs, and hands are bright red, and some of the knuckles are cracked open. Blood trickles out, but I welcome the pain. It makes me alive. What seems like hours later, but is probably only thirty more minutes, I quit my regimen and take a bath to get rid of the sweat.

Turning on the water to scalding hot, I inhale the sweet aroma of lilacs wafting up from the tub. My body glistens while I vigorously use the loofa as I try to wipe off the stench of Aiden. I relax for a moment, soaking in the calming effects of the lavender fragrance.

While in the bathtub, I try to conjure weights or tension bands. Neither appears. Aiden knows I'd use one and chuck it as his evil head, which reminds me of my next task for today.

Lifting my refreshed body from the water, I dry off and dress in a clean pair of yoga pants and a T-shirt.

My sister told me that it's finals week at school. I'm missing the exams, but who cares? I miss my friends and the routine of going to classes. What really hurts me more is that Aiden has robbed me of my junior year. Isn't this supposed to be the best time of a teenagers' life?

And he's taken that from me, time away from my family, from my friends, and from Shay. Okay, that last one sounds a bit shallow, but he's the first real boyfriend I've had and he's my soulmate. My heart truly aches from being away from him.

I move the bed back to its original location and conjure paper and a pen. But the pen never appears. Great. I try for a pencil. Nothing. How am I supposed to make a list without a writing instrument? Aiden must have a list of all known items that cannot enter this room. A pen or a pencil would make an excellent weapon for stabbing his black heart with.

Sorting through other potential items I could use to write, I try markers, crayons, and paint. Nothing appears. Well, a tube of black paint does appear but no paintbrush. I picture using that to gouge out Aiden's eyes. No wonder those are on the list.

I rub the paper between my fingers, gazing onto the floor where my cell phone lays. I never could conjure a reading devise; it had to be no technology.

Hum.

What did they use to write with in the olden days?

Paint. Nope, tried that.

Ink. Definitely a no to that one. The quill tip is a dagger-like object.

Chalk.

Yes!

And a black board and chalk appear in my hands. I've never been so thrilled to see that fat, white tube before. Yeah, there is no way I could do any damage with it. The powder is leaving white residue in my palms and fingers, and when I try smashing it against the board, it falls apart into large chunks.

At least I now have something to use.

Immediately, I draw a line down the center of the black board. On the left, I write "Name" and on the right side, I put "Characteristics."

Name	Characteristics
Fairy	Wings. Time manipulation.
Angel	Wings. Good, but maybe not.
Nephilim	Wings. Strong. Cunning.
Werewolf	No. Never seen him shift into anything.
Human	No. He has black wings.
Demon	???
Unknown	???

Well, okay, that didn't help me at all. I move my hand to wipe the slate clean but stop. Maybe I need to keep it and add to it when I think of anything else. I erase it anyway in case Aiden is spying on me.

But what else do I know about each Order? I look at my board again. Apparently, not much. I think back to everything Kieran and Shay have told me about themselves and their Orders.

I recall the afternoon after the warehouse incident where Kieran told me about angels. That was nine weeks ago.

He told me he's a guardian angel and a member of the Third Hierarchy of Angels. Archangels are members of the Second Hierarchy of Angels. Seraphs are in the First, and each level has particular gifts. As a guardian angel, Kieran could create Protection Orbs around himself, but not others; he can disappear or be ghost-like and can fly. He uses angel Light as a weapon that draws out evil. To know if a being is an angel, they must allow humans—Ordinaries—to "see" their tattoo by using Light. And rare people, like me, can see through their Light without assistance. Both angels and demons have wings and a special symbol. Males have theirs on their upper arm while females get theirs on the undersides of their wrists, and it's called a Triquetra symbol.

Fairies have a different kind of mark. They have either a blue lily if they are of the Winter Court or a green lily if they are of Summer, like Sidelle. And werewolves have a paw print.

Shay has the same Mark and has wings. As God's warriors, he has enhanced human traits: speed, hearing, and strength. Plus, he's a member of the Order of Naturals—beings who live longer lives.

I guess that sort of narrowed it down since Aiden does have wings. He must be a Fairy, Angel, or Nephilim. Come to think about it, I've also confirmed a tattoo on his arm. It was during gym and the whole class, even me, stared at his perfectly sculpted body.

14
Shay

Saturday, six hours after Zoe's disappearance.

Two hours later, we make the descent into Las Vegas. I feel the downward pressure, making me stir from my sleep. Through the small window bright lights illuminate the strip. We land fifteen minutes outside of Vegas Boulevard at Bellator Executive Suites on their own private runway.

I shouldn't be surprised on how well the Bellator family has done. They are one of the oldest packs in North America, and their ancestors date back to the 1600s from England.

Outside the runway is a black SUV awaiting with its doors open. Vash glides down the mobile stairway and onto the red carpet. I follow, making sure I have my duffle bag. The driver steps forward and grabs Vash's bag and extends his hand to mine. I relinquish it and watch as it's placed in the back. Vash whispers something into the driver's ear. He nods and saunters back to the office building.

"I told him that we don't need his services today, and I'd like to drive," Vash informs me.

"Yeah, I don't think he needs to witness anything that I end up doing."

"I'll do my best to ensure it doesn't come to that, or that I need to call my cleanup crew."

I nod my gratitude and climb into the passenger seat.

"Since it's early and the clubs are still in full swing, let's hit a few bars to see what the climate is like," I suggest. "It's been a while since I've been here." My eyes follow the massive towers and blinking lights head of us, even though we're a few miles away.

"I've secured two rooms at The Cosmo for us," Vash says.

"Thanks. I haven't even thought about that. My only thoughts have been to come out here and see what anyone can tell us about Zoe, or who has her and why."

"Do have you a specific bar in mind? We need to start somewhere."

"Yes, I know of a demon who might help us. I spared her life some time ago, but I don't know if she still hangs out here or not. She used to be a regular at the Purple

Zebra, right outside of The Flamingo."

"All right, yeah, I've heard of that place."

Vash creeps the massive SUV down Las Vegas Boulevard, dodging drunk party-goers, and takes a right onto a service road between The Flamingo and O'Shea's Casino. He stops the vehicle in a no parking area and gets out. "Let's go," he says.

"Won't you get a ticket?" I'm hesitant to leave my bag in the back, especially if it gets towed away. "Let me grab a few more items out, just in case."

Vash clicks the back hatch open, and I rummage through, grabbing more daggers and knives, sheathing them into holsters that are strapped to my thighs.

"No. Every cop in Vegas knows this vehicle." He kicks the license plate, drawing my attention." It reads: BELLATOR. "We'll be able to park it wherever, right in front of main doors, alleys, delivery spots, and yes, even the fifteen-minute parking places. While the city has granted the company use of the fire lanes and handicap spots, we don't ever park there. People with needs use those spaces. As long as I still have two working legs, I can walk a few feet."

We approach the violet doors of the casino, and my heart beats in time to the music. The place hasn't changed much, if any, since the last time I was here. The larger than life purple-striped zebra still greets us at the door. Zoe would love this place since all the cups and glasses are various shades of purple along with the neon lights, the menus, and the advertisements. I make a mental note to bring her here after we win the war. But first, I need to find her.

We stroll to the bartender and plop down on two bar stools. His back is turned to us, fixing someone their drink. We wait.

As he turns around, his eyes widen slightly and he huffs. "What can I get you?" he shouts over the blaring music. His mask of slides back into place hiding his recognition of what we are, which is why he doesn't card us for the alcohol.

"I'm looking for Oriana," I say. "Know where she is?"

"Nope. Haven't seen her in a long time. Years, maybe."

"You wouldn't lie to me, would you?" I stand, leaning closer to him.

"Me?" He lowers his voice. "Never Nephilim. Just doing my job, keeping my head down." He sets a beer down in front of us, even though we hadn't ordered it. "Who's this? Haven't known you to get a partner. Thought you were a solo worker."

"I usually am but not today."

"Don't play with me, Demon," Vash growls. "Oriana. Where she been hanging?" He doesn't have to shout as I can hear his chest rumble.

100

The bartender's nose flares, but he keeps any quips to himself. Wise choice.

"Fine, you don't have to go all whatever you are on me." Using a white towel, he cleans a spill. "She's been down on her luck lately and got kicked out of the high stakes games few weeks ago. You'll find her at the penny slots." He nods to the right.

"This better be good intel," I threaten. "Or I'll be back after your shift and beat it out of you."

"It's good, I swear. Oriana walked in a couple hours ago. She's drinking today's special. It's the drink that flashes purple and white, in that three-foot plastic bottle." He holds up an empty one.

I nod to Vash, and we leave the bartender to his grumbling. We head farther into the room and scan the crowd. I know exactly where the penny slots are. After people part the aisles for us, I spot her in the far corner. I stalk in her direction, but Vash pulls on my arm.

"What does she look like, and what is she? I need to know so I can prepare myself, if need be."

"She's the one in the rainbow hair sitting on our left. She's a Knight. Pretty harmless, but on a good day, she will fight."

"Okay, you go directly toward her, and I'll come in from a different side in case she decides to run."

"Good plan."

I continue my way toward the Demon Knight sitting in front of a purple zebra machine, hoping that today isn't a bad day for her. The bar is crowded even at this time of the morning. I don't want to have to fight her and accidently injure an Ordinary. With any luck, she'll see reason and give me information, or we can somehow get her into the alley.

I glance over her shoulder to see how much money is in the machine. She's betting high, and her balance is in the low thousands. But since this is a penny slot, her total is a bit over ten bucks. She's placing her last bet when I tap her on the shoulder.

"Get your hand off me," she yells but remains staring at the screen. "This machine is taken."

"I think you're done." I dig my fingers into her shoulder.

"I said…" She spins around to face me. "Oh, it's you. I was having an okay day, but it seems that it's gotten a bit worse." She scans me up and down. "Haven't seen you in a while. You still holed up in Minnesota?"

"Yes."

"What ya doing in Vegas?" Oriana swivels back to the screen and presses the "Bid" button.

"Searching for you." I lean against the machine, pressing closely to her.

"Well, you found me, so now you can get lost." She waves her hand.

"Hey, now, is that how you talk to someone who spared your life?"

"We're even, Shay."

"Not even close."

"What do you want?" Oriana slumps her shoulders in defeat. "Since you're not going to let me continue playing until you get what you need from me, so shoot."

"Answers."

"I don't have any."

"That may be true, but you might know someone who does."

"What do I get out of it?"

"Your life." Vash steps out from other side of the machine. "Now, let's go somewhere a bit quieter, so we can talk like civilized beings."

"But I'm not done here," Oriana whines.

I move to stand on her other side, one hand leaning against the machine. With my other hand, I press the "Bid" button, and we all watch the pictures go around and around.

"Come on zebra." Oriana bounces in her seat. "Momma needs a new pair of shoes!" I roll my eyes. The first picture stops on a purple zebra. "Oh, yeah. Come on. Come on. Come on." She hits the front of the machine as if that will help her get lucky. The second picture lands on a purple zebra. Dull silver Light glows under my palm that's

103

touching the top of the machine. It's inconspicuous with all the other neon signs flashing, the machines swirling, and drinks blinking in cups.

Vash smirks at her and taps his fingers on the side of the machine. He has no powers, but Oriana doesn't know that.

"Hey, stop doing that." She slaps Vash's hand away. "This is it."

The screen totters between the purple and the pink zebra. The last picture rolls to a stop.

My face mirrors Vash's smirk. She's going to hit the big jackpot.

"Please, please, please." Oriana's head tilts back.

"I didn't know you were the praying type," I say.

"A demon's gotta do what a demon's gotta do."

The light on top flashes like an ambulance and sirens blare. "WINNER, WINNER, WINNER" scrolls across the middle screen.

"Oh, hells." She kicks the stool away and jumps up and down. "I won. I won. I finally won!" She glares around at the other gamblers. Some clap and others scowl.

"See what a little faith will do?" I glance at Vash, and his face is stern. He knows what I did, but I don't care. I ignore him as a security officer dashes in our direction.

"Congratulations, miss," he says. "I need to verify your player's card and will escort you to the Guest Service counter."

Oriana beams. Purple lights reflect across her face. She can't stand still. The officer checks Oriana's card and nods for her to follow.

Vash stops me from following her. "Why did you do that?" he asks.

"I thought if she won some money, she'll be on a high and more apt to answering our questions. If she lost everything, she'd be depressed and reluctant to help." I shrug. "I'm not going to justify my actions to you. I need answers, and she's going to give them to me."

We catch up to them and wait for Oriana to get a payment voucher. She turns and heads back to a different penny machine, but I block her path.

"I think it's time to take your winnings and leave while you're still ahead."

"Get out of my way, Shay."

"No. You're going to answer my questions."

"Hell, no. Now, I'm on a winning streak. I can't stop now."

"Yes, you can," I grit though my teeth.

"I can't—"

"Please. Give me ten minutes." I can see her wavering. It's sad, really. She doesn't have the money to spend, yet this is all she wants to do. How did she get like this? I can't save her if she doesn't want to be saved. But I can save Zoe. "If you don't, I'll make you lose all of it and more."

"You did this?" She holds up her credit voucher. I nod. "No, you didn't," she huffs.

My face shows nothing. She launches herself toward me. I dodge her punches, but she persists. She shoves me hard. I jump, missing her leg sweep. She comes at me again as I step aside. I don't want to fight her in here or at all. People are moving out of our way, and the floor is shaking a bit. Security officers are coming.

Vash is on her in a flash, pinning her arms behind her. "Stop," he demands. "Do you want to be kicked out from this casino? I can make that happen."

"Doesn't matter," she spits back. "There are others who will let me in."

"I can ban you from all of them in Las Vegas. Don't push me."

She hangs her head. "Where are we going?"

"Follow me," Vash says as he releases her.

Oriana glances my way. "After you," I say.

Vash leads us through an emergency exit and out to an alley where the SUV is parked. There are no bystanders milling around, so this is perfect.

"So, talk." Oriana leans against the brick wall.

"Have you heard anything about a demon who is keeping someone prisoner?" I ask.

"You have to be a bit more specific on that. Hell has a ton of beings in its cells."

I inhale and close my eyes.

"How about any Ordinaries being held?" Vash asks.

"No." She flicks her eyes to mine. "Wait, humans? No. We don't take them to Hell."

"You sure about that?" I ask. "Because I was there."

"But you're not a full human; you're a Nephilim."

"True, but because you don't know of any, doesn't mean that other demons don't take them there."

"Look, I can't betray my own kind."

"Yes, you can, and you will."

"They'll kill me."

"If you won't tell us, I'll kill you."

"Shay." Vash nods. "We've got company. There are three Knights coming towards us. Oriana, if you know what's good for you right now, you won't warn them."

She nods.

"What do we have here, Oriana?" the center Knight asks. "Didn't pay your bookie on time?"

The three of them wear matching black jeans, boots, T-shirts, and leather vests. The two on the outside each have a dozen earrings in their ears, and both have their brows pierced. The one on the left sports a chain from his ear to his lip.

"Naw, it's gotta be more than that if a Nephilim is here to collect," the Knight on the right says, flicking out his tongue and playing with a bar piercing.

"Stay out of my business!" Oriana shouts.

"Oh, we plan to." Middle Knight nods. "But it's just that we heard Bellator was in town, and we wanted to see the young pup for ourselves."

"Who else would be driving around with those custom plates if it wasn't actually the Alpha himself?" Tongue Ring thumbs back toward the SUV. "I had to come see if a demon had horns to steal it, or if Vash was here in Sin City."

"From the looks of it, the vehicle isn't stolen," Middle Knight says. "So, you must be Vash."

"Too bad about your dad," Tongue Ring contributes. "I heard he died a painful death inflicted by the Marqs. How many of them were there to take him down again?"

"Don't talk about my father." Vash fists his hands.

"Oh, I think we brought up a touchy subject, hey, Pup?" Face Chain asks, continuing his baiting. "I heard it took about a couple dozen to overtake your lands. It's not an impenetrable as you think it is."

"I'm Alpha, I can take you all on," Vash grits out.

"Vash," I say. "We don't have time for this."

"Is that a challenge, Pup?" Tongue Ring asks. "Oh, come on, Nephilim, have some fun."

"Where's your sense of humor?" Middle Demon asks. "We're messing with you. Aren't we boys?"

The air tingles, and I know that these three demons

don't mean to walk away or let us go without a fight. Face Chain won't stop ribbing Vash. He's barely holding it together; the memory of losing both his parents still fresh in his mind. Vash's body shakes, and I don't know how much longer he'll stay in human form.

And I see it. Face Chain smirks at Vash and then pulls out a Viking sword from behind his back. He charges and swings right for Vash's head.

But Vash is no longer in human form. He's instantly changed to his harder-to-kill wolf body.

"The night is young, and we haven't had any worthy opponents in a long time," Middle Demon says. "You didn't think we would let the Alpha go without a chance to kill him, did you?" Both male demons draw their weapons and step closer to Vash, who is snarling fiercely.

I call my Light and my Nephilim Sword and then join the fight. Metal clashes from our swords as I parry with Middle Demon, but the noise is drowned out by the beating music from the Purple Zebra. Neither Vash nor I can create a Void, so we'll have to keep the damage to a minimum. Thankfully, no other gambler has found their way into this ally.

Oriana is shuffling back to the door while the males battle. "Don't go too far, Oriana, you still need to answer my questions." I slice Middle Demon across his chest; black blood oozes out. These demons are better with their swords than any I've ever come across. Usually, it's the Marqs who carry them.

Vash is still dodging and dashing around Face Chain and Tongue Ring. He leaps off the dumpster and claws Face Chain's arm. The sword drops. Face Chain attempts to pick himself from the ground but stumbles back down. Vash rounds on Tongue Ring, stalking him farther into the ally. Neither of those demons are as good with their swords as Middle Demon.

My attention is drawn back to Middle Demon when he slashes across my cheek. I shriek in pain as my eyes water. My free hand goes up to my face. That split second is all Middle Demon needs. He swings down on my Sword, hard and relentless. I barely block, trying to catch up with his movements. He's fast and good. I have no time to check on Vash and can only think he's doing okay. Howls fill the alley, so at least I know Vash is still alive.

I kick back Middle Demon, but he recovers swiftly. My legs trip over something, and I sprawl on the ground. My grip on the sword falters. A shadow hangs over me. I fumble for a dagger from my thigh. The blade is too short. Middle Demon will have to be closer in order for me to stab him with it. His blade is longer and is about to press into my neck.

Blood drips from Middle Demon's mouth. Silver, caked in black blood, emerges from his chest. The sword lengthens and then is gone. Middle Demon drops to the ground, eyes blinking no more.

Oriana stands with my dripping sword. Using both hands, she swings it against Middle Demon's head and slices it clean off.

"Now, we're even," Oriana says as she helps me to my feet and hands me back my sword. "Don't ever come calling on me again."

I look down the alley for Vash. He's panting hard, but two dead demons lay on the ground with their throats ripped out. His body shimmers back to human form. He's sitting on his knees and when he tries to stand, he stumbles. I run to him.

"Are you okay?" I ask, bending over and placing my hand on his back.

"Yeah, just need a bit of time to recover." He breathes in and sighs, peaking at Oriana. "I saw what you did for me. I am indebted to you. Thank you."

"Shay and I are square. So, I'll tell you what I've heard, and we are square. Got it?"

We both nod.

"Rumor is that someone high-ranking kidnapped someone from a school and is keeping her in a vicious room. That's all I know."

"No name or location?"

"No."

"Then it's a demon?"

"Not necessarily. Now, I'm done with both of you. Leave me alone." She stalks back into the Purple Zebra and slams the exterior door behind her.

15

Zoe

Sunday, twenty-nine days after prom.

I don't know how many hours or days it's been. I've figured out that the TV can remain on if I use a small amount of Angel Light. Aiden said this is live TV, but could it be that what I'm seeing has already happened? I wouldn't put it past him to lie to me.

The screen shows me Kieran leave the Angel Tower, and his wings twitch erratically. He leaps to the skies and lets his wings pull him in what seemingly is a random direction.

As soon as he passes through the Veil, he's heading toward the southern states in the U.S. Kieran materializes on the outskirts on the southern edge of a city and it's pouring rain.

I wonder where he is? Why he's there?

The rain is coming down so hard it's pelting his body and soaking his wings. The wind whips around like a tornado, blowing tree branches and almost bending them. Downed power lines lay in standing water in the ditches. People are stranded inside their vehicles, on top of their houses, and some made it to safety in the trees.

The sky is an unholy black as the wind carries whispers of death.

Kieran is high in the sky, and I can see white caps crashing, destroying the sandy beaches.

The river that runs eastward from the center of the city crests over its banks and threatens to wash away parts of the city. Everything floods. The water rising at an unprecedented level. Thunder cracks the sky, casting an evil shadow over everything.

In the lower lying areas, cars are being swept away. Houses are bending and snapping. I fear that the town's inhabitants will all die.

Instantly, Kieran appears next to the Summer fairy who is standing in the parking lot river.

I know those two have a special connection. Did she call him to her?

"This is crazy, Sidelle!" Kieran shouts.

"I know. Something is going on here," she responds. "As soon as it started raining, I felt in in my wings. Nature isn't supposed to be like this. No warning, nothing." Her arms are extended high into the air, and a green glow surrounds her.

"It's got to be the doings from the Marqs."

"That's what I'm thinking, too. We have to help these people, Kieran," she grits through her teeth. "It's too strong; I can't slow the rain or the winds. Maybe if more Summer fairies were here, we could combine our glamour. If my father were here, he'd probably be able to stop the buckets from pouring onto earth."

"Sidelle, you alone can only do so much. And I'm here now, and we'll both help. I'll let Michael know that he needs to send reinforcements because you and I aren't going to be able to handle this many people. We can use the stadium for all the displaced persons. We'll open the Astrodome next door, too, if we need it. You start transporting as many people as you can and get them here. I'll work on getting supplies and will help you rescue the humans."

Ah, my friends are in Texas. I watch Kieran press on his chest. Light pulses and then vanishes.

A semi-truck with a water bottle logo catches his attention. The road to the stadium is blocked, so he works on getting it cleared. Using his gold Light, Kieran removes fallen debris from the two-lane highway. Gently, he pushes the vehicles toward the shoulders to make room for the driver. Floating toward the truck, he whispers something in the driver's ear.

In front of the massive sport arena, Kieran gets a few police officers and firefighters to route and direct traffic. They need the entrance to be clear and act as the drop off point. The city must use this for emergencies because there are people milling around inside, pulling out blankets, cots, and water bottles from closets throughout the hallways.

My fists clench as my anger builds. Who could do this to all those people? I feel sad and helpless for them. I'm sitting here watching their fate unfold and can't do anything about it.

A bright light toward the playing field catches my attention. Angels descend into the space, creating a strobe light effect. Kieran goes to check in with them.

Is that why he pressed his chest? It must be some sort of distress call or something. I wonder if that would work for me?

Sidelle is suddenly next to him on the center of the lawn. She sections off the ground into large squares. "Divide yourselves and stand in one of the sections."

"We're going to send you out in the city. Gather as many stranded humans as you can." Kieran nods to them, as they aren't accustomed taking orders from fairies. "People have cleared the front of the building as the drop off point, but get the Ordinaries here as fast as you can. The Archangels will Mind Wipe everyone after."

"You in this section, go to the northwest of the city," Sidelle says. Waving her right hand to another section, she says, "You take the northeast sections. And the last two groups will take the southern sections. Now, off you go."

"There is definitely something amiss here," he says after all the angels disburse. "When I entered the city, I could see the Gulf stirring. We should check on that and the small communities along the beachfront."

"Okay, boss." Sidelle chuckles.

Kieran shakes his head. Grabbing her hand, they transport onto the beach I saw earlier. The sand has been wiped away. No houses line the shores, either. The water is over the island, and there is nothing left of the community. So many lives lost.

Both of their wings droop.

As they peer back onto the main land, the water line is several miles inland. A tidal wave must have crashed through and destroyed everything in its path. Homes and office buildings are severely damaged from the water's pressure and force. Boats from the marina lay on their sides, at least ten miles inland.

A stark dread fills my soul as many of them find their way to the Heavens. My chest hurts from the sheer number of them being transported all at once. Tears stream down my face. Sidelle lays a comforting arm around Kieran's shoulders, not speaking. I know they feel the same sadness that's pressing on my chest.

There isn't time to wallow in sorrow.

Kieran's wings twitch again. "Do you feel that pull, Sidelle?"

"The one now coming from Italy?" She nods.

"You can pinpoint it?"

"We better see what's going on there. But I have a feeling we're going to find something like here."

"Agree."

They link hands and disappear from wherever they were.

The screen morphs into a new sandy beach, the atmosphere electrically charged. Even I can feel it through the TV. A shadow covers the sunlight and casts an eerie glow over the peninsula. Dark clouds are running across the sky, hurrying to cover the blue with black.

The sand is covered in a thick, gray film. The entire beach has hundreds of thousands of dead fish. The smell must be horrific. The ocean has reclaimed a couple feet of land. The water is receding, but it's still there. An enormous wave is building high into the horizon, creating a wall of water. It's going to hit the beach and wipe out the entire downtown.

Kieran's and Sidelle's eyes widen as they gawk at the approaching wave. Dread plunges into my stomach.

"Go! Do something," I yell at the screen.

"Evil is definitely working against us, Kieran," Sidelle says as she waves her hand across her nose. "All those poor creatures."

"I know, but we can't save them. We need to hurry and get as many people away from here as possible."

They follow the same plan as they had in that other city. They find a building, and Kieran presses against his chest again. Shortly after, more angels descend from the sky, offering assistance.

Many more lives are lost, including trees, animals, and the natural wonders of life.

But we would find a way to prevail.

16
Aiden

Sunday, twenty-nine days after prom.

Oh, the sweet cries of human agony fills my ears and warms my heart—an empty, cold place in my chest where it would be found.

The Marqs are doing exactly what they were bred for, and what I told them to do. It's nice to know that there are some beings that listen to me.

Reports come in from all over the globe of unnatural, natural disasters. Headlines range from violent storms causing mass flooding all along the western coast of the United States, to landslides along Thunder Bay destroying homes by the thousands, to hurricane winds demolishing towns in Asia.

The Knights are doing their part, too. A record killing

spree in New York, Los Angeles, and Mexico City are being reported on the evening news. Burglaries are on the rise throughout the countries of Venezuela, Poland, and Honduras. Ordinaries are losing faith and not attending Sunday mass in the numbers they used to.

My wings feel the growing power of the end times. The start of Armageddon is near.

And I love it and dread it at the same time.

I'm beckoned to the worst events. It can't be helped. All the screams and prayers that go unanswered, the souls that won't sing any longer.

My body is drawn to what's known as the Ring of Fire. The pull tugs me across the U.S. to its western coast, outside Mount St. Helens in Washington state.

I land in Gifford Pinchot National Forrest. Dense trees block my view of any cities or inhabitants. This far inland away from Portland to the south and Seattle to the north, there aren't many towns. But this is an active volcano site, sending forty plus weekly quakes into the surrounding grounds.

What the Ordinaries don't know is that all volcanic fire is connected to the underworld. The River Stixx runs beneath the Earth's Veil, and each volcano is an off-shooting branch. Eventually, like all things, heat builds with enough activity, and it needs an outlet. That's what causes the eruptions. And there are the Marqs who can make them erupt more frequently, like they are today.

The ground and atmosphere warms as I near the volcano. Marquises demons float around the area, bowing as I pass. A row of them stands around the base, barely touching each other. Their powers create an invisible, but continuous line.

To me, it's a red shimmering path connecting their black robes by the sleeves.

Tremors rise through the ground.

Beneath me, scorching magma inches its way to the sky.

The Marqs chant, enhancing their powers.

I close my eyes, breathing in the smoke, and wait for what I know will come.

Ash floats on top of the crater.

Popping sounds fills the air. It's like a semi-truck is driving over loose gravel. The earth parts way, making room for the lava creeping up through the throat of the volcano.

My wings flutter in anticipation.

It's almost here.

The chanting from the demons grows until the volcano's anger dims their hums.

I feel pressure in my chest, as if I've been shot by a canon. I step back as the sky flares with red fire and black smoke. Ash rains, burning a path on its way down the sides. Molten lava spews high like a rocket and slows, eating its way as a stampede of rocks move out of its trail.

I'm sure the blast can be seen from miles away.

Everything in the lava's path is gone, buried deep under the red coat. It flows like water, spreading its reach across the land. Trees are knocked down. Animals run for their lives. If the lava doesn't get them, the thick black smoke will.

The eruption is so fantastic and wide, the burning fires stretch miles, but not enough to affect Portland. Winds blow from the east. The city will soon be covered in soot.

This is the start of the chain reaction. All through the north and along the coast up through Canada down to the Alaskan boarder, fires spit from their volcanic slumber. To the east in Japan, I sense Mount Fuji ready to burst.

I immediately appear, so I can watch the destruction of the narrow island.

The Marqs have already ended their chant, and I've made it in time to witness the awesome eruption as it slithers, covering the entire island and sealing every living being with death.

The blast is so powerful that my wings cannot hold me in place. The lava radius covers more than 100 miles. The ocean answers the volcano's cry with its own sizzling and dancing as the molten liquid joins into its body.

Every time a volcano flares up, I feel it in my wings. More than 450 volcanoes erupt within the same hour.

The deafening silence of souls brings a smile to my face.

I'm euphoric when I return to the vocivus room to spy on her.

Zoe's ending her stretches and is about to meditate. I know her routine by now since I've been watching her for the last couple of weeks.

Her powers are emerging faster than they should. It's still weeks before her birthday. There is nothing normal about this girl.

She doesn't seem to know I'm there. I have caught her a few times glancing around the room as if she could feel my presence. But that's impossible. There is no other angel on earth like me. I have eons of practice to mask myself. A newbie like her couldn't possibly detect me.

Could she?

Doubts creep into my mind and thus ending my glee from my trip.

I need to get that feeling back; it's like a drug. I should find another soul to annoy, but she is right here, and I love baiting her.

Without further thought, I interrupt her quiet time. Her eyes are closed as she sits on the bed, yoga style. I tuck my wings behind me and wait against the wall. My appearance is barely visible.

I watch the steady rise and fall of her chest and it becomes erratic. A muscle on her face twitches. She tucks a stray her behind her ears. A loud sigh escapes her lips.

"Hello, Aiden." She opens her eyes. "Come to torment me some more?"

"I'm hurt." I mockingly place a hand over my heart, that she can't see.

"Then you've come to gloat about something."

"Boy, you are getting to know me so well."

How did that happen? Maybe she's becoming astute to her surroundings. I shouldn't be here. I shouldn't be visiting her like this. I should leave her alone.

"I know nothing about you, actually."

"What would you like to know?"

"You are different today." Her eyes become slits. She's suspicious. "What's changed?"

I let myself become visible to her and remain in my ghost-like form. "If you don't want to ask me anything, then I'll leave."

"I didn't say that."

"I'll give you a chance to ask me three questions. Anything you want."

"Anything?"

"Yes. I might not answer the question, but that's the risk you'll have to take. Think of it as an early birthday gift. Now, what's your first question?"

"Why did you kidnap me?"

"Getting right into the meat of this." I motion for her to follow me to the couch and chair and for her to sit in one of them. She chooses the sofa. "You told me in your backyard that you were the Redeemer. If that's true, when you turn eighteen you'll get wings. And if you fight for Heaven, you'll also receive a Mark. If you get those two things, you are the one in the prophesy; the lone girl who will start Armageddon." Needing to solidify my body, I cross my ankle over a knee. "The cage that Sammael is being held in will open. He'll lift the Veil between Hell and Earth and allow demons to pour into your realm. You and your friends will try to stop that from happening, and I can't allow that." I stare at her. "Next question."

"You're a demon?" She doesn't miss a beat. Her head tilts to the side.

Should I answer that? She'll know more about me. What could it hurt? I think of all the possibilities. She could tell her friends, but they'll find out eventually and tell her. The demon world is a bunch of back-stabbing traitors. Someone will leak something.

"Yes," I say.

I'm sucked into watching her brown eyes try to sort something out. She fidgets with that stray piece of hair that always comes untucked from behind her ear.

"Are you the Prince of Hell?" she finally asks.

"I'm called many things by many beings."

"So that's a yes?"

"And that is a fourth question and I won't answer."

I fade from her view.

That was close, too close. Zoe is smarter than I thought.

Time to start phase two of my plan. I think Quinn's ready. It's been six weeks of solid training with her. She's mastered the control of her wings. If I didn't know better, I'd say she was a natural at this. I chuckle at the thought. All Nephilim are good at a lot of things. They need to be superior and at the top of their game all the time. It didn't surprise me that Quinn wasn't any different.

She learned flying with ease. I showed her defensive maneuvers and aerial tactics. Never once did she question me. I think she wanted to be special and part of something bigger.

Little does she know that she's in the center of things and critical to my plan. Today, I'm going to show her the art of weaponry. I pull out my phone to send her a text.

Me: Come over after school

Immediately, my cell chimes with an incoming text.

Quinn: OK, can't wait to see what we're doing today

I couldn't stand the thought of going back to that dreadful place they call a school since I managed to secure Zoe in the vocivus room. Oh, hells no. High school was the last place I wanted to be, so I dropped out. Who is going to stop me? My sister? Nope. I outrank her, and if she runs to daddy, well, I'll deal with that later. And really what's he going to do about it since he's still stuck in his cage? If and when he gets let out, I'll worry about that later. I'll take my chances that he doesn't find out I disobeyed him.

The basement is stocked like I'm ready for World War Three. Racks and cases are filled with daggers, knives, swords, and guns. As I wait for Quinn to arrive, I select a variety to use for training.

She will need to be proficient in using them all and more. I don't expect her to grasp everything today, but I also need to see which weapon calls to her. So far, her Nephilim Sword has not appeared, and I don't know why.

On the far wall that runs the length of the house, I place bows and arrows on top of a small table and drag straw targets to the opposite end of the room. Right above the bales we're using for the arrows, I hang paper targets and set up a table with guns, amo, and magazines. Using a tiny bit of Light, I conjure a ten-inch thick foam board and place it behind the paper, propping it up against the wall. In one of the spare rooms, I tow a sword-training dummy and hang a sword rack. Gently, I set a long blade, broadsword, katana, and a claymore onto the display.

Now, the basement is ready for her training to begin.

"Hello? Aiden?"

"Down in the basement," I say.

Footsteps echo as Quinn steps down the stairs. She stops on the last step and gazes at everything. "Whoa," Quinn says. "Are you getting ready for the apocalypse?"

Oh, hells, she's intuitive, too. Maybe I have underestimated her.

"No," I quickly say. "But today we start your next phase in training: weapons. So, I laid out a bunch to see how you do with these. Maybe if you find something that fits you, it will force your Nephilim Sword to appear."

"Do you have a Nephilim Sword?" Her fingers graze over the table of smaller daggers and knives. "I'd like to see it."

"I do. When you need it, it appears." I reach behind my back to where an invisible holster crisscrosses, holding mine. I draw it from its scabbard. The black blade glimmers from the ceiling lights, making shimmering dots dance all over the room like a disco ball. One hand covers the hilt and my other balances the blade.

Quinn reaches to take the sword from my hands, but I quickly pull it away. "You can't touch it. You'll burn yourself. This one is special to me as yours will be to you. Part of your essence will be taken to create it." What I don't tell her is that mine was also dipped in the River Styx's Hell Fire, so the blade can cut through any Nephilim or guardian angel. "Since you have an interest in the bladed weapons, let's start there."

I proceed to advise her about each blade, length, and what sort of fighting they would be good for. She picks up each and makes stabbing motions, feeling each one in her hands. We move onto the knives and practice throwing them at the targets.

Thump. Thump. Thump.

The perfect timing of each toss finds its marks in the bull's eye. She's a natural, just as I thought she would be.

On her own, she selects the katana and removes it from the sheath. The blade is long and has a slight curve. I watch her feel the balance and swing it a few times. She moves gracefully, as all Nephilim do. Her head turns toward me and I nod.

Curling my finger, I wave her into the spare room where the dummy is set up. "Take a few whacks at the body so I can see your swing."

"Like this?" Quinn asks. She cuts the blade across the mannequin's jelly chest, taking a step back and driving the blade into a shoulder.

"Good." I slide behind her and lock my hand around her wrist, guiding the sword. My body is pressed against her back as I lean forward and force her to do the same. "Throw the force from your center and not just the arm. Your core is where balance resides." I step away and let her practice more swings. "Widen your stance a bit."

"Is this too much?"

"No, perfect. You're catching on quickly."

"It's like I was born to do this."

"You were. You've always been a Nephilim; you just never knew or were trained. Most are found at a very young age, and their training starts immediately. But we don't have that luxury."

"Why not? It's not like I'm ever going to need to use this, right?"

"Actually, word on the street is that there's evil present, and everyone must choose sides. All warriors will fight."

"As in good versus evil?" I nod. "But good always wins; plus, that's the side we're on. How could we lose?"

This is going to be epic. In the first time in history, good will not prevail. I won't let it. And with Quinn at my side, Zoe and her friends won't ever know what hit them.

17

Zoe

Friday, June 1, thirty-two days after prom.

I'm losing track of the time. Days and weeks have passed since I've been kidnapped, and my cell phone ran out of juice a while ago.

Aiden only has physically visited me in the vocivus room twice. The last time was when he confirmed to me that he is all the evil my mind has made him into and yesterday.

What changed? He seems different somehow.

I felt his presence in the room almost daily. I wonder why he's spying on me?

I'm still consistently being fed.

My life has become a monotonous existence.

With nothing else to do, I flip on the Light to the mirror

and catch up on what my friends are doing. It makes me sad that I'm not with them and if I think about it for too long, seeing them all makes it worse.

I haven't watched the mirror in a couple of days, ever since I saw the mass flooding and Sidelle trying to stop the water all on her own.

Sidelle appeared near a body of water, and I didn't know where or what she was doing, until the water came down as a torrential downpour and didn't seem to want to stop. The streets flooded with vehicles being swept away. I witnessed people drown and others become stranded within their homes as the water rose at least ten feet. My heart broke, and my only consolation was that they weren't alone when they died. I was there in spirit. My heart ached for all the people who were saved or rescued.

But now I want to know. No, I need to know what else is going on in the world. I wonder what Shay's doing while the weird weather events kept Sidelle and Kieran busy.

Today, a desert appears on the screen with a city's lights in the background. It's dusk or dawn, I can't tell which quite yet. Reds, pinks, and yellows color across the vast sky. The sun peaks above the horizon, casting much needed light on the area. The famous "Welcome to Las Vegas" sign is still lit. Warm light crawls, brightening up everything in its path. Blue skies above gently kiss the land. I briefly wonder who's in the Sin City and why.

Heat waves rise from the ground, creating mirages of

hope. It's too early in the morning for such temperatures. The wind picks up and blows sand and tumbleweeds across the flat landscape.

The sun is soon high in the sky, and the city's lights flicker. Some shut off and stay darkened. It's like the timestamp on the mirror is in fast-forward mode, moving ahead hours at a time. The earth cracks of dryness. Flowers wilt. Grass turns brown and shrivels.

Hardly any people are parading around as the Vegas strip is scanned over. I thought it's a city that never sleeps, but today it's too hot. In the alleys and under bridges, the homeless die first. Their skin leathers to dark brown; their bodies cannot stand the heat any longer. Hospitals are filled to the brink of patients needing to cool down. The generators can barely keep up.

More lights turn off as if to say, "I'm dying."

I'm still wondering why it's showing me this city when a black SUV comes into the frame. The license plate says: BELLATOR.

Vash?

The windows are so dark I can't see in them, so I don't know if there's a passenger or not. They are driving out of town, nearing the airport. But they don't go to the main terminal; instead, they head toward a smaller one with a waiting private jet.

Of course.

The passenger side door opens and out steps Shay.

He's wearing all black. Gosh, he must be baking in that. His hair is a bit ruffled and strapped across his back I can see his Nephilim Sword. In fact, his arms and legs are also strapped with knives or daggers. He rakes a hand through his blond hair and pulls off his black shades as he wipes his brow with the back of his hand.

Vash speaks to him and Shay nods. They meet in the back of the SUV and unload two bags. Someone grabs the gear and places them into the belly of the plane. I watch them board and close the door.

The screen changes back to the city in a panoramic view.

The extremely dry air has cracked the earth open. It looks like a turtle's shell. Valleys are forged, and the earth breaks apart.

My heart sinks at the thought that the land is dying from the extreme lack of water.

The stars of twilight give no reprieve.

Now, there are no humans on the streets or sidewalks.

The final lights are turned off, and the city is blanketed in darkness, expect for the eerie glow from the moon.

The mirror zooms out, and more cities are turning dark. Power is being lost on a massive scale. Soon, it could reach Los Angeles.

Small towns are showing people huddled inside their homes, eating what they have left on their shelves. Water from faucets drip into bowls as they ration it within their families.

The reservoirs are dry.

People will die of heatstroke, thirst, and hunger.

I have no idea how many days it took for the heatwave to claim so many lives, but the mirror is littered with tiny dots floating toward the Heavens. I stop counting because I know what they are and what it means.

The purple Light flickers off, and I sit on my own bed in darkness. My shoulders heave from crying. And I cry harder, thinking that's what those people needed, water from my own tears.

How can Aiden let all this happen?

"Aiden, you get your sorry wings in here this instant. If you know what's good for you at all, you better not ignore me." I stand and get ready to glare or fight as soon as I see the black of his feathers. "How can you do this? Why are you keeping me here?" I scream at the top of my lungs, letting all my frustration and sorrow release from my body. "I know you can hear me. Stop being a scaredy cat and face me."

"You rang, my Sweet?" Aiden's form appears. "You can lower your voice. I think all of—oops. I almost told you where you are. No one else can hear you but me, and you only have to whisper for me to hear you." He leans against the wall. "Now, what did you want?"

Usually, I can see through his body but not now. Is he a solid form? "I know it's you who has been destroying the cities with flooding and droughts." I take a menacing step closer to him.

"Oh, and don't forget that all the world's volcanoes erupted and spread toxic ash into the skies and smoking lava coats the lands." He wags his finger at me.

"Why? Why would you do this?"

"It's in my nature." He shrugs. "Why not? I can, so I do."

"But you haven't always been evil. You weren't when we first met."

"You don't know me, or what I've done in the past."

"Doesn't matter. It's what you do with the present to change your future that matters."

"You're such an optimist." He picks his perfect fingernails, bored.

"And you're a pessimist."

"I am what I am. Nothing will change that. Not even if I wanted it to."

"That's not true. If you want to be different, you can be."

"Not for me."

"All those people and animals."

"They die. It's the circle of life."

"But you ended their lives early"

"And who's to say that it wasn't their time?"

"I saw the masses of souls leave Las Vegas." I shuffle a couple steps closer. "I know what it means. They died, and it's your fault."

"It is," Aiden agrees. "You don't understand."

"Tell me and help me understand."

"It's not that simple."

"Yes, it is." I stand in front of him and reach out, grabbing the sides of his lips. "You move your mouth like this." My fingers land on his smooth face and do not go through his form. A numb, tingling feeling spreads down my arms and into my chest. "See, it's that easy." If sparks could fly out of my fingers, I think they would.

My eyes seek his.

Black hooded orbs stare down on me.

They flash red, and he glances away, shaking his head. He steps back.

I drop my hand.

"No." His brows scrunch. "Not for me," he says again. Resolved, his wings extend, forcing me back a few more steps.

Our moment is over.

Anger blinks across his face.

"Now, stay in here and be a good girl. Everything will be over soon."

Aiden disappears from the room, leaving me ... how? And what was that when I touched his face? I only know one other person who affects me like that with a strange electrical current.

18

Shay

Friday, June 7, thirty-nine days after prom.

I board the private plane, sweating like a pig. We've been at this for a month. Trying to find another demon who knows where Aiden is keeping her. No one is talking. Either they really don't know, or they're more scared of the one calling the shots on their end. My guess is the latter.

It got hot quickly here in the southwestern states, even though it is still early in the morning. Sleep tries to take over my body. I need rest, but I can't stop thinking about what Oriana said, "It might not be a demon who is keeping her."

Does that make Aiden not a demon?

The same seat I sat in before beckons to me. The soft leather caresses my body and pulls me under.

I dream of Zoe and I in Las Vegas but not hunting for demons. It's a vacation for us. She's never been outside the state, and I know Sin City would be on her bucket list.

She's happy perusing in and out of the different casinos, each having its own style and décor. We walk together, take in the lights from the Stratosphere, eat a fantastic meal at the Bellagio, and take in a show at MGM.

It's perfect.

Someday, we'll have that chance.

"Shay." Vash shakes me awake. "You've got to see this." He points to the TV.

We watch the news clips scroll between flooding in Texas and volcanoes erupting all over the world. Thousands of lives are being extinguish by mother nature. Picture after picture portrays death. Interviews of survivors telling their stories break our hearts. The land is devastated beyond fixing.

"Do you think the scorching temperature we left is also part of this?" I ask.

"Could very well be. I've been trying to get a hold of Kieran or Sidelle. Neither is picking up their phones."

"That could be bad, or they are busy trying to save as many people as possible and don't have time to call us." I slip my phone out of my back pocket. "Flip to the local news around Vegas. I have a feeling that the city is also affected."

Me: I'm sure you have seen the news. Vash & I left LV and are heading home. Don't worry about us. Keep doing what you're doing & we'll regroup later.

Vash changes the station and finds a news flash about severe drought invading Nevada and the surrounding states. Cracked land, empty food shelves, and the hospital overflowing with patients are all shown. Hundreds are still dying from dehydration.

My phone pings from an incoming text.

Kieran: Yep. Busy here. Try to text more later.

Vash's phone also chimes, and he shows me the text.

Sidelle: Was in TX trying to stop the flooding but didn't help. Tried to save as many people as we could in Italy. K's with me. Now, we're in Australia. B back soon.

We're both distraught. We hadn't known how bad it was. I was so focused on Zoe I didn't look around me. And now, all those souls are gone.

The pilot interrupts my thoughts.

"Sir, we're running into slight turbulence from heavy winds. Visibility is less the lower we go, but it's unstable in the higher altitudes. We can see smoke down there."

Vash jumps to the intercom and presses the button.

"Take us down to the nearest airport." He stares out the

window. "Now."

His urgent voice startles me, and I spin to my own window. The plane is descending. Below us, fires rage across the heartland. The sky is thick with black smoke billowing upward. From this height, I can see the damage the flames are making. It's covering thousands of miles. We bank right, and fires burn as far as the horizon goes.

All the crops are ruined.

In a matter of minutes, we are landing on a small runway.

"Sir, we're at Emporia Municipal Airport. Wichita is to our southwest and Topeka is north of here."

"Thank you," Vash says.

"I've called ahead and ordered you a vehicle. It doesn't seem like it's arrived yet. I'll bring your bags around as soon as we're done taxiing."

"Okay."

"What are we going to do here?" I ask. "We can't stop the fire from spreading."

"No, we can't. But we can help the hospitals, drive people to the city, and help them protect their homes. Anything. They'll need capable bodies here." He looks directly at me. "I know you're anxious to get back to Minnesota, but without Kieran and Sidelle, there's no use having a meeting without them. We can be here for a day or so and head out early tomorrow morning. Maybe Kieran

142

and Sidelle will also be back from Europe by then."

I nod. It's all I can do. I know we must help these people. The smaller towns won't have the medical needs or manpower. Plus, Vash is right. We have no other information to go on except that Oriana confirmed that someone kidnapped a girl and is holding her in a vocivus room. We can spare another day or two. Zoe would want us to.

Clutching my cell phone, I swipe it to "on," so I can draft a text to Kieran.

> **Me:** We're in Kansas, outside of Wichita. Fires are spreading across the Midwest. Vash and I are stopping to help. Be back in MN in a few days.

Immediately, I find a response.

> **Kieran:** OK, Sid and I will wrap up here. She can't stop the rain, but it sounds like you guys could use her glamour to put out the fires.

Vash and I wait inside the plane. The air is too thick with smoke to be outside. In a few minutes, Sidelle and Kieran appear outside the plane.

"You rang?" Sidelle asks as the door drops to let us out. "Word on the street is that you guys need my help." She winks. "We weren't doing anything. You know, hanging around the massive pool falling from the sky that someone created. And they didn't even serve us any drinks."

"I showed Sidelle your text about the fires; we came here." Kieran rolls his eyes. "All the angels are stretched thin helping the entire world with all of the mess that's going on, so it might be only us here to cover the Midwest." He fists his hands. "I suspect that this is what Aiden wants."

"How so?" I ask.

"Whoever is pulling the strings here needs us saving the Ordinaries, so we can't focus on finding Zoe. It's the perfect cover. Misdirection. And it's working. Between the flooding, droughts, volcanoes, and now fires, every Order is stretched thin." He turns to Vash. "We met up with Alpha Nickola in London, and she confirmed that Knights and Marqs are breaking through the Veils' gates in record numbers. They've sent as many as they can afford to Stonehenge to squash any more coming through. But many are breaking across the barrier using some fewer known locations. Knights have been spotted near the Drombeg Circle of Ireland; Marqs are rising out of the ground near the Carnac Stones in France and on the Balearic Islands of Spain. Europe is overflowing with demon activity."

"We can't think of that now," Vash says. "We can only do what we can do here."

"What are we waiting for?" Sidelle asks. "Why are we still standing around doing nothing when there are a ton of folks and land that needs saving?"

"No vehicle," I say and rotate my hands, imitating driving. "Vash and I can't appear and disappear all over the world. We need human technology to get from place to place."

"Well, duh, silly boy. That doesn't mean that Kieran and I need to stay here and wait for you to drive to wherever." She cocks her hip out. "So, what's the plan? K and I have our work down to a science, but from the looks of this place, that won't work out as well. We're not even near any cities."

"But we are in the middle of nowhere, and you can call for rain and extinguish the fires. Or at least try to. If that fails—"

"It won't. I've got this."

Sidelle strides a few steps away from us and raises her arms. She stops and calls to Vash, "The pilot?"

"He's fine," Vash answers.

A slight breeze picks at her black hair, but nothing as forceful as the gusts of wind in the south. Clouds increase over the blue sky. Darkness blankets the lands, and it hides the sun's rays and mixes with the fires' smoke. Her body glows bright green with enough glamour to force rain to be squeezed from the clouds. It pitters down, caressing the ground. Hissing and popping sounds are heard around us as the coolness of the water hits the raging fires.

Smoke billows as the heat dies.

The prairie grasses are saved; it's not a total loss.

The rains continue to fall, but Sidelle's glow is growing dim. She's tiring, using all her reserves. Her footing falters and her arms lower. She's swaying. Kieran catches her body as she collapses into his waiting arms.

Our vehicle finally makes its way toward us, and Vash and I pile into the front, as Kieran gently lays Sidelle across his lap in the back. I glimpse behind me and watch him stroke her hair. Our eyes meet, but neither of us says anything.

Turning back to Vash, I ask, "Where next?"

"We need to see how far the rains went and to make sure the cities are safe."

Vash turns the ignition switch, and we drive down the two-lane highway toward Wichita. All around us I notice that the ground, crops, and grass smoke. Heavy, soaking rain saturates into the land. During the hour-long drive to the city, it continues to pour.

Maybe this is our second lucky break.

19

Shay

We make our way southbound along County Road Fifty, turn left onto Inter-state 135, and head into Wichita proper. The most logical place to stop and regroup is the Botanical Gardens on the west side of the city. It should be private enough from human eyes. Plus, the radio station we listened to on the way said that the city is in lockdown due to the excessive heat advisory.

As we pull into the parking lot of the gardens, Vash secures a map, and we head into the Shakespeare Garden. Teak benches surround a beautiful, two-tiered limestone fountain. Hawthorn trees line the perimeter. Wild flowers fill in between stone paths.

We pass under a large trellis on our way.

It's magical, and I would hate to see this place burn.

The heat has risen, and the winds have picked up. It's not raining here, but the char smell lingers in the air.

"How bad is Europe?" I peel off my black jacket and use the bottom of my T-shirt to wipe my face. "Vegas was really hot and thinking back on it, unnaturally so. I should have known something was wrong. But I was too anxious to get back to Minnesota."

"It's the same as here," Sidelle says. "Strange weather. High temperatures, lots of rainfall." She pinches one of the yellow daisies from its stem and plucks the pedals, watching them fall in the breeze. "Why did you go to Las Vega, anyway?"

"I was looking for someone."

"Did you find them?" Kieran asks.

"Yes, and some trouble along the way," Vash confirms.

"I was looking for an old friend who owed me a favor. Oriana is a Knight who I've crossed paths with before, and I helped her out of a jam. She hears a lot of stories from the demons that pass through the city. When they relax or are drunk, they get loose lipped and they talk. So, I knew that she would probably know who and maybe even where Zoe is being held."

"We found the demon at the Purple Zebra," Vash says. "And convinced her to leave her gambling habit for a few minutes to talk with us outside. Some Knights found us in the alley and wanted to make a name for themselves by taking out an Alpha."

"But we wiped the floor with them, eventually," I say. "Oriana said that someone kidnapped a girl and is keeping her in a vocivus room."

"Really?" Kieran asks. "She's said vocivus?"

"Yes, why?"

"Because Michael said that only angels can create them."

"What are they?" Sidelle asks.

"They're special rooms placed within the Void." Kieran paces to one of the benches and sits, shoulders slumped. "The space moves from Level to Level, so they are hard to track. Only the creator knows exactly where it is and can bring anything into the room or can exclude any item. Powerful Light can be used to bring items in, if it's not already in the room. The only way out is if the creator lets them go."

"Well, we know that Zoe is being kept in that type of room by Aiden," I say. "Now, we have to find out where and if there's a way of breaking her out."

"Yes, and we need to continue helping the Ordinaries with this mess. The angels are doing all they can, but once a soul dies, they cannot bring them back. Massive amounts of souls are making their way into the Heavens lately."

"What about my people?" Sidelle suggests. "If we can get my father to open a porta, Summer will help. I know they will. They can take care of the rains to dowse the fires, and maybe my father can stop the downpour that's causing the flooding."

"Let's try it." Kieran slaps his hands against the bench and stands. "It's all we've got for now. Sidelle, go see your father and get as many fairies as he can spare. I know you probably don't want to, but you may need to contact Finn, too, and get help from Winter."

"I'll go see my father first, and if I cross paths with Finn, I'll update him. I haven't seen him since the battle in Winter." A green shimmer envelopes her body and she disappears.

"All right, what else do we have?" Kieran asks. "Shay, why don't you get some rest? We'll hang out here for a while and see if Sidelle comes back. You look horrible, and you'll need your strength when we rescue Zoe." He claps me on my back. "There's going to be an upcoming battle if the weather keeps up like this. The next phase will probably see animals dying in mass numbers like on the beaches of Italy."

"Yeah, okay. I'll see if she's sleeping and can Dream Walk to me." I lie on one of the benches and close my eyes. My mind fights me, but eventually my body relaxes and I'm asleep.

I find myself standing on a beach, like the last time. No footprints mark the pristine sand. "Zoe?" I call out to her, in case she can hear me. The gentle waves lap against the shore as the bright sun warms my face. "I'm here, waiting for you." It's relaxing, and I wish I could stay here forever.

I'm mentally and physically stretched to the limits. It's been almost a month since I've held Zoe in my arms, and we're no closer to finding her. She's going to turn eighteen in a couple of weeks, and I won't even be able to be with her on her special day. It's not fair.

I'm pouting like a petulant child. I can be selfish for this minute. No one is around and seeing me fail. I can have this moment. My strength is waning.

God, I miss her.

"Zoe, I need to see you. Please come visit me in my dreams."

Today, I have my wings out. They twitch as if someone is watching me. I turn around, but no one is there.

Millions of tiny sparkles light and merge together, forming an orb. As the circle solidifies, a shape appears. A girl with long, brown hair emerges. She's wearing yoga pants and a purple T-shirt. Her smile breathes fire into my body. Her athletic build is running across the sand towards me. "Shay!" the person yells.

I know that voice instantly as her body solidifies. "Zoe!" I lift my body with my wings and gather her into my arms. "I'm so happy to see you." My wings wrap around us like a protective bubble. I kiss her feverously, not allowing her to talk.

Finally, we break apart.

"Shay, I've missed you so much." She places her head on my shoulder. "Tell me everything. But first, what day is it?"

"It's Friday, June 7."

"My birthday is in two weeks. My phone died probably four weeks ago. Tell me something good." She leans up and gives me a soft kiss on my cheek.

"I love you." My hand wraps about her waist and refuses to let go. I pull her down to the sand, never breaking contact. I proceed to tell her everything that is happening on earth. I describe the natural disasters, and what we're doing about it. About all the souls that have died. And what Kieran thinks will still happen. I end the story with Sidelle's trip back to Fairyland to enlist the help from Summer.

"Aiden lets me see where you guys are at and what you're doing through a special mirror," Zoe says. "There's been sound on and off. My heart broke the day I saw all these colored orbs release into the Heavens, the day of the flooding. I guessed what they were, and now you've confirmed it." Her eyes tear. "With everything that is going on, you guys haven't had time to look for me."

"No, we haven't. Zoe, I'm sorry. We're all doing what we can. When I was in Vegas, someone corroborated that you are being held in a vocivus room. And we think that Aiden created it especially for you. Only he can let you out, so it doesn't matter if we know where you are, we can't break you out of it." I hang my head.

"It's okay, Shay. I know that all of you guys are doing

everything to find me and help the humans. They need it more than me. I'm not dying in that room." Zoe bumps my shoulder. "Well, maybe a teensy tiny bit from boredom, but I'll survive. There are people out there around the world who are not that lucky."

"You're amazing, you know that, right?" I kiss the top of her head.

"Have you guys figured out what Aiden is?"

"Kieran said that Michael confirmed that only angels can create vocivus rooms. But I tend to disagree with him. I know he was the one who tortured me, and the place had to be somewhere in Hell. So, unless there are angels in Hell ..."

"He's a demon."

"How do you know?"

"Because he told me. I guessed, and he didn't deny it. He said he's tortured beings for a very long time. Plus, he kidnapped me. No angel would do those things, right?"

"Not any that I know of. But the person I met in Vegas, she's a Knight ... well, she isn't all bad to the core. She's helped me out of a few jams in my life." I watch as Zoe's lips flatten. She's mad but won't contradict me. "Look, whatever Aiden is, it's up to you to get him to release you. You're going to have to figure out his plan and get ahead of it."

"I know. I'm realizing that, too." She sighs. "He's not all bad. I don't think. If he was, why does he visit me? He asks me a lot of questions about me growing up, my future, and the way I see the world. If he wants to kill me, he would have done it already."

"No, he wouldn't. He needs you to be eighteen, so he can see your wings or your Heaven's Mark. He won't do anything until then." We both contemplate that and look out toward the blue water. "We still have time. But Zoe, you need to get him talking. If he's chatting you up, he's doing it for a reason. You need do the same. Maybe he'll slip, and you can get yourself out. You'll be coming into your powers soon." I squeeze her hand. "I wish I was there for you to help you. I know Kieran wishes that, too."

"It's enough that I know you both are thinking of me. But okay, I'll get Aiden to open up to me. Somehow."

"Good. Now, let me hold you until you have to go."

Since it's my dream, I think of the sun setting. Bright oranges, reds, blues, and purples canvas the sky. The full moon shines on the opposite side while the sun sets. Twinkling stars dot the horizon.

The waves lapping the shore are the only sound besides our breathing, which is in sync with each other. The sun finally sets, and the ocean stills, leaving only the beating of our hearts.

20
Zoe

I need a distraction from Aiden and my thoughts about him. The screen pulses, waiting for me to view it. The scene shows me a sleeping Shay on a teak bench. I know he was just with me in a Dream Walk. He's been mumbling ever since the dream ended. His body has been moving on autopilot.

Everyone seems to be waiting for something to happen. Vash is pacing, and Kieran stands perfectly still.

"Hey, Vash." Kieran nods. "How do you think Shay is handling this?"

Yes, sound!

"Better than I would be." He's sitting on the fountain ledge, running water over his fingers.

"I can't say if I would be or not. I've never known love

like what they have."

Oh, K. What Shay and I have goes beyond what normal people have. But what you and I have will always hold a special place in my heart. You've been, and forever will be, my best friend.

"You'll find it someday, Kieran." Vash pats his should. "It's whoever you're meant to be with. I know you love Zoe, and you thought you were in love with her at some point. But you'll know when it happens. The earth will literally move and tilt on its axis. Your heart will pound every single time you see her. Your mouth will spew incoherent words when you're around her. Mushy thoughts will consume you. And they'll be what you think about when you wake, right before you go to sleep, and everything in between."

"That sounds wonderful." He closes his eyes.

"It is."

Kieran is thinking about something or someone. I hope it's the latter. Maybe something will go beyond friendship with Sidelle. They're both Eternals. But she still has Finn whom she keeps at arm's length.

"Kieran," Vash says. "You have a huge heart and generous soul. And we all love you for it. Someday, hopefully soon, you'll find what Shay and I have. It'll come. I know it will. You, of all angels, should know that."

"Maybe I'm destined to be alone."

"You're never truly alone though, are you?"

"No. I guess not."

"You are closer to Him than any of us are or will be. Find comfort that He knows best."

"Thanks."

Neither of them say anything for a long time.

A blue light floods the area, coming from the trellis. A mirror-like surface covers the inner circumference and out steps the Winter Queen. She's dressed in a tight fitting blue gown that flares out near the bottom. Her black hair is swept into an intricate up-do. A sneer mars her beautiful face. A step behind her is King Oberon. He's regal in his green robes.

Oh, so that's whom they've been waiting for. The Fae Royals. Are they offering help?

"I hear that you need our help," Queen Mab says. Yes, do they ever. "Revenge is a dish that I'll be serving as the appetizer, for the main meal, and dessert. I'll obliviate the earth of its demons," the queen continues.

"Calm down, Mab," Oberon says as he tries to lay a hand on her icy shoulder.

"Do not tell me to calm down, Oberon. You didn't have hundreds of your subjects' lives extinguished from your realm. Did you?"

"No, I didn't. And I'm sorry I wasn't there to assist sooner. Like I've told you before, if you would have made the distress call sooner, Summer could have helped."

Fury rocks the queen's expression.

"We sent word to my father as soon it was possible," Sidelle says as she steps through the porta. "It's not his fault."

"Don't you dare speak to me like that," the queen hisses.

"Sidelle is my daughter and while I'm here, you will address her in kind." Oberon scowls at the queen.

"Thank you for both coming to earth's aide," Kieran say. "Has Sidelle filled you in on the goings on?" He addresses each royal. They both nod. "Good, I don't have to tell you what's at stake here. Besides all the human souls departing, if things continue to unfold, there will be no earth left, and Sammael will breach into Fairyland and do the same to yours."

"What do you need me to do?" Oberon asks.

"We need to stop the rain that's causing the flooding and landslides. Sidelle managed to address the wildfires that have been burning across the Midwest."

"The souls we cannot replace," Oberon says. "But we can restore the earth as it was before the devastation. I will do all I can."

"What do you need me to do?" Mab asks.

"The volcanoes need to be silenced," Vash says. "And any demon you run across can be killed."

"Ah, the new Alpha. Vash is it?"

"Yes."

"Very well. At least you and I are on the same page. I'll do what I can for the earth, too."

The earth suddenly shakes. Vash loses his footing on the ground. Shay rolls off the bench, now wide awake.

"What's happening?" Shay asks.

"Earthquake," Oberon says. "We have these in Fairyland. It's never a good sign. The earth is fighting back the only way it knows how. With the excessive water and everything burning, the land can't sustain itself. It's trying to reset, but by doing that that all the crops will be destroyed. Worldwide famine will take hold. Not only in the third-world countries, but in your own backyard." He stretches his arms wide. A deep, emerald green, swirled with browns and tan, surrounds him. His baritone voice chants an old-world language. He opens his eyes, but they are not his own chocolate coloring. Instead, they are solid white.

The ground continues to shake; decorative stone walls crumble as trees topple over. The limestone fountain begins to crack. Water seeps through, drenching his feet. A shock wave is emitted from the King of Summer. His eyes flash open, returning to normal.

"The evil runs deep to the earth's core," Oberon says. "There are many who work against us, and all is fixed for now. We shouldn't have any more quakes. A few small tremors, but nothing that will cause damage." He fixes Queen Mab with a stare. "We are needed to mend some of the wrongs done here, and we are needed in the far north."

"What did you see, Father?" Sidelle asks.

"The Marqs are on the move toward northern Canada. I didn't see their plan, so we should have enough time to stop the flooding rains here and find them."

"How far north?" Mab asks. "I can go there now and head them off."

"We can go, too," Kieran suggests.

"No. It's too dangerous. There are too many of them and not enough of us."

"This whole mission has been nothing but danger for us," Shay says. "It's what I was created for."

"I may need Mab's assistance," Oberon says. "My glamour is straining now because of the effort of stopping and shifting the fault lines back to the way they were. I won't know if I can handle it on my own or not. And if she goes, and I can't stop the evil here, she'll be called back. It's better to wait thirty minutes and we all go."

It's a good enough plan. I silently send prayers toward my friends. The TV screen fades to black.

21

Aiden

Thursday, June 15, forty-seven days after prom.

Those lucky protectors have managed to quell some of my efforts. And now they have called the royals from Fairyland to assist.

But it's no matter because in the human world, it's only weeks away from her eighteenth birthday. My wait is nearly over. She should come into her full powers, and we can get on with it.

There have been so many disasters around the world that even the Reperio Teams were pulled from their searches to assist. No one had the chance to find me, dig into my sister's or my history, or retrieve my prisoner from her locked room.

I watched as her four friends toured around the world

saving people from their deaths. It was glorious to witness so many souls die. And yes, some went to Heaven while others were met to face their equal in Hell.

My wings flutter. I'm anxious, and I haven't had this feeling in many years. If ever.

I can't stay away from her, but I know I must.

When her soft fingers touched my face, something passed between us. I saw it written in her eyes. Sympathy maybe? I know she feels something for me. It's pity. She wants to fix me, but there isn't anything wrong with me.

But her touch ...

My thoughts shouldn't be on her like that. I need to keep my wings on straight.

There is no messing around when it comes to my father. He will be released, and he'll unleash his power onto this world. Then conquer the next.

She's not my soul mate. I repeat the mantra in my mind as if I'll start believing it.

She's not my soul mate.

Zoe is not my soul mate.

No matter how many times I repeated it, wishing it weren't true, hoping it wasn't true, it is real.

These past few days with her ... something is changing in me. She evokes feelings that I haven't felt in eons. Feelings I never thought I'd feel again.

An inner battle rages in me. My head chants that I must

kill her to release my father from his prison, so he can come into his full power. But my wings keep telling me to release her and be damned with the consequences.

I can't.

I must.

Which part of me will win?

Still struggling with that inner battle, I find myself wandering back to Zoe's room. When had it become her room and not my room or the vocivus room?

I'm going soft. What will the other demons think of me? They'll know I'm weak and use it against me. Zoe will be used against me.

Oh, hells.

Somehow, my body has dragged me to stand behind the speculo. I had told Zoe that it worked like a one-way mirror and it does. I've stood here watching her go about her business for hours. Even in her sleep, I've spied on her.

How have I become a stalker?

She's felt my presence in the room, even though I've remained invisible. It made her feel uneasy and that bothered me. So I tinkered with the mirror to allow me to view her, but only when she's not watching the real world.

I'm pathetic.

I'm the Prince of Hell. A seventeen-year-old girl isn't

going to be my downfall.

From now on, it's going to be all business and that's it. No more being mister nice demon. No more chatting with her. And absolutely no spying.

I nod to myself and turn away, but my body won't take that step to desert her.

The speculo isn't turned on, and I'm drawn to it like my soul to Hell. I'll take a quick peek, and then I need to get an update from my minions. Yes, this is exactly what I need to do. Throw myself into work and forget about her.

When I gaze through the screen, Zoe is doodling on a small chalkboard. Tiny bits of chalk are scattered across the bed. Pink dusting is smeared along the side of her face, near the piece of hair she always plays with. I even notice that some of her hair is colored in spots. She must have wiped her face and forgot that she had chalk all over her hands.

I can't see what she's drawing, but from here they look pretty good. I could be biased, though.

Thinking back to all the times I snooped in her bedroom at her house while she was attending school, I don't recall seeing any hand drawn pictures. Maybe it's a new hobby or an old one she's picked back up again.

I watch her stretch like a cat, and she hunches back over her drawing. Without looking for a specific color, her hands fumble for chalk. She's deep in thought, and her fingers work feverously outlining and shading.

Now, my curiosity is peaked. I must see it.

"I didn't know you could draw. Do you want to be an artist after high school?" She doesn't look away from the chalkboard. I lean forward more, and my knees hit the bed. "It's nice. What's it supposed to be?" Just when I think she's not going to respond, her brown eyes lift from her bed and find mine.

"Thank you," she whispers. "It's not done yet because I don't have all the materials I would like to get the coloring correct, but I'm making due." She flips the board in my direction, so I can see it better.

For a chalk drawing on a twelve by twelve piece of board, it isn't too bad. Zoe's managed to draw a beautiful waterfall with flowers lining the cliff. The blue water dives into a dark green pool, swirling around a lagoon. Palm trees line the outer edge.

"Watch." She waves her hand across the picture and it comes alive. The leaves sway, and the water bubbles as it creates an eddy.

"That's amazing."

"Do you draw?" I continue to stare as the spinning colors. "Aiden?" Her voice pulls me out of the picture.

"No."

"Listen to music? Do you read? Go to movies?"

"What's with the twenty questions?" My voice is harsh,

more than it needs to be.

"I ... I need to talk with someone and you're here." She shrugs. "You don't have to answer anything. You can sit and watch." Grabbing a different chalk, she starts filling in the sunset. "I don't know how long it's been, but I'm craving companionship. I miss my friends. I miss talking to people. I know you're not a person, but you do talk. And I miss ... people."

Oh, Hells.

"I don't have time for indulgences like that." I soften my voice. She sniffles and wipes her nose with the back of her hand. "I have a job to do."

She better not cry in front of me. I see her inhale.

Oh, Hells.

Her shoulders slump and her head shakes.

She's going to cry.

She doesn't look at me, but fat tears drop onto her picture, smearing the colors. When she finally glances in my direction, her eyes are red and puffy. Tears line her cheeks.

She's finally broken.

"But all those movies and CDs in your room—"

"All for show."

"Everything in your room, too?"

"Yes."

"Oh." She moves off the bed and shuffles toward her

bathroom. "Was anything you said to me the truth?" Her hands hold the edges of the sink. "She's not your sister, is she?"

It's a statement, not a question.

Seeing her like this when I know how strong she is breaks me. "Everything you know about me is a lie." I close my eyes and inhale. "Sarah is not my sister in the conventional way."

"California?"

"I've been there but not to live."

"It's on my bucket list to go there."

I can't watch her lose it. I'm supposed to be a badass. I'm the Prince of Hell, I remind myself again. This soft stuff — these feelings — don't happen to someone like me.

Her head hangs low over the porcelain sink. She's grabbed a tissue and turns her body away from me. With one more glance her way, I'm done.

I leave her alone.

22
Zoe

Saturday, June 23, fifty-six days after prom.

Over the days or weeks, I honestly didn't know, but Aiden starts to visit me more frequently. At first, it's only once a day, but it soon progresses to twice. He arrives at every meal and watches me eat. He never consumes anything, but is curious at some of the dishes I have come up with. He's let me decide and conjure my own foods when I want to eat. After a few more days pass, he stays for hours at a time. I enjoy the time we spend together and really look forward to his visits.

Zoe, he's the enemy.

He has opened up more and talks about himself; most of it is pretty vague. He doesn't talk about his past life. I do most of the talking, which is fine with me. I steadily grow to like his silent company.

Weeks have quickly gone by. Neither Kieran, Shay, Sidelle, nor Vash have come to rescue me, and today is the day before my birthday. Tomorrow, I turn eighteen. How exciting. I'll officially be an adult. But then I remember where I am, held captive by Aiden, as if I could really forget. My joyous moment vanishes.

But now, I have a new mission.

Getting him to stay longer and talk about himself. Only I can do this. Build his trust and use it to get out of here.

Sunday, June 24, Zoe's eighteenth birthday.

The next time Aiden enters my room, I'm ready. The other day is totally forgotten. He happened to see me at my lowest but never again.

I'm stronger than that. He will not break me. Yes, I had a momentary lapse, but hey, I'm allowed to every now and then.

A crying woman is a downfall for most guys. If the waterworks didn't affect him, I'd have to think of something else.

Not everything I told him was a lie, though. I do miss people, and I worry about my friends and the world. He had to see me at my most vulnerable. He had to think that

169

he had finally broke me.

I didn't have to wait too long. It must have been only a couple of hours since I was already doing my cool down.

His sudden appearance doesn't startle me anymore. I've come to relish the soft tingling feeling that courses through me right before he arrives.

"Are you wishing for anything specific as a birthday gift?" Aiden asks when he appears. "Besides getting out of here."

"No, not really. I'm healthy and made it to my eighteenth birthday. Yes, I wish I could see my parents and friends, but at least I'm alive."

"No Seraph Sword on your list?"

"Nope." I shake my head.

"You know you'll either have to find one, or it'll come when you get your wings."

"I didn't know that. If I don't get one, how do I find one?"

"You'll know. Why is California on your bucket list?" He leans again the wall, arms crossed.

"I've never been." I shrug. "It's wine country."

"You're too young to drink."

"I know, but after I turn twenty-one, I want to experience it." I stop stretching and end my workout. "Plus, there's San Francisco and the trolley cars, San Diego Zoo, Disneyland, and Hollywood. There's so much to see and learn about historical events and places."

A silence weighs heavily in the room.

"California is what you got out of our last conversation?" I ask. "That's what you want to lead with now?"

"Yeah, about that ... I didn't mean to upset you. It's just that I'm not what you think I should be. I can't."

It's as close to an apology as I think I'm going to get from him for making me fake cry. "I'm not going to say that it's fine because it's not. Yesterday was a fluke, and it won't happen again."

Soft instrumental music plays in the background. After my meltdown earlier, I tried Conjuring a radio and an iPod. I even tried a record player, but nothing happened. On a whim, I thought of music playing through a speaker and it did. The idea came to me while in the makeshift bathroom. The longer I stared at the lack of pipes, the more my mind wandered to other possibilities.

"Your father isn't really your father, is he?" I ask. "He must not be very nice to you if he forces you to do things for him that you don't want to do."

"Who says I don't want to do them?"

"Do you? Do you enjoy doing all the tasks and being his lapdog?"

"It's not like that."

"Really? Because that's how I'm see it. If it's not that way, how is it exactly?"

"I don't see him all the time."

171

"Yeah, I remember you telling me that when we first met."

"What I mean is, that he's around, but not available to me."

"I don't understand."

"It's complicated. Think of it as a colossal conglomerate and he's the CEO, CFO, and the board members. He doesn't always have time for his employees."

"That's how you think of him? An employer? Well, there's part of the problem. He's your father. He loves you and wants to see you do good."

"No, he doesn't." His hands clench. "He's selfish and only wants one thing in the world."

"And that is?" I prompt.

"More power."

"He couldn't have always been that way. What about when you were a kid?"

I think back to my own childhood and the two loving parents I have. We had many wonderful times together at our cabin up north, they came to every recital I had, and we ate dinner as a family every night. He didn't have any of that from what I could tell.

"A very long time ago, he was giving and considerate until something happened and he changed," Aiden says. "I've only ever known how he is now."

"Maybe be does love you in a warped way."

"I doubt it."

"You don't need him. You should find people who will love you and accept you for who you are."

"It's easier said than done."

"Doesn't have to be. It's all up to you and what you choose to do. Who you surround yourself with. Who you want to become."

"No." Aiden shakes his head and leaves the room.

I sit on my bed and contemplate everything that Aiden has ever told me. It's all been a lie up until now. The person he lives with next door isn't really his sister. Maybe she's a friend. He made the analogy of his dad being a CEO of a business. Could it be that she's a co-worker?

And going along with the business idea. His father must be someone powerful and who craves even more power. He runs his so-called family like a dictatorship. Like the mob? And the word father could be interchanged for the boss, and all the workers are siblings.

Nephilims are independent, freelance loners.

Packs have each other but use Alphas as their leaders.

He's definitely not a fairy. And their terminology is a court system.

Leaving ...

Angels and Demons.

But which is he?

23
Shay

Sunday, June 7, thirty-nine days after prom.

I am suddenly ripped away from Zoe, sleep forgotten. My body lands hard on the paved ground. For a moment, everything is spinning in my mind. My friends are still there, and two newcomers are in our group.

Sidelle has returned from Fairyland, and she brought, who I assume was her father, and a woman. The King of Summer towers over everyone. His presence is foreboding. His dark brown eyes tell another story, one of sadness and love. His companion is swathed in old power.

She, the beautiful lady, stands regal, as if nothing could penetrate her cold exterior. Blue glamour radiates from her and seeps deep into my wings. Her features are stark. Anger hovers behind her raging blue eyes, and her stance screams danger. I can only presume that she is the Winter Queen.

And now we are traveling with them. I catch the end of Oberon's display of power. The blast that sunk into my soul will haunt me forever. He has fixed the earth of its sorrows.

Nephilims are created by both earth and Heaven. We straddle both lines of existence. I wonder if he feels what I felt. It's like hearing a mother's wail of a lost child and the years of mourning that follows.

The earth knows that Oberon is sending his magic to heal her. She thinks she is too far gone to be helped. But he insists and then she relents.

The king opens a porta, and we all walk through, back to the remote deserts of Las Vegas.

"Let's make this quick, so we can be on our way to Texas and go north," Oberon instructs. "Mab, please give me your hands." She hesitates but does as he requests.

They face each other and lock their palms together. Their powers meld. We step back and give them space, since we don't want to be blasted with the force of the healing glamour. Both chant in a foreign language. Hers is harsh with forced breaks. His is fluid and sing-songy.

In a matter of seconds, the cracked dessert floor folds back together. Small pools of water soak into the ground. The fierce winds cease to blow. Some of the cacti stand tall again.

And we're back stepping through another porta. Our party doesn't say anything. We watch in silence and let them work, so we can be done with this and head off the Marqs.

They do the same along the southern coast, pushing back the waves smashing against the shoreline. All the sea life that lay dead on the sand are gone. The royal powers dry the heavy rains and the dark clouds lift. Rays from the sun dot the buildings with hope.

Everything is as it was before.

Oberon opens another porta, and we step through it. The land is lush green, trees full of new leaves block the sun's light, and birds flutter in the sky. Evil has not marred this pristine land—yet. We stand in a field of tall grasses. Somewhere close is a stream or brook, but I've seen enough water to last me a while.

"Are you sure about this place?" I ask. "It doesn't appear that anything is wrong. The animals wouldn't be out in the open like this if there were. They usually know the first sign of trouble coming."

A herd of deer watch us with curious eyes. Their ears flicker, alert for any foreign sounds.

"They're here," Mab says. "I can feel them."

"So can I," Oberon agrees. "Be watchful and ready for anything."

An eerie tranquility crawls over the field. Mist weaves between the tall stalks of grass. The birds silence their songs of freedom. Leaping for safety, the deer leave us alone with our thoughts. The wind stills.

The temperature plummets. Frost forms along the boughs. And the mist rises, blanketing us in gray.

Dark figures emerge from the ground. It's like zombies rising from the dead. I guess in a way they truly are. Demons were something before they became the evil beings they are now.

Shadows hide their flowing bodies. With their hoods drawn up, I can't see their black holes where their eyes should be. They hover above the ground, encircling us.

"We meet again," a Knight shouts. A small group crouches in the distance. "We were wondering when our paths would cross."

"Your fate was sealed when you marched into my territory and slaughtered my subjects," Mab screams back.

"Oh, was that your land? We heard about that incident. Too bad I wasn't there to witness all that death."

"Don't worry. I saved my strength for you and your kind." Mab stalks forward a few steps. "None of you will be leaving this field. And your Marq friends will never return."

She raises her arms high into the air as blue glamour shoots out from her palms, flying directly into the awaiting

Knights.

They scatter like gnats and charge us.

We spread out, so we don't accidentally hit each other.

Kieran is on my left and Sidelle to my right. Vash instantly changes into his wolf form and charges into a group of Marqs.

Oberon fires his green magic from behind me and barely misses my head. I shoot a glare in his direction. He ignores me.

Mab, who is positioned in front of us, throws a flurry of three-inch long ice daggers. They zip as fast as an arrow and find their marks. A few Knights fall but more advance from the tree line.

The ground shifts. The rest of us use our wings and hover. Vash is the only one who is grounded, but he's light on his paws and easily maneuvers on the uneven terrain.

An orb encases Oberon, pulsing to the motion of his hands. With fire raging behind his eyes, his power is gathering. The circle grows larger and larger with each beat.

I step out of his boundary. I have no idea what he's about to unleash.

Sidelle uproots trees, swinging them behind the Knights and catching a few off guard. She looks to her father and nods. Mimicking his stance, she, too, creates a sphere around her. And as her magic gathers and pulses, it

178

matches Oberon's.

Kieran spins high into the sky and pours his Light onto the field. Bright light cuts through the mist.

Marqs close the distance between us, leaving Vash to battle them.

"Kieran," I shout. "Clear a path for me through the Marqs, so I can get to the other side and help Vash."

A stream of golden Light flares and shines on the outer edge of the forest. With my Nephilim Sword extended, I forge my way through, cutting and slicing anything in my path until a Marq stops me. It smashes its arm across my chest, sending me flying backwards.

Two more advance on me. I won't be able to break their defenses. But I'm not going down without a fight. With renewed strength, I swing my sword to the demon on the right. Using my legs, I kick the other back. But my leg goes right through its body, throwing me off balance. I tumble onto my knees. Before I can spring back to my feet, a forcefield goes through me.

Turning my head, Oberon and Sidelle have unleashed their combined power. My chest aches slightly, but that's nothing compared to how the field looks now. All three fairies are standing in a crater the size of a couple of football fields. The ground is partially frozen, and the other part is dead brown.

The remaining Knights are clutching their own chests

and dropping one by one.

I shake my head, clearing my daze and sprint towards Vash. His breathing is labored, and a red gash oozes blood on his shoulder. One of his ears is bent at an odd angle.

"You okay?" I ask him.

He nods.

"Man, what was that? I think someone trampled my sternum." I place a hand over my heart. "We can't rest too long; there are still Marqs all over the field. But at least whatever the fairies did, it wiped out the Knights. You go, and I'll take care of their bodies."

Vash nods and sprints back into the fray.

I check each Knight to make sure they are good and dead by slicing my blade across their necks. Within a matter of seconds, their bodies evaporate and return to Hell.

When no more Knights litter the ground, I also return to the battle against the Marqs.

Light blasts from all directions in a swirl of green, gold and blue. Vash's brown form darts in between the Marqs and takes down as many as he can. His enormous paws swipe at their black cloaks. Black demon blood drips from his claws and lands on the grass. Vash's coat is drenched in red and black swirls.

The ice queen is encased in a blue sphere and continues to volley ice spears at the Marqs. Blue sparkling lights outlines their flowing capes. Old magic gnaws at them, dissolving tiny patches of them. With enough magic, her targets begin to fade.

King Oberon uses the same tactic, but with his combined energy and that of his daughter's, they crush their victims faster.

Kieran still hovers above, shining his Light into clusters, and Vash takes them down, one by one.

By the time I'm across the field, the battle is over.

24

Zoe

Wednesday, June 24, thirty-nine days after prom.

"Happy eighteenth birthday, Zoe," Aiden says as he enters the room. He smiles as if it is his birthday and not mine. If all goes well today, I will get my wings and the completion of the tattoo at the exact time I was born.

"Nothing happy about it, Aiden," I state. "I'm still here as your prisoner. I could think of so many places I'd rather be than here with you. Where am I anyway? You can finally tell me, you know. It's not like I can tell anyone where I am. I haven't been rescued since you brought me here."

"Ah now, Zoe, don't be like that. I have been a gracious host to you. And today, I am feeling extra generous. After all, it is your birthday." He raises his arms and sweeps them in an arch over by the wall opposite the door. Instantly, a window appears. I'm afraid to look out of it. I don't want to see any more of Hell than I need to. But when I glance out of the window, it's a picture of the ocean.

"The same rules apply to the window as the mirror. Think of the landscape you wish to view, and it will appear." He smiles.

Wow. Aiden very rarely smiles. I guess he doesn't have much to smile about. He does work for Satan, after all. That's what I've deduced. If he weren't out to kill me, I would think Aiden was an extremely good-looking guy.

It must be close to twenty-six minutes after three in the afternoon, the exact time I was born. My body feels weird; it tingles, as if it has fallen asleep. A gut-wrenching pain shoots through my body, forcing me to the cold floor. I curl into a ball and whimper, praying to God to let the pain subside or hurry up the process in giving me my wings.

Aiden stands in the corner and watches, not saying anything. I bet he has never witnessed anyone getting their Mark, wings, or becoming a seraph angel.

How could he? I am the first born of earth and Heaven.

My body trembles as sweat pours from every pore on my skin. My right arm throbs with shooting pain from my shoulder down to my wrist. I'm not sure how long I lie on the floor. My bones ache like I had the flu for weeks. After what seems like an eternity has passed, I peel open my eyes and look at my right wrist. There on the inside, iridescent purple wings surround my existing silver Triquetra symbol with a golden sword down the center.

I stand on trembling legs. When I look down at myself, I am no longer in jeans and a T-shirt, but in a simple white shift dress with purple ribbons tied around my waist that crisscross over my back. I turn my head to look over my shoulder ... yes, I have sprouted wings.

They are bright white with flecks and streaks of purple throughout. I have seen Kieran's and Shay's wings on several occasions, but mine are larger than theirs. Even folded, they extend above my head, and the points touch the floor.

I think about them moving, and suddenly they do. I think of the word "expand," and they obey my command and unfurl to their full length. I am totally enamored with them. They are so beautiful.

I thought that when I received my wings, they would be heavy and cumbersome, but they aren't. In fact, they're light as a feather. I giggle at my own pun. I move my hands and arms out in front of me, turning them over and inspecting them. A soft white glow emits from them. I hike up the dress to view my legs, and I remember I'm not alone in the room.

Aiden.

He stands so quietly watching, waiting. I see him even

more clearly than before. He is beautiful with his dark blond hair and brilliant, mysterious aqua eyes. Even this far away, I can clearly see light blond streaks in his hair. I haven't ever noticed the small dimple on his face, until now. He is smiling; he rarely smiles. He needs to smile more. I like it when he does.

Where did that thought come from?

Tiny dust motes float in the air. The stagnant air smells of death. Has he used this room to kill others in? My heart sinks at the gross though.

He stands, staring at me.

When our eyes lock, he nods approvingly. His shirt disappears and out snaps his magnificent wings. They are as large as my own, black with speckles of blood red feathers throughout, and on the very tips are a smattering of white ones.

He stalks forward, stopping short of me; his eyes are wide and still locked on mine. His mouth is open, probably in awe. The black feathers are iridescent, like a prism of every color. His wings are glorious like mine. His body also radiates the same bright, soft white glow.

This close, he looms over me. My eyes move up to his bare chest, momentarily distracted by his wings.

Oh, boy.

He is toned and sports defined abs. He has beautifully sculpted long arms and lean legs. I never really noticed, nor appreciated, him before. I was too stuck on him wanting to kill me.

The glint of something in his eyes says otherwise.

I look back at his wings, curious about why they're that color. I look back to my own, compare my white feathers with his white feathers. They are the same. I wonder if he still has some good left in him. He's had many opportunities to kill me, when he first took me and every day since. He hasn't.

Why?

I feel my body being drawn toward Aiden and his wings. I extend my hand to him. I want him to close the distance between us. He stands perfectly still. Minutes go by, or maybe it's only a few seconds, but he doesn't move.

Finally, when I determine he isn't going to make the effort, I lower my hand but his wings twitch. One of them moves forward and meets my hand.

I knew what it took for him to make that small action. I don't know firsthand what it feels like when someone touches my wings, only the account Shay told me. It's like someone touching a part of your soul.

Does Aiden still have a soul?

As soon as my fingers touch them, I see flashes of images. Confused as to what I'm seeing, they are coming at me too fast: white wings, someone falling, black wings, and ... and then, nothing.

Blackness.

Aiden starts to retreat from me. His wings snap close and disappear into his back. He's about to take a step backwards, but I quickly move my hand from where his wings were to inches away from his face. I'm not sure if I should touch him. I don't know how he's going to react. He probably hasn't had anyone touch him like this in years, maybe even centuries.

My hand lingers, silently asking permission. I know this is a very intimate situation, and he needs to make the next move. He steps back, his eyes still locked onto mine.

His expression changes, softens. He steps forward, lowers his head, and closes the distance between my hand and his face. As soon as we touch, the room is filled with Light, and a very intense shock courses through our bodies. It's so forceful we both fall to our knees. My hand drops from his face. Our eyes are frozen with shock.

I know I wasn't meant to see his thoughts. Nor do I know what this could mean. I've only ever felt anything like this before, and that was with Shay.

"Aiden," I whisper.

Immediately, he's jolted out of his momentary shock when I say his name. He quickly rises and turns his back to me. He's withdrawing. Again.

No! I must know ... I must touch him again.

"Aiden," I shout at his back.

He turns his head to look at me.

My eyes plead with his. I mentally think, "Come back. Don't leave me here alone. Help me sort this out. I'm scared." I add, "Please."

I have no idea if I can project thoughts to him or if he can even hear me. He turns away but doesn't advance any farther.

"Aiden. Can you hear me? If you can, I beg you to say something. Anything."

"Yes."

His response is so quiet I almost miss it. I would have if there were any other sounds in the room besides our breathing. He fists his hands at his sides and spins back toward me. His eyes are lowered to the floor when he approaches. He stands close to me, too close. His body heat warms me. I reach my hand to touch him. He towers over me, forcing me to look up at him; he stares at my extended hand. He places his hand into mine. The same jolt rocks our bodies and leaves me panting.

He flashes out of the room.

"Aiden ... do you know what it means?" I yell.

"Yes," he mentally responds.

Great. We can mentally speak to each other, and now I am certain that we are soul mates. Shay and I had the same shock thing happen to us when we touch, and Kieran said it's a sign of being soul mates.

How in the world could Aiden be my soul mate if I am an angel of Heaven, and he's a something of Hell? My hands shake at the thought. Maybe because I am a Seraph, the mind speaking was part my abilities, and I could mentally speak to everyone? Maybe it isn't something only between Aiden and me. I've never tried speaking to my best friend with only my mind.

I wonder what other abilities I will have. I already figured out I have enhanced vision. My body doesn't feel any different than before, but there is no way to test any other theories, being locked in this room.

A bazillion questions flitter around in my mind.

But at least now I have a window.

Happy birthday, Zoe.

25
Aiden

Oh, hells!

How can I be a Soul Match to Zoe? She already has one with that Nephilim. There's been no case in the history of angels, or demons, to have two matches in the same lifetime. Or has there?

I must find out more information about Soul Matches. I can't be hers. As the Prince of Hell, there is no one for me. I'd have to betray my own kind. Could I do that again?

I disappear into the lower realms of Hell. A coincidence it's the same level as the torture chambers that held the Nephilim. When demons run out of ways to inflict torture, there are always the old scrolls to help inspire new ones.

It's a small library of sorts. What demon takes time to read? I do. There is knowledge that comes from the scrolls and books. I can't just use my surveillance information.

I hope to find what I need here because the Angel Archive will not let me in. I burned that bridge a long time ago since my Fallen Days. Perhaps Quinn can get me something.

I take a few scrolls at a time and toss a couple of potential books onto the small table. The demon magic in this room prohibits me from removing any items. Although I wish I could take them and be more comfortable in my chambers, it's a rule of my father, and he's the one who can set the boundaries around the room. I cannot break them.

A small light is conjured into the lamps and sconces around the table and room. Then I set to work.

Hours pass and I'm about to call it quits for the time being, but one of the last scrolls on the shelf beckon to me. Carefully lifting and unrolling the ancient parchment paper, I gloss over the tiny, black markings. This one is by far the oldest I've ever come across. It's one taken from Heaven, and somehow, it's made its home in Hell.

I sit back down at the table and conjure more Fire Light so I can make out the letters and symbols. It's old language and will need to be translated. I don't think I've ever read this dialect before. And of course, I can't ask my father.

Leaving the scroll on the table, I stand and skim the dictionaries and reference books. Grabbing one of the oldest looking ones, I return to my working area. I begin flipping and reading various pages since there isn't an index. In the later third of the book, I stop on a page that has a similar marking to that on the scroll. I compare each, but it's not quite the same. I'm getting closer. My wings feel it.

Turning the page, I find an exact match. I look at each marking in the book and gently take the scroll and match the symbols. It's a shortened alphabet, based more on sounds and images. I conjure an ink quill and paper to translate each mark. It's painstaking to do each one, but finally I reach the end of the scroll.

From what I can decipher, a Soul Match happens when angel Light aligns to another soul. It recognizes that the being is their equal in all ways. Equal could mean genetically, like twin siblings—that has never happened before. I've never heard of any two angels, demons, or Nephilim who have an identical. I suspect that it could be more likely with the Nephilim since they are part human, and having twins or multiple births is more common for them.

Soul Matches are also non-genetic, too. Light is attracted to like and profound characteristics: a deep-rooted love, generosity that knows no bounds, or spirits willing to take the ultimate sacrifice.

To date, there are no known cases of two Soul Matches

to the same angel, demon, or Nephilim.

When a Soul Match is found, electrical current courses through each beings' body when contact is made with each other. The more connection of the outer shell, the more intense the current will be.

Side effects: reading each other's thoughts, becoming in tune with them—physical and mental whereabouts, and/or manifestation of the same Angel Light or Fire Light. On extremely rare occasions, the transfer of information and knowledge can occur where part of the Soul attaches to the other.

There are no known reversal treatments once the Soul attaches. Also, there are no known reversals to slice the Soul Match.

Nothing is said about bonds occurring between species.

Oh, hells no.

26
Zoe

I don't waste any time devising an escape plan. I realize that my friends will never find and rescue me. I must do that on my own.

Some birthday I'm having. The rest of my Heaven's Mark appeared, and something weird is happening between Aiden and me. Plus, I got wings.

Freaking wings!

They are gorgeous, an iridescent purple and white. I can't store them away. They flutter around me as I sit on my bed.

Up until today, I felt my powers getting stronger. It was the only way I knew the date of my birth was coming.

I've been held prisoner for almost seven weeks.

Aiden. There must be something I can use. We are

connected. I don't know how or why. I still my thoughts, only thinking of him. We could be siblings, or maybe we were created from the same angel.

What has changed in Aiden these past weeks? Why now allow me to touch him? He must have known this was going to happen. Did he give me a loophole to escape? Is he helping me?

So many questions and no answers fill my mind.

I stop pondering and use his absence to work the room. My Light surges throughout my body, ready for release. Every particle of myself is made of up angelic power.

With my wings extended out and on the ready for anything, I pace the room, touching the bed, couch, and chair. Eventually, I want to brush my hand against the windowsill. I hesitate in front of where the invisible shield is. My fingers creep toward the glass. My hand is engulfed with purple Light and goes straight through the barrier. I'm touching the window.

"Yes."

I peer out to view the scenery. It's aqua-blue water surrounded by white, sandy beaches. Birds of all sizes soar in the air and speckle the sky as far as I can see. Dolphins play in the ocean. Occasionally, one jumps and splashes down. The scene changes. I'm pouring everything into creating a dense forest and then a vast mountain range.

A smile forms on my lips.

I pace the rest of the room toward the mirror, my Light

still pulsing through my body. I press it against the clear wall and it shatters at my touch. With my hand extended out, I sweep the air like I'm feeling for hidden objects, making sure that nothing else is concealed to me. The only thing I can't break are the four exterior walls; they remain solid under my palms.

I take one last look around the room. I know this is the last that I'll see it. My head turns back to the window; the view has not changed.

This is insane.

But I won't stay here any longer. If this fails, then I'll think of a Plan B. For now, this is all I have.

Running toward the window, my wings extend out. Light consumes the room. It hums just under my skin. I make the final leap and crash through the glass. Like the mirror, you had told me. Liar.

I freefall to the ground but quickly remember that I have wings. They carry me up on the winds, and I soar through the air. I'm sure I'm a something to see. A human body flailing about crookedly flying through the sky. I sink, spin, and tumble all the while trying to get myself righted and soaring straight.

My wings pump up and down and bring me higher. My back is already sore, but I fight through the fatigue. I look back and see a long island with two orange towers sitting on one end and a bridge connecting them. The open window I flew out of is in the exact middle of the bridge, the only dark spot on the building. It reminds me of someplace I've only seen in commercials.

I disregard it because I know it's not real. It's a place I once saw and thought of in my mind.

My body passes through an unseen forcefield, my vision is gray for a couple of seconds, and I see everything from a bird's eye view.

Mountains line the sky to my right. My geography is limited, and I could be anywhere in the world. No snow is seen on the ground, except on the mountain tops. Europe has the Alps. I recall that Asia has the most ranges, the Andes in South America, Alaskan Range, and the Appalachian Mountains in the continental US. My mind flips through countries like a rolodex. Why hadn't I paid more attention in class?

I fly lower to the ground, but not enough for humans to recognize a person with wings flying in the sky. With one thought, my body becomes invisible, and I decide to risk zooming toward the ground in hopes to find something familiar.

Using a circular pattern, I spiral outward, but nothing pops or nudges my memory until a landmark that is one of the wonders of the world comes into my view on the left: the deep valleys of the Grand Canyon. That would mean that the mountains to my right are the Rockies.

Now that I kinda know where I am, my mind recollects that Arizona would be to the southwest, New Mexico to the southeast, and Utah and Colorado to the north. Which would mean I'm close to Four Corners.

A narrow river winds through the countryside and flows westward. Is that the San Juan River that joins the Colorado River? I follow the twists and turns until four tiny rows of buildings come into view. It looks like a bull's eye inside a square. As I get closer, five spikes rise, each spear waving colored material. I spot the U.S. flag immediately, the red and white strips dancing on the breeze, and fifty white stars against the blue background blink as if to say "hi." I land in the middle of the four flags.

I wish I could tell you I landed gracefully, since I'm an angel. I can't. I tumble onto the hard ground, trying to roll to lessen the impact. My face flattens. That's going to leave a mark.

On the ground is a three-foot cement disk, and in its center is a smaller one. Four state seals with their state name mark the center of each corner. Red benches line each pie shape. A couple dozen Ordinaries mill around, taking pictures of each symbol as they wait their turn to straddle the very center circle, so they can say that they've been in four states at one time.

It's a good thing I'm still invisible.

With one more passing glance, I take back to the sky and head northeast to Minnesota.

27

Aiden

"AI-DEN!"

I cringe when my name is bellowed. The directive bounces between all levels of Hell. There is no hiding. My father is summoning me. Why am I the second in command when Sammael and I have the same angel rank?

If only the king would stay locked away in his cage forever. I've been dreading this day; his release. Things have been pretty good thus far. The Knights are creating havoc in the Ordinaries' world, natural disasters are in abundance thanks to the Marquises demons, and my plan is being executed nicely. I'm assured that Father is going to mess up my plans now that he's free to roam the levels of Hell.

I should check on him though, in case there was a

malfunction to the prison's door. I can only hope. The Archangels locked dear old Dad in a cage since the Fall, but that doesn't mean that his powers were sealed. The Seraph Angels weren't strong enough to strip him of his Light. He said that he managed to draw some of their Light with him when he got locked up, which is why they can't come to earth or even roam between the Levels. Yes, the King of Hell can still do quite a bit of damage. And I do not need that additional heat raining down on me.

If there's a God, my father will still be imprisoned.

I chuckle at my own joke.

I vanish from the library and reappear in Hell's throne room, where my father is shockingly not seated. I must make sure, though. Using Fire Light, I send it across the large, dark room inspecting every crevice for the king.

Could it be?

The black throne sits empty. The room is cold, even though Hell's Fire flickers against the tall obsidian pillars that line the outer edge of the room. The king's stone chair sits atop a dais. A thick layer of dust is undisturbed. The rot of death lingers in the stale air.

"Aiden. I know you hear me." The voice booms as the Fire Light's flames rise. "Do not make me wait. I gave you a command."

"I am in the throne room, awaiting your orders."

"I'm not there."

That only leaves one other place where he'd be. Shaking

my head, I disappear and reappear outside the door of my father's private chambers. I pull out the large silver key that hangs around my neck, the only one of its kind, given to me as a safety precaution so many eons ago. Who knew that today would be when I use it? I had hoped this day would never come.

I slide the key into the lock and hear the click. I push the black walnut door open.

The room is the same as it has always been, ever since the Fall. I haven't been here since then; there has been no reason. Cobwebs hang down the mirror and across the shelves of various weapons. Dust and dirt covers everything. Everything except ... the gold cage the King of Hell sits in.

I stare at my father. Neither of us says a word.

Humans think that the prison the Archangels placed my father in is similar to what they have on earth. It's not. The king can roam free in a predetermined space—much like the vocivus room that Zoe is in. But this room is much stronger since all the Archangels infused their Light into it to create it. Even if all the demons banned together and did the same with Fire Light to counter the effect, it wouldn't be enough.

I infused my Light in make Zoe's room. If she becomes strong enough, she will be able to break it.

That can't happen, not yet.

There's the fact that the demons wouldn't band together

to assist their king, too. They want him kept in here as much as I do. Demons live by their own code and do things that only help themselves. Even if I need them to do something, they have to have something in exchange for it.

Because of that, Sammael will exact his revenge not only on the angels as many demons are on that list, too. The world doesn't need the king's wrath.

Sammael hunches over a large desk, pouring over paper documents. He still rules Hell and must address all situations that arise. Sometimes the Hell Hounds escape or don't return. A lost soul wanders to the wrong level. Once in a while Hell can have visitors; it's rare but does happen. He is the only one who can lift the veil between earth and Hell and allow entrance without having your Light stripped and your wings burnt off.

But that's what happens when angels try to enter without an invitation. Demons can leave Hell when the veil thins on its own accord, though. Like back in the Great Fire of London, or 1871 in Chicago, or when Mount Vesuvius erupted in 1944. Dozens of demons fled the confines during those times of natural disasters. Or so we let the Ordinaries believe. The veil naturally thins every couple of centuries. There's a balance to all things. Evil cannot be bottled forever. At some point, the top will blow, as in the case of volcanoes and Hell purges itself.

My father still does not address me. He continues to read whatever the parchment is about. No technology can be brought into the vocivus-like room, so in order to conduct Hell's business, everything must be written down and presented to Sammael.

I breathe in deeply. My father knows I'm there. It's a game to him. But I will not speak before my king acknowledges me.

"Am I keeping you from something?" Sammael doesn't look at me.

"No."

"Good. Maybe you can tell me why I'm still on this side of prison?"

"I have no idea."

"That's not what I hear." Sammael raises his head and looks in my eyes.

"What is it that you hear?" I meet his gaze.

"Are you questioning me?"

"No." I shake my head ever so slightly.

"I didn't think so. It's been a long time since you've seen me. I don't want to think you've gone soft on me."

"I haven't."

"Now. Tell me about the girl you have hidden away in a vocivus room."

"I don't—"

"Stop. I know you do. Nothing goes on in my own kingdom that I don't know about. And that goes for you. Especially you since I left you in charge of finding her. So, tell me exactly why I am still a prisoner? Is she not the one?"

"She is."

"And how do you know?"

"I watched her transformation. She has the tattoo and enhanced angel Light, but she doesn't know how to use it or what else she can do."

"You're sure it's her? I've been waiting a very long time to finally be released."

"Yes, I'm sure."

"Then how in Hell's name am I still on this side?" Sammael stands and tosses all the items on the desk to the floor.

"I don't know."

"You say it's her, but it can't be since I'm still locked up."

"Maybe it takes time for her to come into her full powers and you'll be free." I walk forward a few steps and inspect the shimmering, gold barrier. It's definitely still intact. Power makes my wings flutter. I step back. I've learned my lesson the day Father was locked in. We both had tried using Fire Light to free him. All it did was zap my powers for a long time.

I would never feel that loss of my Light again.

"Could be." Sammael's voice interrupts my thoughts. "I've been pouring over the scrolls for any documentation about the prophecy. It starts with Glory. So, I know that the Ordinary will be blessed by my Father. Babe born. Self-explanatory. First and last. Meaning that it can't be angels or fairies. Heaven and unto Earth. Could possibly mean that the one will be born of earth but also of Heaven. Receives the highest in jubilation. This could be that the angels will help. Enlightens will unite; they shall band. Never have they joined forces, so we must stop that. Triumph be if darkness is driven back. Help found who love, the world will stand.

"We will lose if we don't find this being," he continues. "I don't understand this last sentence, but I guess we'll see how it plays out. You will return to the library and bring me any book that mentions the prophesy, her, or the Archangels."

"All right."

"That was too easy. What's going on with you?"

"Nothing. I will do as you ask and bring you everything, so you may continue your research. Is there anything else I can do for you?"

"No."

Maybe there is a God looking over my dark soul. I know up to the very tips of my wings that Zoe is the one who will set my father free.

So why hasn't it happened yet?

28
Zoe

Oh, it's good to see corn belt country as I fly above the fields making my way to Minnesota. The gusty winds blow me off course, but I straighten and fight against the breeze until it bends to my wishes. I remain invisible as the Twin Cities' skyline appears on the horizon. By the time I see the IDS Tower soars into the clouds, my back is sore, not used to using muscles to flap wings. Freaking wings! I'm almost there.

Home.

Turning north, I know these cities and tick them off one by one as I pass them. A countdown to when I can be with my family and friends. And when I can finally land and rest.

I'm free at last.

Over the long journey, I've managed to learn how to use my wings. With nothing else to do but fly, I've spun, twirled, and dived into spirals, taken sharp turns, circled, and delicately floated on the air currents. Flying became second nature to me.

I should check in on my family first, but Kieran's house pulls me in. My feet touch the ground outside his house; I sway, then fall to my knees, not used to using them after my long flight back from Four Corners.

Making myself visible, and my wings invisible, I burst through the front door. The house is silent. Everything is in order and nothing is disturbed. I run through the halls and to the weapons room. The door is ajar, and the shelves and cabinets are bare. It's the only disheveled room. Someone must have been here and left in a hurry.

"Kieran? Shay?"

I wander to the backyard. Paschar is gazing down at me with her wings reaching upward. I don't know how she works or communicates with others. Cupping my hands, I scoop up water and let it run through my fingers onto her feet just like how Kieran had done it.

She blinks and tucks her wings behind her back. A soft female voice fills my head. *"Hello, Zoe. I'm glad you made it back to us. Everyone has been concerned about you. They have been distracted in your search by all the natural disasters, but rest assured that you are still in their minds."*

"Thank you for telling me that. I know I've been worried sick about everyone."

"They will be back soon. I believe that they are returning from Denali National Park."

"All right, I'll be back. I'm going home to my parents."

Paschar nods and returns to her original position.

I sprint around the house and down the street. My feet automatically take me up the three steps to my door. My raised hand hovers on the handle. I inhale a deep breath, turning the knob.

"Mom? Dad?" The house is dark. Where is everyone? The ticking clock tells me that it's early in the morning. They should be here, unless ...

What day of the week is it?

I check the calendar, and it's flipped to June. It's what I feel is still my birthday, but it might not be. I left my dead cell phone in that room. Running up to my room, I open my laptop and glance at the bottom right corner of the screen.

It's still June 24.

"Yes!"

I click on the clock icon and open the calendar. Today is Wednesday. Breathing a sigh of relief, I know where my family is: soccer practice with Stella.

Looking around my room, it's just as I left it. Makeup is scattered along the counter in the bathroom. The door to my walk-in-closet is still ajar. A single heeled shoe sits at the foot of my bed, the match someplace else. Dresser drawers are half closed, tops skewed and peeking out.

Remembering what Aiden told me about my Seraph's Sword, I should pack some clothes and toiletries. We'll be leaving to go fine mine, as soon as my friends come back.

I dig for my purple backpack in my closet. Yes, I'm back and could conjure anything I need, but there is something about wearing my own clothes that just feels like home. I toss in jeans and T-shirts, knowing that they're more durable than yoga pants, as well as throwing in undergarments, socks, and a hat. Going to the bathroom, I drop a toothbrush, paste, and face tissues into the bag. Makeup, I can live without. Being in battle isn't a fashion contest. And frankly, I could care less what I look like anymore. I have much bigger problems to deal with besides wearing the correct clothes and always trying to fit in. I don't need that added stress.

I drop my bag in the hallway.

My feet take me out of the room and down the hall to my parents'. Their bed is neatly made; nothing else is amiss. Then I amble to my sister's room. Her laptop is open as the screen saver flips through pictures of me and her and some of our whole family. A few of her favorite stuffed animals line the bookshelves. New band posters are pinned to the walls.

I leave her bedroom and march down the stairs, skimming my fingers along the photo frames.

Once in the kitchen, I scribble a note and leave it on the table, telling my family that I'm back and at Kieran's, leaving his house number because I no longer have my cell phone.

Picking up my pack, I wedge in a few water bottles and protein bars, head out of the front door, and wait for my friends to return.

I sit in my favorite room at Kieran's house, the den. We've had some major meetings in here. First, he told me about the Enlightens, the Orders, and the coming war. During another meeting, I met Vash and he told me about werewolves and the packs' fight against demons. So it seems to make sense that I'm here now, waiting for them to return.

The sun shines bright through the floor to ceiling windows. No clouds hinder its rays. It's like the sun is rejoicing my return.

My wait isn't long. I hear the exhaust from Shay's Bel-Air rumble into the driveway. I leap off the couch and rush to the door, throwing it open. The three steps and sidewalk are a blur as I launch myself into surprised arms.

"Zoe? Is it really you?" Shay mumbles into my ear. "Oh,

my god! I can feel you. You're really here." He steps back to look at me. His mouth crashes against mine as his arms tighten around my waist.

"Ahem."

We don't break apart. I block out the rest of the world and inhale Shay and his musky lavender scent with a hint of something sweet like a strawberry.

"BFF time." Kieran nudges his way between me and Shay, forcing us to part. "It'll only take a second, and you can go back to being lip-locked. I just need to get a hug."

Blood floods my cheeks, but I toss my arms around Kieran's shoulders. "It's great to be back. I've missed you guys."

"Some more than others apparently."

"No, I've missed you, too, K."

"How did you escape?" He turns and leads us toward the house. "Come inside and tell us everything."

"Where are Vash and Sidelle?" I ask as Shay takes my hand.

"I dropped Vash at his house, so he could spend time with Cali. We'll call him, so he knows you're here. I'm sure they both will want to see you."

I nod. The bond between wolf mates is strong. So entwined with each other that if one dies, the other will follow. That's how Vash became Alpha of his pack. His father died during a demon battle.

"Sidelle went back to Fairyland with her father and Queen Mab."

"What?" I stop mid-step.

"Yeah, we've got a lot to tell you, too. Happy birthday, by the way." Shay kisses me again, and we stop in the hallway. "I've missed you so much, and I'm thankful that you're here and you made it out."

"I know." I press my body against his and lay my head on his shoulder. "I don't ever want to be away from you again."

"Have you gone to see your parents? They must be thrilled that you've returned to them."

"I stopped over there first, but they're not home. I left a note to call here when they get back from practice. We have some time yet."

"Guys?" Kieran calls. "Will you two be joining me anytime soon?"

I cringe, knowing that we have more important things to discuss. Locking hands, we enter the den. Shay pulls me onto the couch and lays me against his chest. For a minute, I stare at my best friend, glad to be here and see him again, even though I know what's coming.

"I watched you and Sidelle battle the storms and saw the deserts dry up," I say. "Aiden told me about the volcanoes."

"How?" Kieran asks.

"Through a special mirror. It allowed me to see you guys."

"Sounds like a speculo."

"I could check in with my parents and Stella. I couldn't answer, and I'd like to think she knew I was there."

"So, you know what we've been trying to handle here," Shay says. "Including the crazy weather and the fight in Denali. Sidelle got her dad and Mab to come through a porta and help with the rain. Oberon managed to stop the flooding and landslides. And he told us that the Marqs were on the move in northern Canada. That's where we met some Knights and Marqs."

"Zoe, have you found out anything about Aiden?" Kieran asks. "Shay kept us informed about your Dream Walking."

"It's all a sham. Everything he's ever told me was a lie. Well, there's always a bit of truth to it, but nothing significant. He works for his father; Sarah, his sister, is not really related to him. I think he's an angel and not a demon."

"Why do you think that?" Shay asks. "Did he say he was?"

"No, just a gut feeling. The things he's said, what I've read between the lines."

"He could be a demon, then."

"Maybe."

Silence hugs the air as we process everything we said. Shay kisses the back of my neck, sending a tingling feeling down to my toes. My back itches and I squirm.

"Oh, my gosh." I bolt upright. "I have to show you something." I stand and think about my purple wings: their length, the way they shimmer, their feel. Light zips through my body, and my wings snap out from my back. "Look what I got!"

The boys' mouths drop open. The room is flooded with pulsing purple light. My wings gently flap.

Before either can speak, the silence is broken from a phone's ring.

29

Zoe

"Hello," Kieran says into his cell phone. "Yes, she's right here. Just a second." He mouths, "your mom." He then says louder, "Here, Zoe."

"Mom? You got my note. Yes, I'm leaving right now and will be home in a bit. I missed you, too. Mom, it's okay. I'm here now, but I can't run across the street until you hang up. Yes, I love you, too." I toss the phone back to Kieran. "I have to go home."

"We'll reconvene tomorrow."

I turn to leave and hide my wings.

"Zoe, it's good to have you back." Kieran steps beside me and embraces me. I feel and see his gold Light pulsing just under his skin and know just how much he missed me.

"I'll take you home," Shay says.

The twenty-nice steps it takes to get to my house isn't fast enough. My parents are standing in the driveway when I open the door of Kieran's house. Dropping Shay's hand, I run to greet them. They don't close the distance. My mom is clutching Dad. Stella hovers in the doorway.

I plow into my parents and cling to them.

"Welcome home, Zoe?" Mom asks as she pushes me back.

"Yes, I'm really missed you guys." Tears run down my face.

"Zoe." Dad's arms tighten around my shoulders. "Oh, Zoe. We thought ... we thought that you'd never come home again."

"No, Dad, I'll always find my way home to you guys. You're my family." I motion for Stella to join us. "Stel, come give me a hug! I've missed you so much."

"Zoe!" She hurls her body down the steps and flings her arms open. "I'm so glad you're back. I've missed you like crazy."

"I know, Squirt."

Mom's shoulders shake from crying, and she can't get any words out.

"I know, Mom. I know." I squeeze her waist and lead them all back in the house.

"How was Europe?" Mom asks.

"Long. I'll tell you guys as much as I can, but for now, I

just need to hold you guys."

Once my parents settle down, we stop crying, and of course after Mom made me a quick sandwich.

"Go rest, but then you're going to have to give us something."

I excuse myself to go rest. I couldn't tell them where I was, who kidnapped me, or why. Plus, Kieran or Shay needs to tell me what, if anything, they've told them, so our stories line up.

Taking the steps up to my bedroom, I stop in Stella's room and grab her cell phone to text Shay.

Stella: Zoe here. Can you come over later? I'm going to rest for a bit.

Immediately, I get a response.

Shay: I'm already here.

I push open my bedroom door and find Shay leaning against the windowsill. God, I've missed him.

He's dressed in all black: boots, jeans, and T-shirt.

"Close the blinds," I say as I shut my door. With everything that I now know of Aiden, the last thing I need for him is to spy on me through his own window. "I left my family downstairs because I didn't know what story you've told them. They haven't asked me anything, but they will. I'll probably have to go into the police station and give a report or something."

"No, Zoe, you won't have to do that." Shay opens his arms. I step into his embrace and place my head in the crook of his neck. "Kieran's taken care of it. As for your parents, just tell them that you went on a trip. A few days after ... when ... Michael stopped by and Mind Wiped them."

"Is that why my Mom was acting all weird?" I look up into his aqua eyes. I've missed them so much.

"Probably. He used only a bit, just enough to cloud memories. They know you've been gone, but it's like a day to them."

"And Stella?"

"She was a bit harder to wipe because she believed so strongly." Shay brushes my hair from my face. "Michael told her that you're on a summer trip, and it was a deal of a lifetime, and that's why you missed your last weeks of school."

"I don't think she bought it. I watched her in the speculo. She knows something."

"Possibly. I'll let Kieran know." He presses his forehead to mine. "Can I see your wings again?" He grins sheepishly.

Every time I need my wings, they appear faster. I don't need to really think about them anymore. They are a part of me now.

Purple light bounces off my walls as I extend my wings to their full height. They tower over Shay. Memories of my first encounter of his wings rushes to my mind. Heat bubbles to my face as Shay's stare penetrates straight to my soul.

We stand across from each other as he inspects my wings. He makes a slow circle around me just as I had done to him.

He glides his fingers lightly on my wings.

I shudder.

His familiar smirk appears on his lips.

Not only is purple light pulsing in the room, it's met by a faint silver color. Shay's T-shirt disappears and is replaced with brilliant, white wings springing from his back. With my enhanced vision, the silver specks aren't just silver, but varying shades of gray, too.

We stand with our wings out, and I wrap mine around us, shielding us from prying eyes.

Footsteps make their way up the stairs.

"Shay, get into the closet. Someone is coming."

"You can hear that?" His wings disappear as he steps into the walk-in closet.

"Yes. I don't know if they—" I tilt my head. "—Dad will come in here or not, but I told them I was going to lie down." I flip the switch to my light off and leap into bed, pulling the covers over my body and making my wings disappear.

The door cracks open, and a head pokes through.

"Zoe?" Dad whispers and doesn't say anything more. "I'm glad you're home." He quietly shuts the door.

We wait a few minutes and listen to the retreating footsteps as they head back downstairs. I hear the TV volume click and know that they are settling in for the evening.

"The coast is clear, Shay. You can come out."

"You must have gotten enhanced hearing, too?"

"Yes, so now you're not the only superhero in the room." I give him my best smirk. "Plus, my vision is better."

I scoot over and peel back the covers, so Shay can join me in bed.

"I love your wings," he says. "I knew they would be purple." I turn on my side and nestle into his. "You've learned a lot, haven't you?"

"I had to. No one else was there to teach me."

"I'm sorry, Zoe."

"For what?" I prop myself up on my arm. "It wasn't you who kidnapped me or held me prisoner for two months."

"I know, but I should've been the one to be with you and teach you how to use your gifts."

"I'm here now, so we can start tomorrow. I need tonight to be just us." I kiss his cheek.

We remain silent, and I return to his side, content to listen to his breathing. I can tell he wants to say or ask me something. His silver Light swirls like an aura.

"I know you went to Las Vegas." I bit my lip. "And in our last Dream Walk, you had mentioned that you were looking for someone, and that someone said she knew of me being held by someone high up."

"Are you jealous?" Shay asks. I can feel his smirk and his eyes staring at me through the darkness.

"No." It's a bit too quick. My face flames. I have no right to be mad or jealous of him. "I'm not. Really."

"I was looking for Oriana. She's a Knight who I've helped a couple of times years ago. She keeps up on most demon gossip, and I thought she would know something. That's all it was."

I don't respond. I'm afraid if I do, something will blurt out that's irrational. I bite my tongue.

"How did you escape?" Shay asks.

"Aiden arrived in my room and watched me transform—"

"I want to hear more about that, too, after your great escape."

"As a parting gift, he created a window. I guess you could say that it's like a speculo mirror because it showed me landscapes that I wished to view. It could fill the room with sound and smells. I kept it on an ocean scene so different fragrances would waft in. Sometimes I'd hear waterfalls. Birds chirped or would fly by." I trace swirls on his bare chest. "After my wings appeared, Aiden left to go take care of something. It got me thinking that if Aiden could conjure the window that I should try escaping. Before all this happened, I had to dig for my Light, but now it's always there, just within my reach. Power surged through me. I took a chance that the window would shatter, and I could fly away."

"You're so brave." Shay kisses my forehead. "It must have worked because you're here with me now."

"Yes, it did. The moment I broke free of the room, I felt it. My wings flared with Light, and I launched through the protection barrier. I flew around, trying to get my bearings. I was in Four Corners, and I made it home. That long trip is where I learned how to make myself invisible and how to fly."

"We should go tomorrow to a vacant field or something, so you can show me what you've learned. Maybe there is still some things I can teach you."

"I'd love it if you would." My mouth finds his in the dark. "And maybe we can figure out more of my powers."

"Do you think he let you go? I mean, I'm really glad you're here, but your escape seems too easy."

"Yeah. I thought that, too. Maybe he did, or he forgot to ward it against me. Or maybe he can't contain me."

"I won't ever leave your side again. That, I promise you, Zoe." Shay tightens his grip around my waist. "So, tell me about your transformation. I want to hear all the details. Don't leave anything out."

"Well. It must have been the time of my birth because I felt power run through my body. It was like nothing I ever experienced before. My Light was always a floating dot that shot around inside, and I had to look for it. But this was different, my whole body tingled, and Light danced around every part of me." I shiver thinking about it. "My back prickled, and purple wings sprouted. My hearing and eyesight became enhanced. I could hear Aiden's voice in my head." I sit up onto my knees. "Wait. No. I could hear Aiden before my change. We touched twice in that room, and both times an electrical shock coursed through us. It's the same shock that you and I feel but different. I questioned it in my mind. I know I didn't voice it, but Aiden answered me, telling me that he knew what it meant. But he disappeared and never came back."

"Do you think he's your soul mate, too? I've never heard of anyone having two in the same lifetime." He rakes his hand in his hair. "I guess it's ... possible. If he is, he's going to have to go through me to be with you."

"I honestly don't know. We'll have to ask Kieran tomorrow. Oh, let me talk to K in my mind. Maybe it's an angel thing."

My body relaxes, and I kick out my legs and sit yoga-style. I only think of Kieran. His blue eyes, the soft smile he wears, the wavy blond hair, and his gentle soul. It's like I'm tuning into his frequency.

"K, can you hear me? Let me know if you get his message. I'm testing something."

We wait for a response, but nothing comes back to me. I lie back down on the bed, and Shay wraps his arms around me as my body again molds to his. We fall asleep in the protection of each other's arms.

30
Aiden

Thursday, June 25, one day after Zoe's escape.

I slink away, leaving my father to pour over the old tomes and scrolls I just dropped off. It has gotten me thinking why he's not released yet. Zoe's birthday was yesterday, and yet he still sits in his prison.

Something is definitely wrong. Maybe she's not the one who will fulfill the prophesy. The fairies have been wrong before. It's rare but does happen.

Before continuing with Quinn's phase three training, I decide to check in one last time with Zoe. She should have her full powers by now.

As soon as I approach the vocivus room, my body tells me something is not right. I appear inside the room, and Zoe is not in it. Broken glass lays scattered on the floor from the window. A breeze blows in smelling of stagnant, musty air.

She finally managed to escape. And it only took her a day. She's going to be strong. Maybe as strong as me. I wonder briefly how she got out of the room. Did she sit and think about the window? Did she use trial and error and try breaking the glass? Did she use her Light for her getaway?

I guess it doesn't really matter how she got away. She's out, and I know exactly where she'll go first. Phase three of my plan is underway.

Training with Quinn has been very productive, now to lay the groundwork for slipping her back into Zoe's life. I'm hoping that Zoe remembers me telling her that Quinn is a Nephilim. Knowing Zoe and her friends, they'll take Quinn under their wings and guide her.

"What are we going to do today?" Quinn's eyes shine with excitement.

She's been doing really well, but there still is sadness in her. I know she wants to get her Nephilim Sword, and I'm befuddled as to why she hasn't received hers yet.

"Nothing you're going to like." I drive into the school's parking lot.

"Why are we at school? It's summer."

"I know, so it'll be empty, and we can use the track and field."

"Yeah, I don't think I'm going to like this."

I park the red Spyder, and we proceed to the fence. It's not locked because I came early to make sure. I don't need more questions from Quinn as to why we're breaking in. Also, we don't need prying eyes watching us, so I had created a repel ward around the field. In case someone does wander over here, they'll see and hear nothing. But if they try to come onto the field, they won't be able to. The invisible fence will deter them and strongly suggest that they don't need to be here today.

"Let me guess. I'm going to do a lot of running and jumping and stuff today," Quinn says.

"Yes, that's the plan. We need to build up your endurance, so you can survive upcoming battles."

"Are there some coming?"

"Soon, but we'll get to that later today. Think of it as your prize for completing today's phase and doing well. You need to pass my inspection before I can throw your name into the hat for the next assignment. Now is the time to impress me. Don't hold back because it's between life and death out there after training."

"I understand, I think." Quinn stands on the grass and begins to stretch her hamstrings and arms. "So what's first?" She doesn't need me to tell her anymore about warmups; it's become second nature to her. The time it takes normal Ordinaries is cut in half with Nephilim. After a couple of minutes, she's ready.

"I want you to run until you can't stand anymore. Push past it and keep running until I tell you to stop. I need to know where your endurance ends and push it further. It won't be timed. Do a couple of laps at a sprint and start running at full speed."

She nods, walks to the track, does some leg lifts, and trots down the lane, gradually picking up speed.

The first lap around, I note her pace is about two minutes. Pretty quick considering she's sprinting. By the third lap, her legs are moving in a blur. I know she's pushing herself to her limits. This is what I'm really interested in. She should be able to do at least six or seven laps at this speed. Quinn rushes by me on the fifth lap and on a whim, I decide to join her. Maybe feeling my presence pushing her on will tip her over the edge.

"Hey, babe," I say as I catch up to her. "Thought you could use some inspiration on these next laps."

"Thanks," she huffs. "I think I'm about burned out, so anything you can do to distract me will help."

We continue running like the Hell Hounds are chasing us. Lap after lap, we go around and around. I notice her waning, but her mouth is set into a grim line. She's powering through. We've just completed the eleventh lap, well over my expectations.

Quinn slows a bit, and I zoom past her, looking back to make sure she's okay. Her pace is still declining to a jog and then to a fast walk. I wait for her at the finish line as she shuffles past.

"I did it. How many laps was that?"

"Twelve, which is very good." She collapses on the cool grass. Her chest is heaving. I give her a couple of minutes to recoup but not long. "All right, time to get up." She blinks at me like I've grown horns out of my head. If she only knew. "Come on, endurance training, remember?"

"I don't think I can walk." She rolls over on her stomach and pushes herself up onto her knees. "Okay, maybe I can." She presses forward and stands. "Can we do something with my arms for a bit? I just need a couple extra minutes."

Driving her past exhaustion today is probably not the best idea, so I relent.

"All right, let's use those arm muscles you have hiding." I lead her to a table of spear and javelins. Even though men and women use different lengths and weights, I only have the men's equipment displayed. "You'll use this," I say, selecting the javelin, "to throw. While this is about distance, it's also about aim. See those lines? Don't hit them. The head, which is the tip here, must land within the sector. The body, or shaft," I say, running my hand the length of the pole, "cannot land on its side. Got it?"

"Yes, I think so."

Quinn picks up the javelin and bounces it in her hands, feeling the weight, balance, and length. I didn't tell her about pose, form, or actually how to throw it. Gripping the shaft, she takes a couple of steps back. Bringing her arm backward, the javelin flies forward. With deadly accuracy, the head buries itself into the ground by a few inches.

"Again." Thinking it might be a fluke, I watch as she hits the sector in the same spot. The javelins are poking out of the grass, side by side. "Again." The same thing happens, repeatedly. "Back up a few yards."

A cluster of spears now nestle together. No matter the distance, short or long, she's hitting the mark. I'm impressed.

"Huh," I say.

"That's good, right?" Quinn waves her hand toward the javelins.

"Yes." I nod. That's all I can say. I'm a bit awestruck. "How are your legs feeling? Think you can run a bit more?"

"Yeah, they aren't too sore. I won't be setting any marathon records." She shrugs. "Whatcha thinking?"

"That you should run across the field." I point in the direction to one of the end goals they use for football.

"And what are you going to do?"

"I'm going to try to hit you." I pick up the duffle bag from the ground and unzip it, revealing knives, a slingshot, bean bags, and arrows. "You better get going because all of these hurt from this close of a range."

That got her moving. She dashes to one of the goals as I load the bow with arrows and launch them in her direction. She easily side steps the first arrow. What she didn't account for is that this isn't a game, and I'm not an angel. Loading multiple arrows, I fire them off in rapid speed, sending a volley of them careening toward her. There isn't anywhere to run, but I'm still careful that she doesn't get, injured or killed.

But I don't stop there. Taking the slingshot, I blast bean bags at her moving target. She's fast, dodging them quickly, but my ears hear her grunting. Some are finding their mark. She is going to be very bruised tomorrow. And even that doesn't make me stop. Quinn rushes toward me and darts to my left as I fling a knife at her. She dodges it at the last second, but more knives come flying her way.

What I haven't prepared her for are the invisible blasts. I know she can't create them, but she doesn't know that. Sending a wave of air in her direction, her body sways, and she loses her balance. She glares at me while stumbling to upright herself. I shrug. No one said battles were going to be fair.

Air detonates around her from all directions as the bean

bags assault her from another. Rubber tipped arrows rain down, a few hitting near her as she covers her head.

A bright orange glow emits from her body. Her wings release. Something glints from the sunlight. She's still running erratically on the grass with the added weight of her wings as I send all the rubber balls bouncing her way.

Instinctively, Quinn reaches between her shoulder blades and clutches her Nephilim Sword. It's there when she most needs it. She bats the balls and bean bags away, swings her blade to knock the knives out of the air. There isn't anything she can do about the relentless, falling arrows, but she does her best to slash at them before they imbed into their mark.

I stop the onslaught of weapons and motion for her to come to me.

"Is this what I think it is?" She stares at the sword in her hands and presents it to me.

"Looks like it." I don't touch it. The blade is long, and around the hilt are orange gemstones, fire opals. The color goes perfectly with her wings. "You've done well today. Better than I expected you would. And if I thought that throwing knives at you would get your sword to appear, I would have done that earlier. I'm sorry I didn't think of doing that."

"It's fine, Aiden. I wouldn't have thought that you putting my life in danger would trigger it either." She bounces while a broad smile shows her teeth. "Does this mean that I can go on a mission now?"

"Yes. I think it does."

31

Zoe

The next morning, I wake to Shay's eyes gazing at me.

"Hello, beautiful."

"Have you been staring at me all night?" I cover my mouth from morning breath.

"No, not all night." He smirks. "Just the last couple of hours. I still can't believe you're here."

"I know. Me, too. But today we need to get moving. K should call a meeting and have Vash come, too, so we all know what's going on and where we go from here." I start to get up.

"Five more seconds and we will hit the day running." He tugs me back down. "I don't know when we'll have another opportunity like this."

I kiss him sweetly, bad breath forgotten.

"Okay, warrior of mine, it's time to go." I nudge him out of the bed. "I'm going to take a quick shower. You text K."

"Yes, ma'am."

I hover near the bathroom door and watch as Shay pulls out his phone, satisfied that he's up and starting the day. There is something about being back in my old bathroom, using my familiar soaps, and shower that comforts me.

By the time I step out of the bathroom, I feel like my old self in my own clothes that I haven't conjured.

"Hey, Kieran texted back and said the meeting is set for two hours from now. Vash needs time to drive here, and Sidelle isn't back from Fairyland yet. He's still trying to contact her." Shay sweeps me off my feet and plants a chaste kiss on my cheek. "Go visit with your family for a while. I'll see you over at Kieran's house in a couple of hours." He shoos me away, turns, and leaps out of the window.

I watch his retreating back. He stops and waves once he gets to the end of my driveway.

There is a soft knock on my door.

"Zoe? Are you awake?" The door creaks open and in pops my sister's head. "Oh, good, you are up. Was that Shay who left?"

"Hi, Stella. Do you need something?'

"No, I just ... just wanted to talk with you. I know you're probably overwhelmed. You looked exhausted last night, and I wanted to let you sleep. But ..."

"Come, sit down." I pat my bed. "This sounds important." I wait for her to begin.

"Where were you?" Her head hangs low. "Kieran said that you were traveling, but I didn't believe him. You wouldn't take off like that without telling anyone." Her head snaps up and looks directly at me. "Besides, he would have gone with you. Or Shay. But neither of them went. Mom and Dad weren't too worried when you didn't show up after a couple of days. Something just wasn't right about it. They weren't acting like normal parents would whose child was missing. No posters went up around town; nothing on the news was said about it. There was a small report about the car accident the night of your prom. But that was it." She tilts her head and waits.

I don't think I can BS her anymore. She's thirteen going on thirty. Whatever I say must sound real. I want to protect her and leaving her in the dark isn't the answer. She was there when the demons came knocking at our front door.

"I'm not stupid," she says.

"I never said you were."

"You don't have to tell Mom and Dad, but you owe me the truth." Her hands fist. "None of your friends knew where you were, so I think you were kidnapped. But I don't know by whom. Do you?"

"Stella. I want to protect you and Mom and Dad. Some

real bad people are coming, and they might try to use you guys to get to me."

"So tell me so I can watch for them."

"It's not that simple."

"Does it have to do with those bad things that came to the house?"

"What do you remember of that night?" Kieran was supposed to Mind Wipe everyone. I'm going to have words with him if he hadn't.

"Everything." Tears run down Stella's face. "I remember everything. Three people came to the house and fought with Kieran and Shay. But I don't think they were even *people*. Your friend, Vash, turned into a giant brown wolf and killed those black ghost-like things." She sniffled. "Sidelle and some boy came and fought in the front yard. You went out there and blew everyone away. Cali died, and you brought her back to life."

"Okay. Yeah, that's about what happened." I turn to face her. "You have to promise me that you won't tell anyone."

"As long as it's the truth. I promise."

"You're right. Those three guys who came to the house that night were not people. They weren't even human. They're called Knights. Demon Knights. But they look like everyday people." I hand my sister a tissue. "Those dark, ghost-like forms are Marquises demons and only very powerful beings like Vash can kill them. He's a werewolf as you might have guessed."

"Like in *Twilight*?"

"I suppose so, but there's no such thing as vampires."

"So, what are you?"

"I'm a ... an angel."

"Whoa!"

"But I just became one on my birthday."

"And Kieran?"

"Also, an angel."

"Shay?"

"Half-angel. The technical term is called a Nephilim."

"Awesome. Thank you for trusting me with this."

"When did you get so old?" I smile.

"I had to grow up fast. My big sister was kidnapped, and I had to keep the family together. So why you?"

"They think I'm the girl who will stop Armageddon."

"Are you?"

"I'm not sure. The devil was supposed to break out of his prison the day I turned eighteen, but nothing has changed. I haven't heard about any really bad news these past two days. Have you?"

"No, just the bad weather, but that's all better now. Do you think I'm an angel, too, like you?"

"Honestly, I don't know, Stella. Why do you think you're going to be an angel?" She shrugs. "I didn't know about myself until a couple of months ago that I might be something other than human." I shrug. "But I do know that there is a war coming, and I must be ready. My friends are going to help me, and I need you to be safe. I'm going to need to be gone for a bit while I look for something important. It might turn the tide on the war."

"What is it that you're looking for?"

"A special item. I'm meeting Kieran and Shay later this morning to go over details."

"I know you'll find a Seraph's Sword, and we'll win over evil."

Wait. I never told her what we are looking for. Or had I? "How do you know?"

"Because I've seen it."

"What do you mean, you've seen it?"

"It's just what it means. I've seen you with a gold sword that has purple gems on the base. You're in a field, or on a lake, which is confusing since how is *that* even possible. You're there with all your friends and you're using one."

My mouth drops open, and I close it like a fish. I process that for a while. Every couple of seconds, I start to say something, but nothing comes out. "You're coming to the meeting with me."

Two hours later we are at Kieran's house. Vash and Cali

are already there when I walk into the den.

"Oh, my gosh." Cali rushes and pulls me into a tight hug. "You're okay, right? He didn't hurt you?" She lets me go and looks at my face. "I'm going to chew his wings off—" Cali turns her head and notices my sister.

"It's okay, go ahead and say it," I say.

Cali shakes her head.

"Glad to have you back with us again, Zoe," Vash says as he quickly pats me on the shoulder, leading Cali to the love seat.

After our quick reunion everyone keeps glancing at me, wondering why I brought my sister. Sidelle is still MIA, and I hope she appears soon. I sit between Shay and Stella on the couch but slightly closer to my boyfriend, who takes my hand and squeezes.

"All-righty-O, peoples! Let's get the party started." Sidelle poofs into the den. "I heard my name and so I'm here." She spots my sister on the couch. "Stella. Um, what are you doing here?" It's the first time I've seen Sidelle flustered.

"I brought her with me," I say. "She knows the basics, but I didn't tell her about fairies."

"Hold up! Are my eyes for realz right now? Zoe?" Sidelle flies toward me and pats my head. A bit condescending, but at this point, I'm just so ecstatic to see her I don't care. She grabs me and pulls me into a fierce hug.

"Hello to you, too," I say.

"Whoa. Sidelle is a fairy?" Stella asks as she turns her head, looking at me for confirmation and awe at Sidelle.

"Yes, but we can talk about that later," I say. "I brought Stella here because she says that she can see things."

The room is so quite you can hear only our breathing. Everyone gapes at my little sister, who is sitting there with a small, knowing smile stretched across her lip.

It's Kieran who speaks first. "A Vate?" he asks.

"I don't know what that is, but I can see things," she says sweetly.

"Do you know it's the future?" Shay prompts.

"Most of the time it is." She shakes her head. "It sounds crazy. But I guess not, considering who's all sitting in this room." She glances expectantly at each of us.

"Kieran." I stand and place my hand on his arm. "The night of our dress shopping three months ago, did you Mind Wipe everyone?"

"Yes." He nods. "Why?" His golden aura flickers.

"It didn't take on me," Stella says. "I remember everything."

"Is there a way to test her of being a ... what did you call it?" Shay asks. "A vate?"

"We haven't had one in a really long time." Sidelle's eyes gloss over. "They are extremely rare and at such a young age to already see things," she mutters.

"You know about them?" I stand beside my fairy friend.

"Yes." Her eyes sharpen and focus back on my sister. "Vates are half-fairies. It's how they draw their visions, by using glamour."

"How is she a half-fairy? And why didn't you know about her?"

I notice Kieran and Shay exchange a glance. Both of their auras fade then brighten back to normal.

"That's not important now," Kieran says. I'll have to ask Shay about that look later. "We've been so tied up cleaning the mess the demons are causing that we haven't been able to find a Seraph's Sword yet. And I've confirmed that Hell's gates are not opened, so Sammael is still imprisoned."

"He'll be out soon, though," Stella says. "I've seen it. The weather is hot, the crops are still growing, and fireworks light across the skies in a celebration."

"Could be Independence Day." Kieran rakes hand through his hair, so unlike him. "Which is only in a couple of weeks."

"And I think I know where we can find Zoe a sword." Stella grins.

32
Zoe

My sister is a fairy, correction, half-fairy. How in the world did she end up being that? I, of course, know the mechanics of it. And I'm also wondering which of my parents strayed. Is Stella from Winter or Summer?

"Penny for your thoughts?" Shay breaks me out of my wondering as he leads me to his car and opens the door.

"I'm just thinking about my sister. What was that look you and Kieran exchanged? Yeah, I saw it."

"Crazy isn't it? You think you know someone, and you find out something like this. But she's still the sweet, younger girl, who despite everything, has a crush on me." He winks at me. "We find it interesting that you are an angel and she's a Vate. Two very unique circumstances in the same family."

Only he could see the bright side of this. Maybe it's not so bad. I didn't want to drag her into all of this. She's so young and innocent. But she's already a part of it.

"Where are we headed?" I ask. My eyes stare out of the window, watching the city change into fields.

"Since your sister has soccer practice now, we can't do anything about the sword. I thought we could go flying and see what else you can do."

Shay drives to the same location where we had our first-second date. I remember it so well: the tiki lights leading to a blanket, him feeding me strawberries, and taking me on flight around the city.

Today will be a bit different since I now have my own set of wings, and it's the middle of the day.

"Can you make yourself invisible like I can?" I ask Shay as we step out of the vehicle. "Don't you think people will notice a person with wings flying around?"

"I've been doing this a long time, Zoe. I know how to blend in. But no, I can't make myself invisible like you." He takes my hand and leads me out into the open field. "It's past planting season, and it's during the week. We probably won't run into anyone out here. Okay, let's see what you've got." His shirt disappears and silver wings flap around him. He lunges and launches himself into the air. "Come and catch me!" he yells. "If you can."

His body is becoming a faint dot in the bright sky. I

won't let him win. Light surges through me, and instantly my purple wings appear. They take me higher into the air, and I soar on the currents, feeling the wind brush against my face and around my wings. The sensitivity of them makes me shudder.

Shay zooms by, startling me. My body flails, and I lose my balance. The ground comes rushing up to meet me, but I manage to straighten myself out.

Tucking the tips of my wings, I shoot myself across the sky, barreling fast toward him. Tears gather in my eyes, blinding me. I can still see his form and using my Light, I seek his silver Light. It's a shining, ball floating a few yards from me.

I turn myself invisible and think of quieting my flight. I'm in stealth mode. No sounds escape me.

Shay's back is facing me. He's looking around on the ground. He knows that I faltered.

My body tackles him from behind, and the force of it sends us careening toward the ground. The impact makes me reveal myself.

"Gotcha," I scream as our bodies tangle, trying to right themselves. "And you thought I wouldn't catch you."

"Zoe!"

The ground is coming into our view much too fast. We break apart. My heartbeat spikes. This is going to hurt. At the last possible moment, I grab a wind current, flex my wings, and soar back into the sky.

I do not need to clean my face of mud. Pride, yes, but dirt, no.

Shay did not make it out as well. His body is splatted on the soil, face down and not moving. I drop and kneel next to him, my smile wiped from my lips.

"Shay?" I ask. "Are you okay?" Gently, I shake his shoulder. "Oh, god, please be okay. I didn't mean it. You were supposed to pull up." I sniffle. "You're the better flyer."

There is no one around. I can't call for help.

Pishh. I don't need others. I have angel Light. It's humming under my skin and moves to my fingertips. Warmth spreads through my hands as I lay them on Shay's body. I send healing thoughts to him.

"You just have to be okay. I can't do this without you. You're my protector." Real tears from sorrow slowly make their way down my cheeks. "You said that you'd always be by my side."

"I will be if you can move a bit."

I scrunch my eyes and free them of tears. Lying my body against his, I squeeze. He groans and I back away.

"I'm so sorry."

"It's okay, Zoe. You're a bit stronger now." He turns and sits up but not without some grunting. "I think you knocked the wind right out from me."

"Shay—"

"Don't worry about it. I know it's not your fault. I'm just surprised, that's all. I didn't think you'd get all of the Nephilim enhancements. We can add strength to the list now." He rubs his chest as he stands. "That's hearing, sight, and strength."

"And maybe talking through minds." I tick off on my fingers. "How do you know about the hearing?"

"Remember last night when you heard footsteps coming?" I nod. "You heard them before I did. I noticed them on the middle of the stairs, but you knew earlier, didn't you?"

"Yes, I heard the couch move, and my dad hit the coffee table. Plus, I could tell by his shuffling."

"Thinking maybe smell, too?"

"I don't know. Never tried it."

"Let's rest a bit." I raise a brow at him. "Fine. I need a break. You see how far you can smell something." He points to his right. "See that farm house?"

"Yes?" I sit yoga-style as Shay rests on his back.

"They must keep animals because of the fences. Use your nose or senses and tell me what they have."

I feel terrible for hurting him but does as he asks. Inhaling, all I get is a nose full of pollen and sneeze. But in there buried deep are flowers, freshly cut grass clippings ... mud?

It's like I'm sitting at a pond near the shore and splash the water line, making ripples. My senses are the ripples and as each band gets farther away, I smell more things: corn, hay, and gas. They must have a barn someplace.

My vision narrows; I can see that all around the property are cats. They run to and fro, darting in and out of the lawn ornaments. Fenced in lays an older German Sheppard. The smell of oats, leather, and a faint whiff of iron lingers.

If the residents raised crops only, would they need leather? Maybe gloves, but the smell is stronger than that. Cattle? I think I'd smell more hay and milk, at least cream or something. The squealing sounds of pigs would tip me off, so that's a no.

"I smell a ton of cats, a dog, and the smell from ..." I inhale. "Horses. I don't know how many, though."

"Not bad, Zoe. Not bad at all."

"Do you know how many?"

"Nope. Just seeing if you did." He chuckles.

I punch his shoulder, lightly.

"Ow." He rubs his arm but grins at me. "I think we can safely assume that smell can be added to your list."

Switching positions, I snuggle against his chest as his legs form a barrier around me. He places his hands over mine. We are content with each other's silence, listening to the birds and insects fluttering about on this sunny day.

"Are you feeling better?" I ask. "I'm really sorry."

"I know you are, and don't worry about it. I'm almost back to normal." He kisses my check.

"Can I try something with you?" I can feel a smile creep onto his face. "Um. It's not anything sexual. Get your mind out of the gutter." I shake my head.

"I'll always be at your mercy." He waggles his brows. "You can try anything with me."

"Shay?" He doesn't respond in my mind, but I have so much to say to him. To tell him everything I felt when we were a part. *"I love you so much. All the days I was gone, I knew you were looking for me. It's our connection and your love that carried me forward each day, not giving up."* His eyes gaze into mine, waiting for me to say something. *"You would go to the end of the world for me and I for you. We'll be by each other's side from this day forward, until your heart stops beating."*

Kieran never returned my mental message to him, but I needed to confirm something. Can I only talk with Aiden? Or is it a soul mate thing? If that's the case, I should be able to mentally speak with Shay, too.

After our flying escapade, I convince Shay that we need a cup of tea. It's been months since I had a decent mug, and there is only one place to get it, which is what brings us to Coffee Grind. The small mom and pop shop looks the same as it always has. The tall glass windows are so spotless, I can see my reflection. A tiny bell chimes when the door opens, greeting customers.

"Quinn?" I spot her in the far corner of, dragging Shay with me. "Is that you? How have you been feeling?"

The Coffee Grind's signature cinnamon dessert scent wafts through the air. The original stone hearth is clean of soot, and freshly cut wood lays strategically on the black, metal grate.

"Zoe? You're back?" Quinn stands and embraces me.

"Oh, my gosh. How was Europe? Everyone was so jealous that you got a free eight-week, once-in-a-life-time trip. I mean, you couldn't pass that up. No one would've wanted you to. But to go alone without even Kieran? Any one of us would have taken that opp." She hugs me again. "I'm so glad you're back. And hi, Shay."

"Hello, Quinn," Shay says.

"Don't forget to breathe in there, girl." Man, I missed her. All the excitement that she carries around her, rolled into a tight, fun-sized body. Lowering my voice, I say, "So ... are you feeling better?" I scan the room looking for anyone lingering to overhear our conversation.

"Oh, yeah, I was only at Mayo for a couple of days," Quinn says. "But the doctors never found—"

"I know what you are. Aiden told me before I left for ... vacation."

"I hope you're not mad."

"Why would I be mad?"

"Aiden ... he came to visit me in the hospital like every day, and we started to hang out and one thing led to another and now ... we're kinda dating."

My mouth opens and closes. I look at Shay, and he's doing the same thing.

He recovers first. "Tell us everything. I know Zoe wants to know." He elbows me in the ribs.

"Yeah, I do." We sit in the loveseat, sipping our chai teas

as Quinn regales us with the past few weeks after her hospital stay, her training with weapons, and her latest exercise program that Aiden is putting her through.

"I'll be right back." Quinn stands. "Do you guys need refills or anything?"

Peering into my cup, I shake my head as Shay does the same. I can tell that Quinn is smitten with Aiden. Neither Shay nor I have the heart to say anything further.

"We have to say something to her," Shay says.

"I know. She's just so happy."

We don't know for sure what exactly Aiden's end game is or if he's truly evil. Yes, he kidnapped me, but he never physically hurt me. And my friend needs to know how about him. I don't want to hurt her, but if Aiden hurts her I'd rather Quinn hate me that to let one of my friends suffer because I didn't say something.

Silently, Shay and I agree to let things play out.

When Quinn returns with her steaming cup of decaf coffee—she doesn't need anything to add to her bubbly personality—she sits on the edge of the high-back leather chair. "I got my Nephilim Sword the other day. It's really cool."

"That's great," Shay says. "Aiden's teaching you technique?"

"Yeah, with other types of swords and weapons in general because when I was learning those, I didn't have my own yet. It just came the other day."

"Quinn," I say. "Just be careful around him. I don't want to see you get hurt."

"I know he's your neighbor, and he's relatively new in town, but you don't know him like I do. We have a connection. Maybe it's like what you and Shay have, or maybe it isn't. But I want to find out."

"Okay, but Quinn—"

"Zoe, maybe we can double date, and you can see what I see in him." Seeing Aiden again so soon is not going to happen in my book. At any point in my life for that matter. I don't care if she likes or dates him. Quinn is not changing my mind about Aiden. He kidnapped me. Granted, I think he might have let me go. But still. Shay squeezes my hand, confirming that he's thinking the same thing. Then again, maybe we should double so I can see what he's up to. "I know you guys had a fight before prom about Morgan—"

"And there's the boyfriend stealer." Morgan glides toward us.

"Take it up with Aiden." Quinn raises her hand. "He's the one who dumped you."

"And I see that Zoe is back." Morgan continues her advance on us. "Word on the street is that you were in Europe galivanting around." She leans in really close to my ear. "But I think that's a cover to where you really were doing. Hiding a baby bump."

"If that's the case," I seethe. "Why after two months of being gone is my stomach as flat as a pancake?" I lift my shirt just high enough for her to see my abs. "And I recall that it takes nine months for a baby."

"You must have lost it." Morgan shrugs. "I'm so sorry for your loss." She squints her eyes. "Not really, it's just something that people say, isn't it? Well, I've gotta run. I have much more important places to be like the beach. Ta ta, losers."

"Oh, my gosh, she just burns my hide," Quinn says. "I don't understand how you can stand her meanness, Zoe. I didn't steal Aiden. He said that he broke up with her. She, of course, was extremely upset about it and wouldn't take no for an answer. She didn't take it lightly."

"She's been like that since elementary school." I watch Morgan leave the shop. "I've learned to ignore her."

"But she does have a good idea." Quinn wiggles her brows. "It's a gorgeous day out, and we're on summer vacation. You don't have a job yet, do you?"

"Nope. I didn't get a chance to line one up before ..."

"So?" She bounces in the chair. "We should get the gang together and go have fun. Celebrate the end of our junior year since you weren't there for it."

"All right," I relent. "Meet at Prairie Lake in an hour?

"Fantastic. This is going to be so awesome. Just like old times." Quinn takes out her cell. "I'll text Rena. You text

Cali." She waves bye and walks out of Coffee Grind.

I nod and stand to leave.

"Do you think it's wise to go swimming today?" Shay asks. "I know you need to have time with your friends after everything you've been through, but we still need to find your Seraph's Sword."

"I know we do, but my sister isn't back from soccer yet, so we have a few hours. Besides, I really do need to hang out with them to feel normal. We won't know when the next time I'll get to see them again." I remove my phone from my back pocket and text Kieran, Cali, and Sidelle.

Me: Prairie Beach in 1 hr. Getting the gang to hang today.

Immediately, Sidelle returns my text.

Sidelle: OK

"You're coming though, right?" I ask.

"Of course. Where you go, I go." We take off and leisurely stroll on the sidewalk, heading for home. "What was it like for you?"

"Don't torment yourself, Shay; there wasn't anything for you to do with all the cities that needed you." We amble hand-in-hand, as always. "Besides, most of the time, I thought I would die of boredom. I talked to myself a lot and at the tail end of my time, Aiden would visit me. So, all in all, I guess it wasn't so bad. I could think of worse scenarios."

"I can, too." He flattens his mouth into a thin line.

Kieran: Are you on your way home? We can all ride together.

I show the text to Shay and he nods.

As we round the corner and turn onto Sandbar Lane, I finally receive Cali's response. She's in, too, but will meet us at the lake since she's still in Minnetonka and has pack business to attend.

The parking lot is full, but we manage to snag an open spot near the end of a row. The park where Prairie Lake butts up against is packed with students milling about, runners on the path getting exercise, and young moms with strollers soaking up the perfect day.

As we near the beach, children build castles in the sand, an on-duty lifeguard supervises the kids swimming, and the concession stand is open with a line of hungry people.

"We can stay a couple of hours, maybe three to allow time for my sister to get home, change, and meet at your house," I say to Kieran as we walk the short distance to an empty picnic table. Shay is carrying my bag that's loaded with towels, sunscreen, and a football. I decided to wear my swimsuit under a coverup; both are purple, of course. "I wonder if Sidelle is here yet?" I scan the thick crowd of people but don't spot her.

"I think she's over there." Kieran points to the far end of the beach where a group of guys huddle around our fairy friend. He scrunches his brows together. "I'll be right back." He turns and leaves us.

"She can take care of herself," I say to his retreating back.

"I know. I'm going to tell her that we're here," Kieran says over his shoulder.

Turning to Shay, I say, "I think she knows we are."

He shrugs and takes the bottle of sunscreen out. "Would you like me to apply this to your back?"

"Sure," I say and spin around so he can spray me. "When you're done, would you like me to do you?"

"If you insist." He smirks.

"Ah." My cheeks flood a deep red as Shay chuckles. He doesn't say anything about my question.

"All right, you're all set." He hands me the can and turns. The bottle is almost empty, and I shake it to get every drop out.

"Let's go and pick our spot then see if Quinn and Rena are here."

We lay our towels out onto the hot sand. I place my flip-flops on two corners and the football on another.

The sun is shining high in the sky. No clouds will provide us any shade today. A half a dozen wind surfers zigzag across the water as a pair of Jet Skis cut through their paths. Jerks. To our left, kids are learning to paddle board.

Laughter fills the air as birds chip their excitement on such a beautiful day. Everyone is enjoying the summer weather.

"Do you think Aiden will come?" I ask. My eyes are closed, soaking in the rays.

"I don't know. If he knows better, he won't."

"Won't what?" Quinn asks. "Rena can't come today; she's working." Her body stands in front of me, blocking the sun.

"Oh, um. We don't want the day to end." I sit up, raising my hand to shield my eyes. "Sidelle and Kieran are over there." I point to the far end of the beach. "And Cali is on her way."

"Heads up!" Kieran dives toward us, sand flying everywhere. "Hi, ladies." He lands on his side and flashes us a smile.

"K," I scream as Quinn shouts, "Kieran."

We immediately stand and shake the sand off our bodies. Shay is smart enough not to say anything, but his mouth is fighting a smile.

Kieran grabs for the football. "Shay?"

He looks at me.

"You go have fun with K. I'll be here with the girls."

"We'll be right over there," Shay says.

"I hope we can do this a lot this summer." Cali plops down beside us. "Hi guys."

"Hey, Cali," I say. "Glad you could make it."

"And miss this gorgeous day and spend time with all of my besties? Never!"

"How was the end of school?" I ask now that all my friends are here, except for Rena.

"Boring as heck without you," Quinn says.

"Yeah, it wasn't the same," Cali agrees. "How was your trip? Do you have any pictures?" She spreads out her beach blanket and sinks down to lie beside us. I notice for the first time that her body is leaner, not that she was fat before she became a wolf, but she's taught with muscle. She's totally rockin' it in her white bikini.

"Um, I took forgot to take any." I shake my head, trying to recover from staring at my friend's body. "And what I did were on my phone, but I left it someplace and never got it back. Someone probably has stolen it by now."

"That's a big bummer," Quinn says.

"Yeah, it was." I look at Cali and hope that she can hear me, even though she's not in her wolf form. *We haven't told Quinn the truth because she's dating Aiden.*" Cali's eye grows

259

wide, and she subtly nods her head.

"So, what is everyone's plan for the summer?" Sidelle asks as she nears us. She left her crowd of followers. I can see why people flock to her. She's tall, her long legs seemingly never stopping. A fashionable short pixie hair cut surrounds a round face with bright green eyes that shine. She's thin, like a model, but has a perfect hourglass figure, highlighting an exotic emerald green swimsuit that has all eyes roaming over her body. "I might travel or go meet up with my folks. I haven't seen my mom in ages. My dad came to visit me, but that was just for a couple of hours while he was passing through on business."

Close enough to the truth. I'm sure Vash has filled Cali in on everything.

"I don't know about me," Cali says. "Try to spend as much time I can with Vash while he's around. Since his parents passed away, he's taken on all of the business and household needs. I'm helping where I can, but it's not enough. His brother, Jackson, has been great, too. I feel really bad for their sister, Era. She's so young and needs parental guidance. I hope that she one day will understand."

She's gotten good about telling a story with just enough truth entangled with it. It was flawless, and I know it's something I need to work on.

"What about you, Zoe?" Quinn asks. "You said that you

don't have a summer job yet. Are you planning to get one? I know that you are saving up for a car."

"I don't know yet. Since I just got back, I'm trying to find my groove. I guess I'll take one day at a time. But like Cali, I plan to spend as much time with Shay and all of you guys as possible. You never know what tomorrow will bring."

This day is exactly what I needed. A few hours of normalcy where I'm not thinking of a war, demons, or the world ending, just being a normal teenager and hanging with my friends, enjoying our summer before our senior year.

34
Zoe

"I've got to go." I watch the sun slip lower on to the horizon. "Shay, Kieran? Are you guys coming?" Both pause their game. "Stella should be done with practice and at home by now."

"Yeah, sure. Can we finish this match?" Shay asks. "It's almost over."

"Yep. I'll pack our stuff."

Everyone on the beach has been staring at the two boys ever since they ended their game of football and started a one-on-one volleyball game. Both had taken off their shirts, sporting their tan skin and six-packs. Sweat glistens on their bodies. Neither is superior to the other. They've been playing for at least forty-five minutes, and this is still their first game.

Some of the other school students tried to cut in, but after a few minutes of watching Shay and Kieran, they came to realize that it was better to stay on the sidelines in awe.

Sun tanning girls also noticed them and casually flipped their bodies on their towels to discreetly spy on my boys. My friends and I have the front row seats. Frequently, we've been sprayed with sand as the ball came too close when one of the boys dove trying to save it, causing us to shriek.

"I wish you didn't have to go so soon," Cali says. "I barely got here."

"Me, too, but…" I look around for anyone too close. "We have to come up with a plan on how to get the sword and how Stella fits into that. She's only thirteen. I can't have her in the thick of things when the baddies come out to play."

"I get it. Today was perfect, if only for a couple of hours. We all need a break just to be numb to it and get a handle on things."

"You should come over, too, and let Vash know what we discuss."

"Wait. What are you trying to find, Zoe?" Quinn asks as she pulls her attention from the game. "Maybe I can help."

Cali looks at me for help. I nod since I shouldn't be the one who outs her. Cali should be the one to spill her own secret. "That's a good idea." Cali begins to pack her belonging.

"Are you coming over, too?" Quinn asks.

"I am."

"Um. I think it's going to be a … how do I put this?"

"I already know what you are, Quinn."

"You do?"

"Yes, and anything you have to say can be said in front of me and my mate. I'll text Vash that I'll be a bit late. Maybe you have some new ideas we haven't thought of yet."

"I'm confused here. If you know about me, then what does that make you? And you said 'mate'."

"I'm a shifter."

Quinn leans in. "A what now? Shifter of what exactly?"

"I can turn myself into a wolf."

"Let's let Quinn mull that over as we pack up. We need to get going. Plus, I want to hear all about you and Aiden," Sidelle says to me. I glare at her. What does that have to do with anything? Sidelle smirks, knowing something I do not. At least I haven't put it together yet.

I think Quinn is too stunned to even make a comment about Sidelle. She doesn't ask why she's coming over to Kieran's house. "All right, it's settled. Let's go to K's place. I'll go pick up my sister and meet you guys there."

We gather the last of our beach items just as the boys end their game and the crowd disperses. A few of the closer girls sigh.

"That was an epic match, Shay," Kieran says.

"Yes, it was. We'll have to do that again sometime. I knew you'd be competitive, and you held you own. Not bad for never playing before." Shay grabs my bag and carries it to the car. "So, what's the plan you girls came up with?"

"Everyone is going to Kieran's house. I'll get Stella and meet you guys there," I say. "We can figure out the next steps." I look at Kieran. "Is that okay?"

"Sounds like as good a plan as any," he says.

"Stella, tell us everything that you've seen," Kieran says. He's sitting in his usual chair.

We are back in the den, and Shay and I are nestled against each other on the couch. He's in his trademark black T-shirt and black jeans.

"Um, hold up a second," Quinn says as she sits in the other chair across from Kieran. "I'm new at all this, so what is Zoe's sister?"

"Hold on a sec," I say. "Before we divulge too much information here." I tap Quinn's knee, getting her attention. "Everything we say in this room cannot leave it. That means you can't tell your parents, people outside of this room. Or Aiden. No one. I need to trust you on this, okay? Promise me that you won't share anything with him." She stares at me. "You're going to hear some things

265

about Aiden that you might not know or like. But Quinn, promise me that you won't say anything about this to anyone."

She looks at me for a moment, then nods. "I promise."

I confirm to my friends that we all heard Quinn's promise and give the go ahead to Kieran to continue.

"We think she's a Vate or Seer," he says.

"How?" Quinn asks. "I mean, since when?"

"I'm not sure," Kieran says. "Stella, when did you start seeing things?"

"It was during the time that Zoe was gone. At first I thought they were dreams, but they were so vivid, and I kept having the same one over and over again. It was like a movie playing on repeat, and each time a small item would become clearer. Gradually, I guessed it was real, and that it was the future."

"Maybe when I came into my powers, so did she?" I ask.

"Could be. I've seen you with a sword during the final battle, so I know you find one." Stella nods. "You must have one to defeat Sammael."

"Is that what you're looking for?" Quinn asks. I nod. "Who is Sammael?"

"First, maybe you should tell us what Aiden has told you," Shay says.

"Not much, actually. He's told me about Nephilims, our abilities, purpose, and he's been training me. He said that it's time I was put on a mission, but he didn't elaborate on what that would be."

"Do you know that he's the one who kidnapped me?" I ask.

"I thought you went to Europe?" Quinn shakes her head. "What, Aiden? No, that can't be right. He would never do anything that terrible. He's been with me almost every single day since I've been out of the hospital. When would he have time to kidnap you?"

The rest of my friends look at each other.

"I thought he was good, too, but I know it was him who took me from prom. He held me in a special room until I got my wings." I sat up and move to the edge of the couch. "But I escaped."

"It just doesn't sound like him, but you would know who your captor was." She shrugs. "I know in my heart that Aiden would never do anything like that. Perhaps he has a twin or something. He loves me and I him. I see the good in him. Zoe, you and I have been friends since grade school. I would never do anything to hurt you or betray your trust. I hope you know that."

"We will agree to disagree on Aiden's integrity. Since I won't be able to sway you, just be careful. That's all. I'm looking out for my friend. I don't want to see you get hurt."

Quinn stays silent and from her facial expressions, she's a bit mad at me. And that's fine. She can be.

"So, Little Stella-san," Sidelle says. "Where do you think we should start looking?"

"Paris, France." Stella pulls out her laptop and powers it on.

"Are you sure?" I ask. "Because that's a long trip to be guessing."

"Almost positive. I've been looking online, and it's the best guess I have. There are a few more places we can look if it's not there." Flipping the screen to me, I see a picture of a stone angel standing high on a pillar. Under it, it says that it's "The Armed Peace Angel" and stands guard over the entrance at Parc Monsouris.

"How are we supposed to get there?"

"You can fly there," Sidelle says.

"I don't have money for however many tickets."

"No, silly." Sidelle chuckles, shaking her head. "We have our own wings."

"Zoe, you have wings, too?" Quinn asks, and then turns to Sidelle. "And you?"

"Yeah, I just got them on my birthday."

"What are you exactly? And what does that make Sidelle?"

"I'm an angel." We are throwing a lot of information out in the open for Quinn to hear. I would hate if she tells Aiden anything, but she is my friend, and I have to trust her. We've been friends since kindergarten. I need to trust in that. Plus, we haven't really told her anything Aiden doesn't already know.

"Sidelle's a fairy," Kieran says. "Can you try opening a

porta, so we don't all have to fly there? It is a very long trip across the ocean. And I don't think some of us will all make it there."

I smack his knee. "Hey, just because I'm new at this —"

"I meant Shay," Kieran coughs.

"If that fails, we probably can use the company jet," Cali offers. "I'm sure Vash won't mind."

"All right, everyone into the backyard." Sidelle ushers us off the furniture. "I need to create an archway, and we'll see how it goes."

We march to the back of the house and open the sliding glass door. Sidelle strolls to one of the trees and gently caresses the trunk. She's whispering something and pats its bark. Quickly, she snaps off a few branches and bends them back and forth, softening them up. She steps to an evergreen and does the same thing.

Once she's done, the branches intertwine together and form a long branch. She calls up some green glamour and molds each end into the ground, forming a tall archway. Again muttering in a foreign language, she waves her hand up and down and across the opening. A cloudy film appears, unlike all the other times I've used a porta.

"It's not working correctly." Sweat drips down Sidelle's face. "It should be, but for some reason, it's not." She drops her hands. "We'll have to take the jet."

"Maybe the wards here are too strong," Kieran says as he pats Sidelle's shoulder.

"How are my sister and I going to take a trip to France?" I ask. "Doesn't it take like ten hours to fly there?"

"I guess we need to figure out who all has to go because Zoe and I could go by ourselves," Kieran says. "The only reason we need the plane is for Vash and Shay."

"I'm not letting Zoe go without me." Shay steps in front of me.

"Shay." I gently turn him to face me. "I'll be okay. Kieran will take good care of me. I need you to watch over Stella while I'm gone. Nothing can happen to her." I turn back to my best friend. "We can fly faster than a plane?"

He nods.

Shay's mouth flattens. I know he doesn't like it. We've always said that we would be there for each other. But with less than two weeks before all hell breaks loose, I really need to kick my search into high gear.

I think he knows this, too. Ever so slightly, he nods. I mouth, "I love you," and then face Kieran. "Why can't we just appear there like I've seen you do?"

"You've never been there in real life. You need to know exactly where you're going and seeing it in photos and movies is different."

"I'm going with you, too," Sidelle says. "We've had eons to learn about every nook and cranny of earth. So you need to do this the old fashioned way until you've lived as long as us and can pop in and out of places."

"Kieran, if anything happens to her—" Shay begins.

"Nothing will happen." Kieran leads me away from our small group. "We'll go there and be back here in a couple of hours. I promise." He motions for Sidelle to step to my other side, turning to me. "Are you ready, Zoe?" He takes my hand. "I need you to concentrate on your Light. You haven't ever traveled this far. Take Sidelle's hand and focus. Wrap it around yourself. Feel it in every cell of your body. Now, think of it expanding like a bubble and include Sidelle and me. Once you have that, picture the Eiffel Tower in your mind."

Heat warms our linked hands. When I look down at them, they glow with purple Light. Sidelle's hand is pulsing with her green glamour. Kieran's has a slight yellow tint.

"You can do this, Zoe," Kieran whispers.

I know I can. My back tingles, releasing my wings. They don't hold back any longer. The force of their freedom affects my angelic power. Purple thrusts from my body, and along with it my wings encase us. And we launch into the sky.

35

Aiden

"Aiden?" Quinn walks into my room. "Oh, good. You're here. Your sister didn't know but let me in anyway."

"Do you need something?" I slam the book closed.

"Am I interrupting you?"

"Nope, just doing some reading about ... never mind." I slide the spine away from Quinn's view. "What's up?"

"I ran into Zoe at Coffee Grind and then decided to spend the day at the beach with her."

I nod for her to continue.

"We went to Kieran's house after." My body involuntarily flinches at his name. I hope she doesn't notice. "Zoe said that you were the one who held her captive. I didn't believe her of course. But why would she lie about something like that?"

I motion for her to sit on my bed, but she remains pacing the room.

"She would know who held her prisoner, right? Well, she said it was you. I just can't believe that. You wouldn't do anything like that. Would you?"

"How could I have done something as horrible as taking someone against their will? You've been with me on most days."

"That's what I told her, too. I know you. You aren't that kind of a person."

"Come here and sit." I take her hand and guide her to the bed, trying to calm her down. "Quinn." My fingers lock with hers. "You do know me, and I would never hurt anyone." She nods. Her body is tense, and tears run down her cheeks. "Stop crying. I didn't do what she's accusing me of."

"I know."

"What did she say exactly?"

"She didn't go into detail about her captivity." Quinn wipes her face. "But she's now off on some mission trying to find a sword. Kieran and Sidelle went with her to Europe to look for one."

"I see."

"Do you know anything about that?"

"Not a clue." My thumb rubs the top of her hand in a soothing pattern.

"I hope she finds what she's looking for. Stella said that

a great battle is coming soon." Quinn moves her body to face me. "Did you hear about that? Is that the mission you were going to tell me about?"

"Ah, well, the cat is out of the bag now. Yes, there is a fight coming. No one knows exactly when, but I have a feeling it'll be in a couple of weeks. Maybe less."

"That's what all the training was for?"

"Yes, to prepare us to win against the opposing side. I assume that Zoe or her friends told you who we would be battling?"

"Someone named Sammael, but, come to think of it, no one ever said who he is. They wanted to know what I've been doing with you."

"Did you tell them?"

"Yeah, why wouldn't I? We haven't done anything wrong. I told them that you have been training me to use my Nephilim skills."

"Are you going to meet up with her again? After she comes back from Europe?"

"Not sure. We didn't make any plans or anything."

"Well." I shrug. "If you do see her, could you find out if she finds a sword or not?"

"Sure." Quinn's voice is hesitant.

"I'm just curious if she does. It'd be cool because then we all have swords for battle." I lean against the headboard, trying to act casual. "Did you have a chance to show her yours?"

"No, they needed to hurry and then off they went. But yeah, okay. I'll pop over to Kieran's tomorrow and find out."

"Great. They'll be prepared for the upcoming fight then, too." I move Quinn closer to me. "So tell me more about Zoe's sister."

"Kieran said that she's a Vate and can see the future. No one seemed to know anything more than that."

Interesting. I check my phone for the time. "I'm sorry to do this to you, but I have an appointment to be at so no training today." Quinn doesn't need to know she has helped me enact my plan. Now, I have to get the fourth part of it going.

Me: Will you meet me for coffee?

I eagerly wait for Morgan's response. Quinn left a couple minutes ago. That was a close call, but I think she was satisfied with my answers.

Morgan: Time?
Me: 10 minutes
Morgan: What's so urgent?
Me: Are you going to meet or not?
Morgan: Fine

Of course she will meet me. I dropped her like a bad

habit, and she didn't like that very much. She's only good for kicks. Well, she does have some redeeming qualities, like … hmm, I can't think of anything. She does give Zoe grief that no one else can do, which I do like.

Driving to Coffee Grind—the only shop that serves a good cup of Joe around this quaint town—doesn't take long. I don't have to wait for Morgan; she's already sitting on one of the high back chairs. The place is rather busy for a late Friday evening. It is one of the few places for all walks of life to hang out without driving into the Cities.

I swagger past Morgan, faking that I don't see her. She needs to get my attention. I feel her gaze on me, but she doesn't call my name. The place isn't big, so a few steps later I'm nearing the back wall. Turning, I spot her and she waves.

"Oh, there you are," I say. "I didn't see you sitting there. You're more gorgeous than I remember. Did you change your hair?" Her eyes cut into mine. "Thank you for meeting me. I wanted to apologize for our breakup. I know you took it pretty hard."

"Are you trying to get back into my good graces?" Morgan crosses her long legs. "Your new fling cut you loose?"

"No, it wasn't like that."

"Then you're not seeing Quinn?"

"Not in the way you think."

"Always so cryptic with you. So, you want to get back

together with me? When did you realize that I'm exactly what you're looking for?"

"I've always known you were meant to be with me." I give her my most dazzling smile, the one that melts souls. "Besides, you and I are one in the same." She motions for me to sit on the loveseat. I snag her hand and pull her body closer to me as we crash onto the cushions. "Will you take me back?" My breath tickles her ears. "Please?"

"I should let you suffer more."

"But you won't, will you? Say you'll be mine again." I squeeze her hand and trace along her jaw line with my other. She's thawing; her body is giving her away. "As a celebration of us getting back together, I thought we could reacquaint ourselves. A nice road trip so we can talk and then when we get to our destination, we can do other things to reconnect."

"Oh, I love where this is going."

Of course she does.

"What do you say? Next weekend we go someplace special."

"All right, but this better not be a trick or anything."

"It's not." I seal our bargain with a scorching kiss. The only way Morgan will know I'm serious.

36

Zoe

My head tilts back so I can take in the full height of the Eiffel Tower. I've only seen this monument in pictures. They don't do it justice, and we don't have time to gawk, as much as I would like to.

"So, where's this park with the statue?" I look around and notice that we reappeared at the Champ de Mars, and the only reason I know that is because in middle school I wrote a paper about it.

"I know where it is," Sidelle says. It's crowded today because it's the weekend, so our sudden appearance goes unnoticed. "Can you make yourself invisible?"

"Yes," I say.

"Good because it'll be the fastest way to get there. Traffic is horrible this time of day. Believe me, I once lived here."

"All right, you lead, Sidelle," Kieran says. "Follow her closely and don't deviate."

I make myself invisible and turn to my friends. Kieran has his wings out, and we take to the sky. Soaring above the Seine River, we head in the opposite direction, past the Le Jardin du Luxembourg and toward the Les Catacombes de Paris. Kieran points the landmarks out as we fly over them.

Up head lays green grass and a small lake within the gardens of Parc Montsouris. Sidelle descends, and we land near a bronze angel with wings opened wide. It's patinaed in green, and her left-hand rests on an unsheathed sword. With her other hand gracefully on her hip and her face looking away, she's very casual in her stance. But the wings are ready to whisk her into a battle.

"What do I do?" I notice that the angel is robed in a long gown. The pillar she stands on is quite tall. Good thing I have wings because a ladder wouldn't reach her.

"What do you feel like you should do?" Kieran asks. "I don't think we'll be of much help."

"Maybe fly up there and touch it, and see if it calls to you," Sidelle suggests.

I do as she proposes and when I'm level with the beautiful angel, my body thrums with excitement. My hand hovers about the one that is holding the hilt. Light cascades around us, and I think I've found my sword. The moment I touch it my palm heats, but that's all that happens. I lift my fingers and wrap them around the handle. Nothing. I gaze at my hand and back to the sword.

"I don't think this is my sword," I say.

"Why do you say that?" Kieran asks.

"Just a feeling. I felt it heat up my hand, but maybe that's from the sun. She's made of metal and basking out here in the summer months; she'll be hot."

Disappointment washes over me. My sister said that there are a few other places to look, so there is still hope. I pull out my replacement phone, late birthday gift from Kierann, to text her and get the next location.

Me: Not it. Where's another place to look?

We walk around the colorful gardens, waiting for my sister's response.

Stella: bummer that wasn't it. I was almost positive it was. OK. Try Rome.

I show Kieran and Sidelle the text. We should have gone there to begin with since it's where the Vatican is.

My Light is brought forth, and we head to Italy. We land at the Colosseum, another place I've always wanted to visit. Finding an angel with a sword here is going to be like searching for Waldo in one of those books.

"Any chance either one of you know where we should start looking?"

"This is a holy city," Kieran says. "We should start at St. Peter's Basilica. It's one of the largest church in the world that stands for Christianity. We'll make our way toward other angel statues."

I nod. It's the best plan for now. I try using my Light to find my sword, but there are too many potential places and too much ground to cover. The streets are littered with crosses, angels, and other symbols of the religion.

It's interesting that as I fly over each building, my brain knows what it is and provides me a brief historical summary.

Keeping ourselves unseen, we fly over the Vatican Museums and the Osservatore Romano to the Apostolic Palace and land in St. Peters Platz. Pillars surround the white rotunda. Statues of martyrs, saints and previous popes stand on top of each, as if guarding the entrance to the sacred place of worship. The whole building is majestic. The gray paved ground doesn't take away from the grandness of the center pillar that soars into the sky, with a bronze cross at its peak

I stumble toward the entrance of the basilica, not watching where I'm going. It's a good thing I'm invisible, otherwise everyone would see me face plant, multiple times.

The inside is as spectacular as the exterior. Patterned marble flooring greets us. Textured columns probably made of the same material as the floor lines the walls. Everything is gold trimmed. Each archway has angels. Alcoves hold massive angelic statues of saints. People mill around, snapping pictures of this impressive space.

"It's not here." Besides being awed like all the other visitors, I feel nothing. "We should move on."

"I don't think the angels would hide it in such a tourist trap," Sidelle says. "Since they went to the trouble in hiding the sword, they'd use some place a bit less conspicuous. Just my opinion, though, from what I know of angels." She nods to Kieran.

"Would I be wrong?"

"I don't think so."

"Okay, where to next?" I ask, taking one last look around the magnificent building.

"I guess let's just cover as much ground as possible," Kieran says. "If anyone notices any sword that could be what we're looking for, text each other."

We leave the plaza, taking flight. I keep myself low to the ground and still invisible to humans. Spiraling outward from the Basilica, I spot what looks like a castle. A Castle of Angels, perhaps. At first I think it's an odd place to have one, but by the state of it, it's old. Part of the walls are crumbling away. The arched bridge that runs over the

River Tiber is caked with green and black moss. Statues of angels escort the tourists to the main door.

Sweeping the pathway, I inspect each angel. None are holding a weapon. As I approach the main building, rising out of the roof is a bronzed figurine. With his right hand, he's unsheathing a sword.

I fly close enough to inspect it. No humans are allowed on the roof. The angel is green from the elements, and the sword's blade shines in the sunlight. It's either what I came to see, or it's been modified.

I hover next to one of its colossal wings and reach out toward the long blade. My fingers graze it but nothing happens. Wrapping my hands around the hilt and letting it bath in my Light still doesn't do anything.

Sighing, I move away and continue my search. The Pantheon, Trevi Fountain, and the Piazza Venzia are all passed. No tingling felt.

Hours pass as I fly over the Baths of Caracalla and outward to Mausoleo di Cecilia Metella. I'm high enough that the whole city of Rome is placed within a circle.

The moon is rising. We've been searching for most of the day. I pull out my phone and text Sidelle and Kieran.

Me: I haven't found anything. I'm at some nature reserve to the west of the city.

I spot of bit of greenery to land on and rest. Sidelle texts back first.

Sidelle: I'll find ya.

Looking around and not finding anyone, I make myself visible and stroll on the vibrant green grass. Rolling hills swell across the land and round hay bales dot the ground. I barely make them out, but my sneeze tells me that I'm correct in my thinking. The ping from my phone disturbs the crickets' song.

Kieran: I think I see you.

When Kieran finds me, I'm sitting yoga-style on the grass when my wings twitch. I've come to know that feeling is when other angels are around me, so I know Kieran is close, even though he's still unseen.

"Nothing?" he asks me as he floats down from the sky.

"No." I shake my head.

"Well, let's wait for Sidelle to consider our next step."

We don't wait too long and from the expression on her face, her search has also come up empty.

"Don't fret, yet," Kieran says. "Europe is a lot older than the U.S. There's tons of places to look."

I stay quiet and unlock my phone again to text my sister.

Me: Next option? Oh, and tell M & D, I'm staying at K's tonight. I'll let them know, too. Just so we have our stories straight.

"Don't count out South America," Sidelle says. "There are tribes there that date back before Europe. And some places in Asia, too."

Stella: Nothing, really? Um, weird. Ok. Off you got to Ukraine. I have a good feeling about this one. OK about the sleep over. 😊

At least one of us does. I show my phone to the others, but before we take off again, I send a text to Shay. I know he's probably worried sick since it's taken way longer than we said we would be gone for.

Me: I'm sorry this is taking so long. Love you, miss you, and thinking of you. I'm safe.
Shay: Quinn came over and was asking if you found a sword yet.
Me: Really? Did you tell her anything?
Shay: I kept it vague.
Me: She has to be reporting back to Aiden.
Shay: That's what I think too

I show them my text. We all shake our heads. "Zoe, you need to rest," Kieran says. "You still need to eat and sleep, too. We'll worry about Quinn later. We really haven't shared anything with her that Aiden didn't already know about."

I nod. "I don't feel tir—"

"Save it, Z," Sidelle says. "Your wings are drooping.

They need a break."

"But you guys don't need one." I stand.

"We don't." Kieran pulls me to him and grabs my phone. "But we've both had our wings for centuries and have had lots of practice flying. You're new at this."

I flex them and they twinge. Frowning, I know they are right. I need to rest, but we need to find my sword and get back home.

"You guys stay here, and I'll go find Zoe food." Sidelle disappears.

"Come on." Kieran drags me under a maple tree. "Let's get you settled in."

The leaves are bright green. The moon is high, and stars sprinkle the sky. Fireflies blink off in the distance. A lone wolf, or a dog, howls in the distance.

The sun is up, and the air is warm. Rolling off from Kieran's chest, I grimace.

"Good morning." He sees that I'm awake.

"Um, sorry about that. I guess I was tired." I wipe my mouth, hoping that I hadn't drooled on him.

"You can tell me I was right later." He stands and helps me up. "But we should get going. I've already texted Shay and told him that it might be a day or two more."

"Thank you." I yawn and stretch my back, releasing my

wings.

"Up and at them!" Sidelle smiles. She knows I'm not a morning person. "Here's a bagel and an apple. Eat up and then we'll take off."

And then we're flying again.

In a flash, I'm glancing over Serbia, Romania, and then Moldova. We land in the only city I know that's in the Ukraine. Kiev.

As we descend from the skies, two glistening spots shine like beacons, beckoning us to them. Two angels are facing each other, as if they are watching over the square. What is this place?

"Do you think it's a coincidence that we're seeking an angel statue in Independence Square?" Sidelle asks.

"I think everything happens for a reason," Kieran says as we land.

Long cement pavers create an ornate pattern on the ground that leads to four levels of steps. The area is in shape of a hexagon, and in the center stands a four-sided temple, for lack of a better word. Each entrance passes through to the opposite side. The archways have two pillars on each side. Gold accents the columns, the archways, and the base of the tower. On top of the tower rests one of the angels.

Upon closer inspection, it's not an angel but a girl. She's wearing a dress while her arms are extended out. In her right hand, she's holding a golden branch. It's like she's wearing a shawl, and the ends are blowing in the wind, which made me think that she was an angel. Gold is accented along her belt, the shawl, and shoes.

If I thought the church in Rome was breathtaking, I don't know what to call this monument.

"It's called the Independence Monument," Kieran whispers. "Isn't it beautiful? I can't believe that Ordinaries made it."

I look high into the sky. She's not carrying any weapons, only what I think is a peace offering.

Directly opposite is a much smaller yellow and white structure. It reminds me of the Soldiers' and Sailors Arch that stands in at the Grand Army Plaza in Brooklyn. On top of the building in front of me is a warrior angel. He's gripping a shield in his left hand and a golden sword in his right. His wing tips are decorated in gold, along with the trim of his cape, breastplate, and boots.

He reminds me of Kieran with his golden hair and halo surrounding his head.

"Is this you?" I ask him, kinda kidding.

"Nope, but I can see how you would think that." He pokes me in the ribs. "This is the Archangel Michael."

"That's not what he really looks like though, is it?"

I've only met Michael a few instances during my life. Yes, he lived across the street as I grew up, but Kieran always said that he was traveling on business. Then when Shay was rescued from Hell, Michael was at the safe house, trying to heal my boyfriend from his injuries. But the few times I saw him he had worn normal clothes, not battle gear like the statue.

"Michael changes his form to what he thinks is the best way to show himself to humans. So actually, this is really close to his true appearance. His wings are longer and broader, plus they don't have any gold."

"Think that sword he's carrying up there could be yours?" Sidelle asks.

"There is only one way to find out." I double check my surroundings, and I float up toward the sculpture. I hover in front of Michael and bow my head. I know that this isn't the real one, but it still feels like the right thing to do.

My hand extends toward his sword. Sparks emit from my fingertips, and the golden sword glows with radiance.

Electrical currents bounce between us. The closer my hand gets to his, the more painful it becomes.

My body glows with purple Light as it's pulled toward and merges with the statue. I'm in the same pose and when I wrap my fingers around the hilt, bright light fires into the sky. I have no idea what other people are seeing, but my own vision is crystal clear as memories flash in my mind.

Soothing music calms me. Voices carry an ancient language. They are muffled, so I can't hear them fully, but

I know what they are saying. Words like joy, love, and harmony.

I clutch the sword as it pulses in my hand. The blade turns metallic silver. Where the blade and hilt connect is the triquetra symbol that matches my wrist. Again, the symbol is repeated at the pommel. Two daggers form the cross-guard, and each of their hilts is shaped into wings.

The blade itself flows with power. It reminds me of mercury and how it shimmers. The edge of the blade has a unique shape, like that of holly berries.

My body is flung out of the statue, and I've barely managed to right myself.

And in my hand rests a long, glowing sword.

My Seraph's Sword.

37

Zoe

Wednesday, July 1.

It has been only four days since we found my Seraph's Sword. But those three days it took were still time away from my family and friends. Who am I kidding? Time away from Shay. Being kidnapped for those weeks made me realize that my time with them should not be taken for granted.

But I also knew that I had to find my sword. I still didn't understand why it hadn't appeared to me when I received my wings, and I had to go galivanting around the world to find it. Maybe someone higher up knew not to give it to me while I was imprisoned. It couldn't fall into the hands of my enemies.

And yes, Aiden is number one on that list. I don't care

what Quinn thinks. If he's good, and I highly doubt it, he needs to prove it to me. And more importantly, to himself.

I guess it doesn't matter now how long it took us. What matters is that we have four days before it's July Fourth. That's when Stella thinks the final battle will begin.

When I returned home, she said that she had another vision. All throughout it was red, white, and blue. I don't think it is chance that my sword was found in Independence Square, and I'd meet Sammael on our Independence Day.

Four days.

In that time, we have to think of a place to draw the demons to. I need to learn to wield my sword and not make a fool of myself. Or get myself killed. The packs around the world have to be contacted, and the fairies need to come out of Fairyland.

So much to do. Plus, I need to tell my parents something to get them away from the battleground. Kieran has assured me on many occasions that once the Void is created whoever is outside of it will be safe. I can't help but think that there might be demon stragglers, and they'll wreak havoc outside of the protection forcefield.

"Again, Zoe." Shay's frustrated voice breaks through my thoughts. "You need to focus so you don't die."

"I know that." My brow is covered with sweat. "I need a sec." Carefully, I place my sword on the patio table. Kieran suggested we use his backyard to train me because it is warded, and his neighbors won't hear anything suspicious. "Do you think Vash will get all the packs to come here in time?" I grab my water bottle and take a big gulp.

"He'll get as many as will come."

I look at my boyfriend. He hasn't broken a sweat yet. I wanted to practice with sticks first only because I didn't want to injure him. Now, I know why he smirked at me. He knew I wouldn't be able to hit anything.

We've been practicing since we returned from Kiev. Shay and Kieran told me I had to get used to the feel and weight of my sword. It really didn't feel heavy, but no one else can touch it. When they try, their hands pass through it.

"What about Oberon and Mab?" I ask.

"They'll both probably come and fight since they helped already." Shay closes the distance between us and stands next to me. "They know what's at stake if this world is lost to evil. We should hear from our friends soon."

"I hope you're right."

"And in the meantime, you need to get better with your sword." He points to it on the table. "You're not going to magically lean how to do this."

"Are you sure? I mean, I never tried before. Flying was sorta easy, except for the landings, and Sidelle can learn how to do things when she Mind Walks."

"All right, we'll try it using Light, but your body doesn't

know the moves. You need to build the muscle retention."

"Let me see if I can understand the moves and if I don't get it, we'll keep doing it your way."

"Sounds like a wonderful plan." Kieran steps out from the sliding glass door. "I spoke to Michael for possible locations on where to create the Void. He suggested Lake Superior. It's the largest body of water near here and less Ordinaries will be around. It should be big enough for the battle. If it's not, we can stretch it to cover one of the other Great Lakes."

"How is everyone going to get there?" I turn around and ask him. "And how are the wolves going to fight on water?"

"Sidelle said that there are a couple of national and state parks near Duluth, so she'll be able to open a porta to there. As for the rest, the Void will take care of it. It'll create an alternate earth that will lay above the lake and be solid ground. It won't be an issue."

My thoughts go back to what my sister told me about the battle field. Land and water. This must be where we make our final stand.

"Is she going to be able to do it?" Shay asks. "She couldn't before when we needed to find Zoe's sword."

"I know, but that was different." Sidelle materializes in a chaise lounge. "I know where these parks are. Tons of trees and nature surrounds them. I draw my glamour from that. Unlike going to urban settings, it's difficult." She hangs her head. I pat her shoulders. "I used to live in France, but that was centuries ago."

"I didn't mean to offend you, Sidelle," Shay says. "I know you know how important it is."

"Oberon will be able to open it from the Fairyland side. He's stronger than me. And Mab will want the fight in the north, since she needs the cold to draw on." The set of her mouth tells us the matter is closed. "So. Whatcha three doin'?" She winks at me, and I know she's back to her old self. "Looks like a bunch of trouble if you ask me."

"I was just about to try using my Light to learn fighting techniques with my sword." I stand and grab my sword, wandering to a chair. Grabbing the pillow, I place it on the ground and sit yoga-style with the sword resting across my lap. "Okay, here it goes."

I close my eyes and feel the Light hum under my skin. The pulse of the sword vibrates on my knees. I think about what Shay has tried to teach me these past days. The way his body moves, so gracefully. How his hand grips the handle, and how his powerful legs dance as his arms thrust outward. The sword is an extension of his arm.

My mind blocks out my friends, the neighborhood noises, and the only think I focus on is my purple Light. I let it wiggle into every cell of my being. It's always there, waiting to be used. But what if I never put it away? Could I use it all the time?

I stand and motion for Shay to join me on the lawn. I'm

using a tiny bit of Light, not enough to make me glow. Shay hunches down, his sword ready. I nod and he attacks, driving me back.

My blade meets his. Metal rings in the air, shattering the silence in my head. My sword is radiant. Swing after swing, I'm blocking Shay's attempts to disarm me. I let out a bit more Light, and I go on the offensive. My hits are finding their marks, and the strength behind them is forcing Shay back.

More Light is used, and we parry with the wing speed of hummingbirds. Our forms are barely visible. Flashes of Kieran and Sidelle sitting on the patio rush by, and it happens. Shay's blade doesn't block mine in time. The tip is inches from his neck. A thin line of blood trails down his throat and is soaked up by the collar of his T-shirt.

My body stops moving.

"Very good." Shay smiles. "I knew you had it in you."

"But I used my Light."

"Yes, you did." He takes my free hand and leads us back to the chairs. "And why not? It's a part of you now. During battle, you're going to need everything in your arsenal. Opponents aren't going to come at you one at a time. There will be many, and they'll keep coming until you're exhausted. And even then, you can't stop."

"It wouldn't be a bad idea to build up your stamina using your Light," Kieran says. "I was created with it and have an abundance because I'm used to it. I'm sure

Sidelle's glamour is the same way." She nods. "It has to be second nature."

"I was telling Kieran while you guys were playing that my father and Mab are in," Sidelle says. "As we speak, they are gathering their forces and will be on the ready. Oberon will open the porta and let both Summer and Winter through."

"That's great!" I say. "Now, we need to hear from Vash and the packs."

Someone's phone chimes. We all check our pockets.

It's Kieran's cell. He looks at the screen and texts back. "Speaking of the Alpha," he says. "That was him. He said most of the packs are coming and preparing to fly here. I told him where the meeting place is, and he'll let the other pack Alphas know. Vash said that a couple male members will be left at their residences just in case. All children and some of the females will also stay."

I nod.

If everyone dies, the packs need to carry on their existence. My eyes sting thinking of my family, of my friends. We could die in four days. The world could end in less than a week.

But I have a plan.

38

Zoe

"Mom? Dad?" I walk through an empty kitchen, wondering where they could be.

"Zoe? We're upstairs."

I climb the staircase and enter my parents' room. Luggage lays on the bed, and dresser drawers are open.

"What's going on?" I ask.

"Are you packed?" Mom asks. "We're leaving early tomorrow morning."

"No. Where are we going?"

She looks at me and at Dad.

"Honey, we always go to the cabin over the fourth. Are you feeling okay?"

Of course. My family is headed to our summer house in northern Minnesota. It's about two hours west of Duluth, so I know that they'll be safe there. And if any demons come looking for us here, we'll be gone.

"Oh, yeah. I'm almost packed. You know me, last minute clothes washing." I turn and shuffle toward my room to start packing for the week-long vacation.

How am I going to get Shay up there? Kieran and Sidelle can make themselves invisible and just hang around. Vash, Cali, and the Packs will meet us north of Duluth, so they can stay in hotels. So it comes back to Shay.

"Um, guys?" I turn around. "Can Shay come with us? His mom is out of town, and he doesn't have any place to go. And I think Kieran won't be around, or he'd stay with him."

"Sure, Zoe," Dad says. "The holidays are for celebration with family and friends. It's nice that you think of them. Plus, your Mom and I will take all the time you want to give us. Next year, we'll hardly ever see you since you'll be an important senior in high school."

"Great, I'll let Shay know." I head back to my room. "And Dad?"

"Yes?"

"Thanks. I love you guys."

"We love you, too."

When I return to my room, I dig out my phone and text Shay to let him know what's happening.

Me: You're coming with us to our cabin!

Scrounging around for my suitcase, which I find buried under a mound of clothes in the walk-in-closet, I toss in jean shorts, tanks, and T-shirts. My cell chimes, alerting me to a message.

Shay: Sounds good. I was trying to think of a way to get us to Duluth without raising suspicion.
Me: Problem solved. You should pack and come over here. Maybe I can convince my parents to let us drive separately.
Shay: OK

Taking a toiletry bag, I fill it with makeup, hair product, and plenty of elastic bands. The cabin already has most of my belongings since we spend most of our summer weekends there.

Reorganizing the luggage, I painstakingly refold everything so more items can be brought with me. Even though I know I won't wear most of it, I must bring enough clothes because a girl has to have choices.

I hear the doorbell and run downstairs to let Shay in. Opening the front door, Shay greets me with a warm smile.

"Hey, Beautiful." He leans in and kisses me. I wrap my arms around his neck as his arms snake around my back, dropping his bag to the ground. "Miss me that much?"

"Always," I pant, leading him back to my room. "Shay's here," I say to my parents.

"Glad you could come with us, Shay." Dad's voice

carries through the hallway. "We're about ready to pack the vehicle."

"Yeah, about that, Dad. Would it be possible if Shay drove me? I'm going to show him around town and some other tourist attractions later in the week."

"Sure," Mom says as she walks out of her closet. "And when you're done with that, you can take Shay to the iron range and Duluth. It's not too far away, and you can view the harbor and watch ships come and go." She comes and leans against the doorframe. "Oh, have you been to the Glensheen Mansion in Duluth, Shay? There's a ghost story involved, if you like that sort of thing."

Shay glances at me and I shrug.

"No, I don't think I've been there before. Sounds cool."

"I have to finish gathering my stuff. Come on, Shay." I tug his hand back into my room. "That's so weird of them. I thought they would kick up a fuss about you coming along, and then for Mom to suggest we go to Duluth for the day."

"I know. It's like someone is watching over us."

"Maybe He is?"

"Could be. Or it could be luck is finally on our side." He sits on my bed and watches me pack.

"Most of my stuff is already up there, so I won't need to bring too much in the way of personal items."

"This isn't too much stuff?" Shay smirks.

"This? Nope. You should see the first and last trip of the season. I think I could fill an entire truck. But I like having variety. You never know when it'll rain, snow, or be cold."

Shay glimpses back to the door and lowers his voice and says, "My car is loaded to the gills with weapons and amo. We won't have enough time to come back for it, so we need to bring it all with us."

I nod and continue to fold clothes.

"Zoe?" Shay and I look up at my sister who is standing inside my room. "I know I should ask to be in here, but I thought you guys would want to know that something is happening."

"What do you mean?" I pull Stella deeper into my bedroom. "What have you seen?"

"Right now, we're in the calm before the storm, and all of Hell will be unleashed and that's not a figure of speech," she says. "There are rumblings that the Knights are gathering near the Canadian border."

"We know," Shay says. "Kieran let the angels know that that's where Zoe'll be for the trap. We need them there, so the Veil can be opened with as little prying eyes from Ordinaries as possible."

"Wait. You're the bait? You can't be!" Stella hugs me. "I have a very bad feeling about you being there. I know you have your sword now, but I can't see beyond the battle."

"What do you think that means, Shay?" I ask.

"Not sure. But I'll protect you. We all will. We knew using you as the bait was risky, but it's the only way to make sure that the demons go up north and not force our hand and take the fight where the population is high."

I sit next to Shay and guide Stella to sit on the other side of me. My hands shake, and my breathing labors.

Shay threads his fingers through mine and squeezes. "I know you're scared, Zoe. You have every right to be. You've only known about angels and demons for a couple of months, you're just learning how to use your sword, and you only recently received your wings. It's a lot to take in. I understand. But your friends are all with you. I know you can do this, and we will be by your side. And we will drive back evil and win this war."

39
Zoe

Thursday, July 2.

We make it to our cabin in Nisswa a couple of hours ago. The weather is slightly troublesome as sheets of rain decide to pour down on us, making visibility difficult. Shay expertly drives his car along the highway with the other vacationers heading to their getaways.

The air becomes colder the farther north we go, unusual for the middle of summer. Dead animals line the ditches. I lose count on how many deer and birds I see, knowing that many more lay on the ground deep within the woods.

The news station we briefly listen to tells us that the entire Middle East is in an all-out war. Truces are being ignored and skirmishes escalate. Thousands are dead from bombings and gunfire. Ships navigate off the coast of Japan and sail for China. Retaliation is imminent. They have threatened to release nuclear warheads.

It's starting. That is all I could think of. The world is already at war, and I'd be battling evil in a few days. Am I ready?

"We should try to get to Duluth a day early," Shay said. "That way we can get the lay of the land, and if fighting starts early, we're there. The angels should be ready to construct the Void as soon as possible. We'll have to make sure that you're seen all over the city. The wards around you will drop, so your Light will shine like a beacon, calling the demons to you."

"Do you think this'll work?" I ask.

"It has to."

My parents take Stella into town to get groceries and ice cream, leaving Shay and I alone. We lounge on the couch, his arm drapes across my stomach. My head lies on his sculpted chest.

Our cabin is small compared to the monstrosities around the lake. It's one of the originals, but it's all my family needs. Fond memories of swimming, fishing, and playing tag with other vacationers flutter in my mind.

The large picture window fogs with the rain that still pelts down, leaving streaks of dirt behind. As soon the weather clears, cleaning is the first task. It always is. Even though we come up to the summer home almost every weekend, a fine layer of dust seems to settle over things.

But it's a tradition that we all enjoy. Time spent with each other. Just like my room at home, I don't have to share one with Stella, but we do have to share a bathroom.

"Maybe we should go to Duluth tomorrow, then?" I suggest. "We can go to Canal Park, eat at Grandma's, walk the shore, and watch ships come in."

"Do some tourist things outside." I feel Shay's head bob. "If the weather worsens, we could get a hotel room, so we don't have to drive back. At least that's what we'll tell your parents."

"Okay." I shift from Shay's body and reach in my back pocket for my phone. Brushing the screen, it turns on and I find the weather app. It's supposed to continue raining all night and into tomorrow evening. The temperature today is also lowering as the day wears on.

Something strange is happening. It's bitter cold in the midst of summer. Yes, even in northern Minnesota it gets into the nineties, but along the north shore, they do get water effect, which lowers the temperature. Not like this though.

This is something beyond abnormal.

My parents come home from the grocery store and ice cream parlor, and then we make burgers on the grill. Dad prepares and flips the meat, Shay is out there too for moral support, while us ladies are in the kitchen prepping the salad, coleslaw, and peeling potatoes to make homemade French fries. That, too, is our traditional first night's meal.

"Have you seen all the horrible news reports on TV?" Mom asks.

"Yes, troubling reports, indeed," Dad says.

I don't say anything and neither does Shay. That was the only downer to the evening.

We continue on nicer subjects and laugh, tell stories of our younger years, and I'm thankful to be with them one last time. My parents don't know what will happen tomorrow but Stella does. She keeps glancing my way throughout the night. With a slight shake of my head, I put her off. I can't get into it with her. Not yet.

After dinner we bring out the games. Stella chooses first and insists we play cribbage. Thirteen going on thirty. We pair off, and I play against my dad. Mom sneaks back to the kitchen, even though Shay tells her to leave the dishes, and he will take care of them after winning against Stella.

The evening draws to a close after a vivacious game of Old Maid. My parents call it a night and suggest we kids not stay up too late. We should be in bed before the sun rises.

I grab lawn chairs and sit out on the porch and listen to the rain pounding on the wood roof. Neither Shay nor I say anything. There isn't anything to say. He knows how I feel about him, and no words can express what I know in my heart, anyway. Besides, Shay can feel my emotions through our soul mate bond. At least I can his.

Around midnight, we hear Stella sneak out of her bedroom and join us. I have a suspicion that she needs to tell us something but is waiting for the right time. Now, we all are sitting in silence.

The calm before the storm.

"Are you ready for tomorrow." Stella breaks the quiet first. "I know you're planning to go to Duluth and get to the field first. Stupid on your part, Zoe." She punches me in the arm. "And stupid for you to let her do something this reckless." Her arm strikes Shay's shoulder. "But I get it. I think it's a good plan." That's all she says. The three of us sit in chairs, look over the lake, and be exactly the way it should always be.

40

Zoe

Friday, July 3.

In the morning, the entire family eats breakfast together. I break the news to my parents who are sitting around the dinette table drinking coffee.

"Today we're going to go see the sights in Duluth like Mom suggested," I say. "Since it's still raining here, and we can't go swimming or fishing, we'll hit the harbor, the lighthouse, and the Glensheen Mansion." I stuff scrambled eggs into my mouth. My mom always makes the fluffiest eggs, just the way I like them.

"You guys be careful on the drive over and if it's raining like this, stay away from the shore," Dad says. "The tide may be ferocious, and we don't want to lose either of you."

"Can I go with?" Stella asks.

"No, Honey," Mom says. "Why don't you let Zoe and Shay go by themselves." She turns, addressing me. "Besides, you'll be back by the end of the day, right?"

"Yeah," I mumble.

Shay is deep in thought over his bagel.

We pack a little cooler of beverages and snacks. Before I went to bed this morning, I remembered to pack a bag of spare clothes and necessities. We snuck that into Shay's car.

My sister sees us off.

"Keep them safe, Stella," I say. "I'm counting on you. If you get any other visions, text me."

"I will. You just come back alive." She hugs me, then Shay. "And good luck."

"Do you think we need luck?" Shay asks.

"You'll need everything you can get."

That doesn't sound good for us. "All right," I say. "Ready to go, Shay?"

"As ready as I'll ever be."

I wave to my parents from Shay's car window, plastering a smile onto my face. They wave back, and I quickly turn my head, so they can't see the tears running down my cheeks. It could be the last time I see them. If the battle goes south and we don't make it. No. I won't think like that.

I'm an angel. And my friends are fairies, Nephilim, wolves, and all the packs in the world are coming here to fight. The Heavens are clearing out and joining us in earth's realm.

"You're quiet." Shay turns his head my way. "I know it was hard saying goodbye to your folks and sister. But you'll see them again."

"I hope you're right." I stare out of the rain-streaked glass. "I was just grateful that we got to spend one evening together as if today isn't the beginning of the end of the world."

"Yeah, it was a great night. I know you love your family. And they love you."

"Have you heard from Kieran today?" I fiddle with the radio, but we're driving in no man's land up here. Reception isn't the greatest.

"Yes, he said that most of the packs are taking private jets into the airfield and will be staying in multiple hotels in the city. They want to spread out just in case they need to do damage control. He and Sidelle are still at home, awaiting word from Oberon and Mab. But Sidelle assures us that they will be there. He'll meet us once we know where we're going first."

I inhale and nod.

The rest of the drive is quiet. We banter a bit but mostly listen to CDs. Before long the two-hour drive is done. I can see the high bridge as we coast down a hill.

Pouring rain is relentless, but we make our way to Canal

Park and grab a bite to eat. We stop at a pizza joint. We sit at a round table waiting for our food when Kieran walks through the glass door.

He waves when he spots us in the corner. "Are you ready, Zoe?" he asks.

"For what now?"

"I need to lower the wards around you, so the demons know where you are."

"Will it hurt?"

"No, you won't feel a thing. I don't think." He frowns. "But maybe you'll feel a bit of more Light now that you're an angel."

"All right. What do you need me to do?"

"Nothing. You can stay seated and give me your hand."

Warmth spreads through me when Kieran touches my palm. It starts at my head and tingles all the way to my fingertips and down to my toes. It doesn't hurt but feels more like a wall crumbling, and I hear bricks falling and breaking apart.

"It's done," Kieran says.

We eat our pizza then walk around. I'm like a zombie, thinking. Of course, I'm scared for tomorrow and what will happen. But as Shay and I stroll hand in hand on the sidewalk, my sense of dread loosens. We end our amble at the shipping pier. I gaze out at the expansive lake, water as far as the eye can see, even through the sheets of rain.

Next, we visit the Great Lakes Aquarium, then Enger Park and Tower, and finally to the Glensheen, all the while taking selfies and posting on Snapchat. It's nice doing normal stuff with my boyfriend and best friend to take my mind off why I'm really here. There are moments though when I think I'm going to break down and cry or actually have a mental break down. But somehow I manage to keep it together with a smile covering my face the whole time.

By late afternoon, the winds pick up, and I need to wear a hoodie. It's crazy that in some of the side streets the water is freezing, and the rain turns to sleet. The roads back to the cabin will be horrible if we had planned to return tonight. I call my folks, and they insist that Shay and I stay in Duluth because of the bad weather. They saw the reports on the midday news.

Shay books us a room at the Pier B Resort. While he checks us in, I text Sidelle to let her know where we are.

Me: We're staying in Duluth for the night. Pier B Resort.

As if she is waiting for an update, Sidelle's response is immediate.

Sidelle: I'll be there in a second. Room #?
Me: 326

Shay carries our bags to our room, and we wait for Sidelle. She appears in the room just as we step through the doorway.

"I've let Vash know that we're all here now," Kieran says. "They are having a pack dinner and then later during the night, they will make for the forest and rest there. Some will stay in the city, though."

"I know you're probably not okay, so I won't even ask," Sidelle says. "Tomorrow if it happens … there isn't anything I can say that will prepare you for what you have to do or will see."

"Just remember that it's you or them," Shay says. "And I'll be by your side the whole time."

"We'll be near you," Kieran says.

"Let's go to dinner and be just a group of friends hanging out." Sidelle takes my hand and ushers me into the bathroom. "Why don't you freshen up, and then we'll go get food. You look horrible."

"Thanks, Sidelle," I say. "It's hard looking like a hot mess."

I gaze at myself in the oval mirror. It's like a ghost is staring back at me. My eyes are a bit bloodshot, and my skin is pasty white. My long brown hair is coated against my cheeks. I didn't sleep well last night, and I doubt I'll be relaxed enough to get any tonight. Splashing cold water on my face and then running a brush through my hair, I lift my lips into a smile that doesn't quite reach my eyes and leave the room.

"I'm ready," I say. Everyone else is staring at me like a booger is hanging from my nose. "Are we ready?"

"You've been spotted, and Knights are converging on the city," Kieran says.

"That's good though; that's what we wanted to happen."

"Yes, it is. They have higher numbers than we initially thought. It's like they've cleared out all of Hell. They aren't doing anything as of now. So we'll let them be until they start messing with the Ordinaries."

"I would send them all if I were Sammael," Shay says. "Leave nothing to chance his freedom."

"Are we skipping dinner and going demon hunting?" I ask.

"No, you're staying here, while we call some pack members." Shay pulls me to the couch. "Kieran and Sidelle will go. You need to eat, rest, and if you can, find sleep tonight. They'll report back so we can be ready for tomorrow." Kieran and Sidelle nod, then disappear from the room. "Now, what would you like to order for dinner? Anything on the menu." He opens the three-ring binder of hotel information.

It's my last night before the end. I have no idea what the morning will bring. Kieran and Sidelle didn't return to the room, leaving me snuggled next to Shay in the large, king sized bed.

"Are you scared?" Shay asks.

"I'd be lying if I say no."

"You have every right to be. You've never been in a battle to the death. I was born for this. Gabriel raised me to know what to expect, while you've only learned about all this a few months ago." I burrow deeper into the covers and press myself next to Shay's warm body. "I'll be at your side tomorrow. You have me and my sword to protect you."

"I know and I'm grateful. You are my center and my rock, and I will draw courage from that. No matter what happens, you know I love you."

"Yes, I love you, too. Now try to sleep, Zoe."

41
Aiden

Friday, July 3.

I arrive to pick Morgan up exactly at the time she requested. My red Spyder screeches to a halt, leaving tire tracks in front of her driveway. Boy, do I love this car. It's almost as fast as flying. Sauntering to the door, it opens before I can press the bell.

Morgan is standing in the doorway, a pink duffle bag slung over her shoulder. "Perfect timing as always." She steps forward and plants a kiss on my mouth.

"Your ride awaits." I reach for her bag.

"So where are we going?"

"It's a surprise." Will it ever be for her. "We'll cruise with the top down until it gets too chilly."

"This has been really strange weather, but we can blast

the heater."

We drive for two and a half hours, Morgan bantering incessantly the whole time. I nod and smile every now and then, so she knows I'm paying attention. I'm not.

Have mercy on my soul and end my existence.

I check into a small B&B right on Canal Park, overlooking the harbor. It's a rustic place that Morgan would not have chosen for herself, but she doesn't say anything. She's too giddy about spending an entire weekend with me. Plus, she thinks we're going to be holed up inside the room the entire time.

No way.

"Let's grab dinner," I say. "I'm starving."

"You're always hungry, but I'd rather have something that's not on the menu." Morgan licks her lips.

"Food." I stand to leave. "Now."

"You're so demanding." She sashays my way, swinging her hips. "I kinda like it."

Leading her back into the convertible, we leave the top up and drive north. I Googled a place ahead of time and already made reservations to the New Scenic Cafe. It's along the shoreline and about a twenty-minute drive. The perfect amount of time to see the lay of the land.

When we arrive, dim lights from hanging chandeliers bathes us in a romantic ambiance. White linen tablecloths adorn each table. The staff wears black with long white aprons.

"We'll start with the seared sea scallops, house salads with ranch dressing on the side, and then the beef tenderloin. Cooked medium-rare," I tell the waiter and close the menu. I order for her, just as I had when we went to Crave before the prom. I know she secretly likes having me take charge.

More chatter fills my ears from her. I'm enthralled by the smoky meat scent that wafts in the air. Plans are flipping through my mind as I gaze out the massive window that overlooks Lake Superior.

"Are you even listening to me?" Morgan's high-pitched voice cuts through my thoughts. "You haven't said two words to me since we arrived here. Where are you?"

"I'm here. Sorry. I have a lot on my mind."

"You can tell me, you know."

"I was thinking about something Quinn said about Zoe."

"Don't even get me started on that witch." She slams her open palm on the table, startling diners close to us. "You're thinking of an ex-girlfriend and my enemy."

"It's not like that."

"Then tell me how it is?"

"Quinn said that Zoe was looking for a very special item."

"Yeah, so?"

"I'm curious if she found what she was looking for."

"Is that why you brought me here to Duluth? Is Quinn here? Is Zoe?" I don't say anything. "Who's here?" She needs to read my silence. "Both? Both of them are here!" She stands and almost tips the chair in her rush to leave.

"Sit down. We need to talk." She smooths out her sundress and takes her seat. "I need you to find out something for me."

"And if I don't?"

"I'll make it worth your while." I shrug, knowing that she'll take the bait.

"Fine. What do you need me to do?"

We return to the bed and breakfast after taking the scenic and long route back to the city. I spy a few wolves lingering in the woods. The packs must be out there. But how many?

I slipped a draft into Morgan's drink when she excused herself to use the restroom just before dessert. Now, she's in a deep sleep as I carry her to the bed.

Early the next morning, I leave Morgan a handwritten note:

Morgan,
I hope you enjoyed your evening. Another surprise awaits you
at Split Rock. I have a few errands to do this morning. I'll see

you at three. I've already set you up a vehicle, and the doorman will get it.

See you soon,

Aiden

Then I walk out of the room.

42

Zoe

Saturday, July 4.

The morning is bleak, and the weather matches my feelings. Neither Shay nor I slept, in spite of my best efforts. We were content to lie next to each other without saying much. It was already said and then some.

A knock on the door tells us that we really must start the day. Shay hugs my shoulders and then rises from bed, opening the hotel door to a cart of breakfast foods.

"Good morning, you two," Sidelle says. "I took it upon myself to order food since I know you lazy bums aren't doing *anything*." She winks at me. "One of everything is here. I know you both will need your strength, especially, Shay."

Placing plates and glasses filled with orange juice and

milk onto the tables, she lifts the serving plate covers to reveal at least a pound of bacon and scrambled eggs, five pancakes, half a dozen sausage links, bagels, muffins, and fruit cups. Off to the side are steaming cups of chai tea latte.

"I ran to the coffee shop in the foyer because I know it's your favorite, and I thought it would help ease your mind with something familiar."

"Thank you, Sidelle. That was very kind of you."

"I do have my moments." She smiles.

"All right, Zoe," Shay says and motions me to join him at the table. "You heard her, eat up."

Never being one to shy away from food, I set a plate of bacon and eggs in front of me. While the eggs are not fluffy like how my mom makes them, these are doused in a white cream sauce. I take a few bites and moan. My cheeks redden, and I cover my face with the latte.

We make a good dent in the food, but I don't think I can eat anymore without it threatening to come back up later.

"What's the plan?" I suggest. "Maybe we should pack food for today?"

Kieran appears in the room. "I thought that we would meet with Vash and then scout the woods," he says. "The angels have set Split Rock as the meeting point and will create the Void from there, spreading it out over the water. We need to be there when it's created because the angels won't have time to keep adjusting it during the battle."

Kieran calls Vash to set up a meeting time and place, so we are well coordinated with our attacks. The assembly point is at Goosberry Falls State Park, and Sidelle informs us Oberon will also be at the gathering.

We do pack food enough food to feed a small army. In fact, it's for all the Nephilim and pack members, so it really is for an army of warriors.

Around noon, I can't sit in the hotel any more. "We need to leave. I have to stretch my legs."

"The meeting isn't for another couple of hours," Kieran says.

"I know, but I can't be cooped up any more. If today is my last day, I don't want to spend it indoors. I need to feel the breeze on my face, the smell of pine surrounding me, and hear the water lap the shore."

"Are you sure you aren't a Summer fairy?" Sidelle asks.

"Pretty sure," I tease.

"Let's get you out of here and be one with nature." Shay ushers me out of our room and down to the lobby. "I need to gas up the vehicle, and then we can be on our way."

The state park is just under an hour away from us, about ten minutes from our rallying point. The landscape is breathtaking. To my left are dense thickets of strong oak trees, red maples, and evergreens. On the other side, as we travel north on Highway 61, is blue water as far as I can see. Lake Superior is the largest of the Great Lakes, sharing boarders with the U.S. and Canada.

As we enter the gated parking lot, the aroma of wood, dirt, and grass fills my nose. This is a perfect setting. The wolves and Summer fairies will be right at home.

We pay our admission fee and roll along the paved road toward the tourist lodge. I can't wait to set my feet on the multitude of walking paths. It's been a long time since I've been here. I remember my family taking a trip here, maybe when I was around six or seven. Mom held my hand, while Dad led Stella to the falls. My sister and I climbed rocks most of the day then waded through the shallow, cool waters.

Now, I lead my party to the same water pool and watch the water cascade over the multiple-level rock formation.

It's early in the afternoon, and people are milling about, but they don't pay attention. Hikers stop and pose for a quick picture before they wander down a new path. Tourists splash the water along the shore, and kids' giggling fills the area. So many are carefree. I envy them.

Shay nudges my shoulder and then points. Turning, I look in the direction and see eyes staring back at my own. A smattering of wolves came early, probably to scout the area for demons.

We head in their direction, going deeper into the forest, needing to be hidden from prying eyes. Twigs snap beneath my feet, and once again I notice that I'm the only one whose soles make noise. It reminds when we were in Fairyland tromping through the Mist looking for a porta. That time, too, I was the lone hiker who couldn't seem to make silent footsteps.

I'm the only sound in the woods, even when the more than two dozen wolves surround us. For a moment, I'm jealous, but then remember the reason we're here.

Vash steps from behind a tree, holding hands with Cali. They smile at us and we embrace quickly. Keeping his voice low and formal, Vash speaks, "We're all set. We've been patrolling since yesterday afternoon throughout the city and the nearby woods." He spreads his arms wide. "I had several other packs meet here early this morning, so we can recon the area. The rest are a couple miles out from the lighthouse."

"Have you seen many demons?" I ask.

"Some have run into Knights in the city, but most have been out here in the wilderness. Marqs are already floating around, too. I think they are seeing the landscape before the battle."

"And numbers for them?" Kieran asks.

"Thousands of Knights. Not sure on how many Marqs, but we've counted four or five dozen so far."

"That many. Are we going to have enough on our side?" I ask.

"Numbers will be about equal, I would think."

"They must be hiding the true Marqs numbers," Shay says.

"I would think so," Vash agrees.

"We'll have more than enough." Oberon walks through a porta. "Mab is on her way with her subjects." He wraps his dark green cape tightly around his shoulders. "Good thing the cold weather is in her favor, or else she might not stay."

I forgot how ancient he is, but he doesn't look a day over forty. He's dressed in battle armor over brown breeches and a green tunic. The wooden weaved crown I've seen him in previously is missing from his head, letting his dark chocolate locks flow freely.

"Hello, Father," Sidelle says.

"Daughter." He nods. "Plan of attack today?" His eyes penetrate mine as if he's waiting for me to answer.

"We were getting numbers from Vash," Kieran says. "Thousands of Knights and dozens of Marqs."

"I assume the angels are coming, too?"

"Yes, Michael is rallying them even as we speak. They'll open the Void as soon as we're there and most of the demons have come."

"Any particular way you want to handle this, Vash?" Oberon asks.

"I think the wolves should focus on the Marqs. We won't know their true numbers until we get into it. But

327

they're our best defense without tying up too many of us. That leaves the fairies and Nephilim to deal with all the Knights."

"Some of the Archangels can also assist with the Marqs," Kieran says.

"The Knights will bring guns, grenades, and anything else they could get their hands on," Shay says. "Nephilims and the wolves will be susceptible for any kill shots they make."

I squeeze Shay's hand.

"It's a good plan," Oberon says. "Remember that, but also know that it's going to go sideways within a couple of minutes and just go with it." He looks at the sky as if reading it. "Mab is here."

And like he has announced, the Winter Queen steps through a glass porta. Her blue skirt is wrapped at the waist securely held with a dark navy bodice. Black boots adorn her feet and travel up to her knees. Her long black hair is tight in a bun on top of her head. Ice cold, cerulean eyes gaze at me, then to the Summer fairies. She is a picture-perfect woman warrior.

Like Oberon, she exudes power with deadly precision. She is a woman of few words, but her face says it all. She's ready to kill, beat, and maim any demon that crosses her path. Retribution for all those she lost when demons overtook her lands.

The Summer King gestures for her to follow and they leave. I guess he will tell her our wobbly plan.

My stomach flips as I realize it's almost time to leave. Turning back the way we came, I trudge through the trees. I don't need to look back; I know everyone is following. We stay silent, each of us lost in our own thoughts, doing our own pre-battle pep talk, or whatever it is we do.

Taking one last glance at the beautiful waterfall and all the clueless people enjoying their day, I march back on the trail that leads to the car.

The short ride to the lighthouse has me on edge. My legs bounce and I fidget, playing with the radio, the window, and my seat. Anything to keep my fingers moving.

Shay places a calming palm on my thigh, sending all his love my way.

43

Zoe

When we near the lighthouse, bright colors can be seen. Some I know the names of, others I can't even describe. Angels' and fairies' wings of various shapes, shades, and sizes sprinkle the land and hover above the water. The dazzling hues not only come from their wings, but from angelic light and glamour.

So many have arrived, answered the call, and I can't help but feel proud and smell victory. The angels are my people. Well, they aren't people. They're angels. So they're my angels.

An array of green and blue tones hover in the woods, staying sheltered in the trees and away from the angels.

Forms emerge from the forest. Howls sound in the distance, adding to the rumbling of the ground. Packs appear and intermingle between the shrubs, foliage, and saplings. Their large bodies tense in anticipation of the upcoming battle.

My friends and I stand on a rock ledge overlooking the lake, the lighthouse to our left.

"Some of the Nephilim are here, too," Shay says. "Michael found as many as he could and get them here."

"Do you know them?" I ask.

"Not too many. They tend to stay in the warmer climates, but there are a couple of us in the northern states."

"Zoe." Kieran points. "It's starting."

Our gaze follows Kieran's finger.

Lake waves roll backwards, making more sand appear on the shoreline. Water slowly moves into a circular motion, creating a vortex. The sky blackens, and the temperature drops even more. Thankfully, the rain stopped hours ago. An eerie sucking sound draws my attention back to the water. It's lowering like a whirlpool that we can't see, the bottom leaving only the top funnel cloud.

Branches break behind us, snapping my awareness to the woods. The wolves' heads turn, looking deeper into the forest, ears prickling for sounds. Growls erupt.

Shadows materialize from behind trees and bushes. Knights crouch then stand to their full height.

We're surrounded.

In the short time I watched the Knights appear, I missed the rising, ghostly forms of the Marquises demons. Hundreds rise from the water and are now making their way toward us. With the angels and fairies beside us, and the wolves behind them, the demons have surrounded us.

I remember the words Oberon told us: "within a couple minutes expect the plan to go sideways." It just has.

The Marqs are almost upon us; the Knights start their advance on the wolves. The only sounds are feet crunching the brush, and the packs' snarls until the DKs brandish their swords. Metal clangs add to my heightened awareness.

Shay brushes him arm against mine as he reaches behind his back and grabs his Nephilim Sword. Taking that as my cue, I summon my own sword.

Kieran's body glows with angelic Light, and Sidelle has called forth her green glamour.

We stare at the approaching demon warriors and stoop into our battle stances. The angels remain in the sky, on the ready.

"Hold steady," Kieran shouts. "Let them come to us."

My eyes search for the Alpha of the Spiritus Pack, who has managed to stay within the tree line. "Vash!" He glances my way and runs toward me. "We need to draw them out and get the Knights closer to the lake, so the angels can create the Void. Circle around and flank them to drive them forward. I'm the bait. Let them see me."

He nods in his wolf form. *"Got it,"* he says through our mental connection. Then he directs the packs in his mind. I hear him shout the orders.

The wolves divide themselves, running to the right and left. The Knights charge forward, pushing through the barrier of the trees. The Marqs are nearly upon our group, too.

It's going to be perfect timing, a double assault as both enemies advance and will arrive at the same time. I look left and then right, not knowing which way I should focus my attention.

"Let's take on the Knights and leave the Marqs to the Archangels and the Royals," Shay shouts. I nod and readjust my grip. "The packs will attack from behind and push them forward. We'll cut them off from joining the Marqs with the help from the fairies."

My body trembles, and the sweat from my hands makes me clench the handle even tighter. I don't have time to rearrange my grip.

A Knight's sword comes down. My blade meets his. The high-pitched sound of metal rings in the air, signaling the start.

Roars and battle cries explode.

I can't even describe all that's happening around me. It's

too much, things happening too fast. My focus is only on the DK in front of me. I raise my sword and meet his again, but then he drops to the ground, dead.

Shay wipes his blade on his jeans and nods to me.

Blasts of Light shoot across the sky, and lake water fizzles as it detonates from the force of glamour.

It's total chaos.

I don't have time to check on my friends; the Knights keep coming. Guns fire in the distance. Something zips near my head and I duck. Then a barrage of bullets flies toward us. I extend my palms outward and use Light to stop them short of reaching me, Matrix style.

I didn't know I could do that. Shay smiles at me, and then we press forward, killing and decapitating any demon in our path.

An earth shattering sound blows, breaking my focus. I quickly glance at my surroundings along with many of us who have paused to take notice of where the blast came from.

Dead Knights litter the ground. Wolves limp injured, but they remain taking on more opponents. Angels and fairies dart across the sky and mix with the black forms of the Marqs.

The atmosphere rocks like a heat wave. An opaque layer blankets the area, engulfing everything in its path, reminding me of a pillowcase swallowing a pillow.

This must be how the Void is created, drastically different than when Kieran created the warehouse Void so many months ago that started this adventure.

As the outer edge of the Void drapes over the woods and lake, the wolves corral the outlying demons, forcing them into the mouth of the Void.

A shimmer passes through me as if I've walked under a waterfall; one minute I see the park and the lake, and the next it's an open field with nowhere to hide. A smattering of trees encircles the field, giving the only protection.

I think the angels created the Void in this way so it forces the demons to fight and not play with us. Confront us head on or leave.

I easily spot the alphas; they are larger than their pack members. Then I locate Vash's dark brown form, paired with a snow white one: Cali. They fight side by side, knowing that if one dies, the other will follow.

Raising my sword high, I barrel through another group of Knights heading my way.

"Zoe!" Shay shouts. "To your left."

I turn my body but can't block in time. A Knight's blade slices my arm. My lungs scream in agony as blood pours out from the gash. My free hand covers the wound to stop the red liquid running down my arm. I gather my Light and heal myself. Something pushes against me from behind and I stumble forward.

Demons surround me, creating a barrier between Shay and me. More Knights wedge their way in, trying to separate us.

Calling more of my Light, it glows on my palms, and I send it out, forcing purple orbs into the chests of everyone around me. I spin in a circle, letting it swirl.

I have no idea how long we've been fighting, but there seems to be more wolves lying on the ground now than in the woods. They are trying to make their way to the Marqs. And since angels and fairies just cease to exist when they die, I don't know how many are no longer with us.

"Create a path for the wolves to get through," I shout and wave my sword in the direction of the path needs to be created.

Shay and I lead teams of Summer fairies and attack from the side. Blue Winter fairies battle from the opposite end, as the wolves continue wrangling from the rear.

Eventually, a narrow path opens and then as Guardian angels come to assist, the trail widens.

We join the pack, bringing up the rear as they start tearing into the Marqs. Deathly howls add to the melee as the wolves do the job they were created to perform: kill Marquises Demons.

Then a shadow in the tree line moves, grabbing my attention. I pull on Shay's arm and point. He follows my line of sight. "What is she doing here?" Shay asks.

"I don't know," I say. "Let's go find out."

We run toward the figure, and it steps out into view.

Morgan.

"What are you doing here?" I ask. "How did you get here?"

"We drove, duh," she says.

"Who's we?" Shay asks.

"Aiden and me. We came to Duluth for the weekend on a romantic getaway, to reconnect. But this morning when I woke, a note was left for me to meet Aiden here at the lighthouse. So I came."

"Why?" I ask.

"Because he asked me to. I don't need to have a reason. He's my boyfriend now. He finally saw the light and dumped Quinn. If he wants to meet here for a surprise, then I'll be here. I was about to leave when I spotted you across the field."

Boyfriend? I thought Quinn is his girlfriend. I knew he was playing my friend. He could be playing both girls.

"And what do you think is going on here?" I ask.

"Nothing. It's a nice area. A little creepy without sounds, but whatever. Maybe they know that people are around. Well, not *people*." Shay and I look at each other. "Witches, doing evil. Isn't that what you're here for? Some sort of séance?"

"I'm not a witch, Morgan." I turn to watch the battle,

337

checking to make sure that there aren't any demons in our area. Morgan can't see them, and I wonder if Aiden did something. "I have no idea where you got that idea from."

"You don't remember? When we were in grade school, you brought that bird back to life. No one but a witch could do that."

"Is that what this is about? Is that why you hate me?"

"Zoe, we have to get going." Shay nudges me.

"I know, just one more minute." My head turns to hear a loud explosion and the ground shakes, signaling the battle wages on without us, and I don't have time for placating Morgan right now. "I'm not a witch, Morgan. I'm an angel."

Her eyes widen, but she doesn't say anything as if she's mulling it over. "And you chose Kieran over me. We were the best of friends, Zoe. You hurt me."

"Morgan, people can have more than one best friend. I've known Kieran my entire life. He's been there for me through thick and thin. And I didn't choose him over you. You left. You didn't give me a chance to explain. Instead, you decided to hate me, called me names behind my back, and turned people against me. Morgan, it was *your* choice to not be my friend." Shay tugs my hand. "Look, I need to be someplace right now, but when we're back in the Cities, let's talk." I reach out to her but she steps back.

"Okay," she says as her head drops.

I think she's going to lift her head and walk away, but she doesn't. Instead, her body slumps to the ground, multiple arrows jutting from her back.

"Oh, my god," I screech. "Morgan! Shay, help me roll her over." We turn her tall frame over. Her eyes roll into the back of her head. I shake her hard. "Morgan. Stay with me." I force my Light into her, but something is blocking it. I can't penetrate into her soul. "Please don't die."

"I'm sorry, Zoe," Morgan mumbles. "For everything I've done to you." And then her eyes close, forever.

"Come on," Shay says. "We can mourn her now, we can do that when the battle is over."

"How did she get inside the Void?"

"I don't know, but she must have been inside when the angels created it or someone, Aiden, probably got her here to mess with you. That's the only plausible explanation I can think of."

"I guess we'll never know."

When we get back into the throes of the fight, I see half of our forces are gone. Hundreds of pack members are on the ground, limping or dead. Noticeably fewer angels and fairies are flying around, and the Marqs are still rising.

My hope dwindles.

44
Zoe

I see Quinn, the unknowing traitor, sprinting toward me. "Zoe!" I'm not sure if she's going to kill me or save me. We've been friends since grade school; I'm hoping for the latter. It's not her fault that she got sucked into Aiden's web of lies. This is his fault and no one else's. She's surrounded by demons, but she's fending them off with her sword, slashing her way to me. "Zoe," she screams again. I shout to Shay to let him know where I'm heading. He's fighting multiple attacks and nods. A pathway is cut between my school friend and myself. Shay follows, a few steps behind.

Bodies fly in every direction. As Quinn slices through the melee, black demon blood drips from her weapon. She shoves past angels and fairies.

I think she's going to make it to me after all. But then a

blade protrudes through her chest. A demon has stabbed her from behind. She staggers the last couple of feet as I close the distance to her.

"I'm sorry, Zoe." Her hand presses against her ribs, trying to stop the flow of blood. "I didn't know for sure who he was." She coughs and falls to the ground beside me. "I tried to stop him," she sputters. Blood leaks from the side of her mouth. "But there is something you should know." I lean in; her voice is barely audible. "Tell my son that I love him. He loves you very much."

"What? Say that again." I shake her shoulder. "Quinn, say it again!"

"Make him happy until his dying days. I won't be around on earth to watch him grow old with you. But I will be watching from the heavens."

"Who are you?" Tears fall down my face. "Quinn? What have you done with Quinn?"

"I'm … Shay's … father."

"How?"

"Disguise … power of combined angels." His form flickers between a man and a girl's as his breathing sputters. "Watch out for Morgan." He takes a final breath, his body remains that of a ghost-like man and disappears from the battlefield.

I can't tell Shay but I must. What did he mean a disguise? Could Archangels mutate into Ordinaries? And if so, was she/he helping us all along? He used Quinn to get close to Aiden. Gabriel had to have suspected who Aiden really was.

My soul hurts as I come to realize that Shay's father is dead. He'll never be able to see his son again. Well, his spirit is not really dead, but his form won't be able to be on earth any more. Shay will miss him. I'll miss him. If he's gone, then does that mean that Quinn is really dead, too?

And Morgan? I can't ask her because she's already dead. Gabriel must not have known that before he died.

I can't linger on that too much longer.

"Zoe? Are you hurt?" Shay kneels besides me. "Was that Quinn? I saw her fall." I nod. "Where did she go?"

"She's gone." I wipe my face and stand. "I'll tell you later. Right now, we must finish this before anyone else dies."

I don't have time to answer Shay's question. A demon swings an axe toward my head. I duck as Shay leaps away.

Pivoting my sword, I block the axe again, but the she-demon is strong. The handle stops my blade, and it slides up and locks against the heel of the edge. She brings my body forward. I scramble for a dagger that's strapped to my leg. Her hand shoots out and swats it from my fingers. She shoves me to the ground and stomps on my right wing.

I scream as I thrash about. My eyes sting, and my vision blurs with white dots. She frees the axe and slams it down on my other wing. Bones crack. The pain is intense. I'm on the verge of blacking out. My eyes shut as I try to block out the pain.

She hovers above me and is about to swing her axe into my chest.

This is the end. This is how I'm going to die.

No.

My Light blasts out, tripping her off balance.

I see movement in the corner of my eye. A silver light swings in my direction and the she-demon falls. Her head is cut off by Shay's blade.

He reaches for me. "Can you stand?" he asks.

My cut wing droops and blood streams out. "I think so, but I fix them. I'm trying to, but they aren't healing fast enough." I lean into him.

"It'll take time since that axe was dipped in Hell Fire. You were a good fighter as a human before you got wings. You'll have to be more careful from now on."

"Okay." I try flapping my wings, but the slightest movement makes me flinch, and I cry out in agony.

"Use your Light and not your strength. And I'll be by your side to protect you." He turns me to face him. "Promise me, Zoe, that you'll be careful."

"I will." My wings disappear. I can still feel them pressed against my back, like phantom limbs.

"I'll hold you to that." He grabs my hand and tugs me behind him.

Shay stays closer to me; he makes his wings disappear. We battle back to back, taking on opponents.

It seems like all of Hell has been emptied, and its inhabitants are here fighting on this field. Things I've never seen before. Ghostly beasts, the size of lions, dart between their masters. Their barks and howls send chills down my spine. These must be the famous Hell Hounds. I'm not sure if I see them now since I became an angel or if I could always see their true forms. I guess it doesn't really matter, though. Two are bounding towards us.

"Ready, Zoe?" Shay asks as he nods to the approaching hounds. "You see them, right?"

"Oh, yeah, the dogs coming straight for us?" I raise my sword. "Yep, I see them."

"They're just like everything else. These are immortal animals. Don't hold back."

"How do we kill them?" I shout. "Do we run?"

"No, we'll make our stand here. They don't die but like the Marqs, they'll return to Hell."

The snarling beasts chew up the ground, and they're before us within a couple of beats. Their massive paws pound into the ground, dirt flying. Large teeth line their maws as drool drips from their mouths.

We don't fight back to back because they separate us. Their giant front paws swipe at us from all directions. I flatten myself to the ground, barely missing my head being taken off. Shay narrowly dodges a mouth as teeth clamp shut where he stood a second ago. With barely enough time to raise our swords before claws strike at us again, all we can do is tuck, evade, and roll. I manage to graze one in the shoulder. Even though they are ghost-like, they are not. My blade hisses upon contact. The hound shrieks in agony.

"I thought our swords would go straight through them," I call out. Shay notices and nods. He follows my lead and slashes at the animals. But his sword doesn't touch them. The air around them breaks apart their form and melds back together. "It's all you, Zoe. They must only react to Seraph Swords."

Shay does what he can to separate the monstrosities, so I can return them to Hell. We run around, trying to get only one to follow me. It works. I run directly at the one chasing Shay. At the last minute, he leaps out of the way.

The hound is tall enough that I only come to its shoulder. Dropping and sliding on the ground, I raise my sword and carve into the underbelly of the beast. Its bellows shake the ground around me. Or maybe that was its partner.

Good thing my dad liked baseball and taught me to slide into bases. The body disappears, leaving me one less to defeat.

I doubt I can use the same tactic again.

"Shay, give me your sword. I have an idea."

He doesn't flinch. On our next pass, he tosses me his blade. I catch it midair and twirl each sword in my hands. Calling my Light, I infuse his Nephilim Sword, hoping that my inspiration works.

I stop in my tracks and turn to face a ginormous mouth, ready to eat me. Brandishing both swords, I dart forward, stopping the animal. It knows what the blade does. Using mine, I swing in an upward motion causing the beast to rear onto its hind legs, my Light pulsing. Shay's sword connects with a paw and cuts it off. The hound limps on its tripod legs. My Light transferred my power into both.

Loud howls send chills to my wings. But I don't stop my onslaught from the dual swords, both acting as my own. They are swinging, whirling, and slicing anything in the vicinity. Some are hitting flesh because more cries fill the air. The injured body is still here. I keep spinning the blades.

I pant and wish Shay could help me, but he's found his own battle. He's in a fistfight with some Knights who wandered into the area.

Taking a breath, I reach deep inside and my Light flares. I slam it into the hound's face. It blinks, and I rush forward, arcing my blade down across its neck. It disappears.

My breathing is labored. I'm about spent. I need a break. We've been fighting for what seems like hours. I don't know how long it really has been. Glancing out over the area, everyone seems to be still fighting someone. It's not over yet.

45
Aiden

I had no feelings when Morgan died on the battlefield. Maybe it was because she was just a means to an end. I never felt any real connection with her. It was mutual between us. She wanted to use me for popularity, and I needed a prom date. And I needed a spy. Granted she had not fared well when I first broke it off with her. I needed to know how dedicated she would be to me. I had seen an opportunity with Quinn. It presented itself and I took it. Anyone would have done the same.

I see a dark shadow standing off in the tree line. She was my Plan C, even after I bailed on her, and after I promised to be right back … in a note.

My scouts told me that Zoe's rendezvous point was Split Rock Lighthouse, a beacon of hope of their win. Morgan was already within the Void when the angels cast it. She did just as I had asked. I knew she would meet me for her surprise. She was Zoe's distraction. I knew how deep Morgan's hatred for her went. And as time went on, no apology would placate Morgan.

Zoe's betrayal of their friendship and witnessing all of Zoe's weird behavior for many years solidified the two girls' fates. Morgan kept thinking that Zoe's a witch.

Both Quinn and Morgan served a purpose. Mine.

No hard feelings. Well, Morgan was a pain in my wings. Always texting. She never got the clue after thousands of unanswered voicemails that we would never be what she wanted. And now she's really gone. Forever.

Then I watch as Quinn is taken down by one of my demons. Those stupid, brainless minions. I shake my head as fury builds. I should have color-coded our side, so my father's warriors know who to kill and who's on our side.

You can't take the monster out of the demon. They love death and bringing it by their own hands.

What's done is done.

A strange new feeling hammers at my chest where my heart would be.

Is this what it's like to be sad?

No. I'll miss her, but it's not sadness. It's …

Well, I don't really know. I've only felt it once before, and that was with Zoe when I made the decision to let her go from the vocivus room.

Both girls seemed to worm their way into my soul.

Oh, hells, I *am* going soft.

Two different girls have managed to break chinks out of my hard, exterior armor.

Shaking the thoughts of them from my head, I peruse the battle. We are winning. We're overtaking the field. There aren't enough angels, fairies, or Nephilims. It's a glorious sight to witness. The downfall of the Ordinaries. Next to conquer Fairyland. Could the two realms be joined without a porta? He would have to find a way. We can't rely on fairies to open the portas and let my father in to rule over them.

My father.

So much death. Destruction. Eternal non-existence.

He will destroy everything that I worked so hard to have and to become.

My eyes glaze over as I dream of my hopeless future if he is released. Back to being second in command. My opinions not heard or acted upon. Minions questioning my every decision. I won't be making the decisions anymore. I'll be back to leading battles on the front lines, skirmishes, and attending court. Oh, hells, I hate the politics. Plus, having to deal with my father forever on an as-needed basis.

Yeah, that's not a future I care to come true.

Now, I know what I must do. I must ensure that he remains locked in the Archangels prison. He can never escape.

Oh, hells.

Scanning the field, I spot Zoe fighting back to back with her boyfriend. Of course, he's next to her. How to get them separated.

I call a horde of demons to me, pointing in Zoe's direction. They immediately take off, knowing what I need them to do.

War wages inside of me. Should I? Can I betray everything I stand for? Everything I am? But what if I'm more like Zoe than she believes I am?

Zoe.

Another piece of hatred falls from my blackened soul.

I stride toward her, blasting my Light at any angel, fairy, wolf, or demon who crosses my path.

"Hello again, Zoe. It's been a long time." The horde has managed to break apart the duo with enough space I easily glide between them.

"Not long enough," she seethes. "I could have gone the rest of my life without seeing you."

"And there's the spunk I've come to love about you. Look. It's just the two of us again."

"I haven't missed you."

"Are we going to do this?" I tilt my head. "Your

boyfriend is otherwise occupied, so I can have you all to myself. I am curious how your training has been. Unfortunately, all of my efforts on Quinn were wasted. Pity that she died."

"Don't talk about her." She swings her sword and misses my face by inches. "You're the one who killed her," Zoe screams at me. "You might not have stabbed her, but you brought her here. And now I'm going to avenge her death." He doesn't know?

I back up from her strikes.

Her other friends are making their way to us. They battle through a path of demons when they see me ready to destroy Zoe. But it only takes one strike on my part.

We parry for what seems like minutes. She has gotten better with the sword since the last time I spied on her. She's physically stronger, too. Her trainers have been pushing her to extreme limits. And it's paying off.

Our blades clash and ring in the air. But I don't fight fair. I blast her with Light and she stumbles. Quickly, she's back on her feet, meeting another Light blast with one of her own. The force makes me falter.

I swing again and draw her close. Our swords lock near the hilt.

We pause, which allows me to briefly look at both swords. Hers is like the one I carry. Upon deeper inspection of her hilt, I confirm it is a Seraph Sword; the etching on the blade is the same as my own. I turn the blade, waving a palm across it. The old language from the angels' glows, and I direct my Light to Zoe's sword.

Similar symbols appear. That confirms it for me.

I parry with her, but she is no match for me. After eons of training, I am better, faster, and have more stamina. Her energy dwindles with every stroke. All I have to do is wait her out. Zoe will eventually grow tired and make a mistake.

Zoe growls with a renewed vigor; she slashes and cuts, driving me back. Her eyes narrow, and her lips thin with determination. It is all she can do to keep her focus on where her blade lands. If she isn't careful, she's going to injury herself, and my plan will be for nothing.

It surprises me that Shay still isn't by her side; the horde really is keeping his hands full. But I thank whomever listening for that small gift.

I watch as Zoe stumbles. This is my chance.

Can I do it? Yes, I must.

I infuse my sword with Light. It clashes with Zoe's and forces her wrist to twist and she drops hers. She scrambles onto her hands and knees, a bit lost, not knowing how she is going to defeat me.

She can't. I'm too strong for her.

A guttural cry escapes her lips. Oh, yes, her wings are damaged. She rolls over onto her back, scuttling backwards. Her eyes are wide with terror, knowing that I am going to end her life. Right there.

I pick up her fallen sword and inspect it to make sure. The text still glows from the Light she has wielded. I look down onto her frantic face.

A war battles inside me. I know I should end her life. It's what my father told me he needed me to do. But if she doesn't live, the King of Hell will escape his cage. The world won't be safe from my father's evil reign, and I will be the acting king again.

If my father ever finds out my true intensions, he'll end my existence for sure. Over the centuries, I've grown to liking the power, the respect, the control. I can't give that up now. Not for anyone.

With my decision made, I stab Zoe with a sword and pierce into her soul.

A blast of Light like nothing I've seen before floods the battle zone, making everyone stop.

I step away from Zoe's body. I can't believe that it worked. I read an ancient scroll from the library that seraph angels carry special abilities.

"What did you do, Aiden?" Kieran runs toward us, screaming at me. "How could you?" He raises his hand to blast me with Light. I easily absorb it. "After all she's done for you. I know you are still evil, but she put her faith in you that you still had some good someplace in your soul.

But she was wrong. There is nothing good in you."

"I'm going to kill you," Shay screeches as he takes down the last of the horde I had sent. "If you run now, I'll find you. I'll avenge her until my dying breath. That's a promise."

Her best friend kneels on her side. I watch as Zoe tries to pat his shoulder to let him know she understands his grief, but her hand passes though. Her body releases her soul. She doesn't look at me; she doesn't know I can see her. Actually, see her.

"Wait, Kieran." I hold up my hand. "Before you end my existence, just wait. Let me explain." I drop the swords.

Kieran is beside himself, yelling and raging. Mumbling to himself and battling between striking me down and leaving Earth to go find Zoe's floating soul. I absorb and deflect all the blows. If he were anything more than a guardian angel, I might be a bit scared. But he's not.

"It'll be okay, Shay," I say. He doesn't hear me. His grief over the loss of his soul mate is too great. "She will rise again, like a phoenix rising out of the ashes."

They don't trust me.

They shouldn't. Zoe has died, and I killed her.

Demons continue to battle around us. Since I am their leader on the field, I blast my own minions with Light, forcing them back. I need to let Zoe have the time she requires to regenerate. A dark red Protective Shield encompasses those who huddle around us and Zoe's dead human body.

I watch as her fairy friend stays by her side. No one has glared or yelled at me. I wish they would.

Have I made a mistake?

After a few minutes, Zoe's body glows with renewed and commanding purple Light.

She has finally come into her full powers.

46
Zoe

I'm dying. I feel my body shutting down. My life's essence is diminishing. I think of my family.

My school friends: Cali, Quinn, and Rena. Yes, I still call Quinn my friend. I forgave her. It's Aiden who I blame for everything.

My protectors: Sidelle and Vash.

And Kieran. The greatest best friend anyone could ask for. He's been there for me since my birth and has protected me ever since. He's family, and I'm going to miss him, but I know I'll see him again somewhere in Heaven.

"Aiden. Why?" I barely whisper as I gaze up at him in disbelief. He doesn't respond. His wings droop, knowing full well what he did. He didn't know about Quinn, that she was Gabriel in disguise.

Would he still have chosen to kill me if he'd known who she was?

His face hardens.

Is that remorse in his expression?

A light flickers in his eyes.

I move my eyes toward Shay. "I'm sorry. I love you." I stare into his aqua eyes, which are filled with love. These are my last words.

He is the last person I see before the emptiness of death swallows me whole.

It's dark.

I feel … nothing.

I draw my last breath.

I am dead.

47
Zoe

My body floats above my earthen form. I watch as my spirit lifts like a ghost and comes to stand next to my best friend.

"What did you do, Aiden?" Kieran runs toward me, screaming. "How could you?" He raises his hand to blast Aiden with Light. He easily absorbs it. "After all she's done for you. I know you are still evil, but she put her faith in you that you still had some good someplace in your soul. But she was wrong. There is nothing good in you."

"I'm going to kill you," Shay screeches as he takes down the last of the horde Aiden had sent. "If you run now, I'll find you. I'll avenge her until my dying breath. That's a promise."

My best friend kneels beside me. I try to pat Kieran's shoulder to let him know I understand his grief, but my hand passes though him. My body releases my soul. I don't look at anyone but Shay.

"Wait, Kieran." Aiden holds up his hand. "Before you end my existence, just wait. Let me explain." He drops both swords.

Kieran is beside himself, yelling and raging. Mumbling to himself and battling between striking Aiden down and leaving Earth to go find my soul someplace in Heaven, or wherever souls go.

"It'll be okay, Shay," Aiden says. He doesn't hear him. His grief over the loss of me is too great. "She will rise again, like a phoenix rising out of the ashes."

I hear my faint voice ask Aiden why. I move my eyes toward Shay and whisper, "I'm sorry. I love you." I stare into his aqua eyes, which are filled with love. These are my last words as my body gives away.

Now as I stand beside my friends, looking down at my own body I listen to them continue discussing my death.

"I had to." Aiden responds, looking down at my lifeless body. "You don't understand."

"You're right," Kieran says. "I don't understand. How could you have killed her? And with her own sword, too."

I look at my own sword protruding from my chest.

"I had to," Aiden repeats. "She can't die by her own sword. Now, she can take the open and available seat next to her mother, Grace."

"What are you talking about?" Kieran asks, angrily. "She looks plenty dead to me. We need her down here ... with us."

"Wait," Aiden sighs. "She will rise again."

Sidelle and Vash stand quietly. I watch them form a circle around my body behind Shay, and I stare into his aqua eyes. He doesn't feel me. Shay kneels by my side and holds my hand. It's weird, seeing myself dead.

I'm dead. It hits me hard, the sword in my chest. I still can't believe Aiden killed me.

"Zoe. Welcome to Heaven."

There is a quiet harp playing music somewhere. It's very soothing.

"Mom?" Her voice reminds me of hot cocoa sliding down my throat and making me all warm and tingly inside.

"Yes, sweetheart. You have finally made it." She's floating next to me, gazing down. Her body glows with a faint purple hue all around her. Soft, pink lips pout as her massive and almost identical wings to my own flutter ever so slightly.

All I see around me is white. I'm lying on my back on the floor, which is made of the softest material. It's like down feathers, silk, and cotton all rolled into one. The sky is fluffy clouds moving in the breeze, even though I don't feel the wind across my face. And nothing else is moving.

There are no trees, grass, or any other animals.

"But I need to finish .. I need to go back there and help them. Without me who is going to stop Sam from taking over and destroying everything?"

"Zoe, you have done well. More than we thought you would do. Your time on earth is complete."

"How can that be? Sam is still out there."

"Sam will always be. No one can ever really defeat him. He will lay dormant until he can strike again. There will be others who will pick up the task and banish him when he returns."

"What about the prophesy, Mom? Was that a lie? I know now I'm not the Redeemer. Am I?"

"You are not. You don't need redemption. But the prophesy is partially about you … and Aiden."

"Aiden? What does he have to do with this? He's a lying, no good demon!"

"Yes. He is that but much more. It is he who needs redemption."

I think back to the prophesy, and something doesn't make sense. All I know is that I need to help my friends. Keep the world safe from Sammael. Live my life and do everything I dreamed of doing.

"I need to go back. Shay ... what's going to happen to him?"

"Is it your choice to return? Are you choosing him of

your own free will? You have already sacrificed yourself to be here with the other seraphs ... will you choose to go back to earth?"

"And if I do? Can I come back here?"

"Yes, but you may have to watch him die if you return to him. That is the downfall of your choice ... You understand?"

"Yes." I did understand ... perfectly. I would remain a seraph angel and watch Shay, the absolute love of my life, die someday. I will come back and take my place in Heaven, but I need to be with him now. I want to spend the rest of his life by his side.

Resolved in my decision, my face must reflect my determination.

"Go, my daughter, return to earth ... to your body. And when you rejoin us, we will again welcome you with open arms. Be safe, Zoe."

"Thank you, Mother. Can you and the other Seraph angels help us?"

"We cannot. We are not strong enough. When we banished Sam to the underworld, he stripped us of some Light. That is how he retained his. We cannot take human form, so we created you."

"I will return to my rightful place. I won't abandon you just like I can't abandon my friends on earth. Not yet."

My beautiful mother's form fades from the whiteness.

I again see my body lying on the ground, surrounded by my friends. I am only gone a matter of seconds. I float next to my body, staring down. I look in my friends faces who are mourning my death. I hover and touch my hand. As soon as I do, my spirit body is pulled into my physical one. I feel my inner mind drift back to my body with an unseen pull. The moment I touch the ground, I materialize back into myself.

My eyes snap open.

I gasp for a huge breath of air.

"Aiden!" He steps back. "Where is he?"

"Zoe?" Shay hesitantly asks. I try to sit up, but my body is too weak at the moment. "Oh, my God. Zoe! You're alive? How can that be possible?"

"Z?" Kieran's head shakes, and his eyes are focused directly on my face.

"I told you she could not die," Aiden says with a small amount of relief in his voice.

The field is still deep in the throes of battle. My friends have managed to drag my lifeless body to the edge, away from the front lines. Dead bodies lay everywhere. To my left, are the Winter and Summer fairies going at it against legions of DKs. They are picking them off in small groups.

And there are the angels who are flying around, dotting the sky and land with color. Their wings brighten the area, like fireworks. They are aiming their forces at the

Marquises demons because they are harder to take down.

Shay lowers himself and hugs me tightly, lifting my upper body off the ground. "I love you," he murmurs into my ear. "I love you so much. I was beside myself ... when ... you died." He sucks in a breath. "Aiden ... he ..."

"I know."

The wolves are fighting on my right and only targeting the Marquises, unless an unsuspecting Knight is in the way. The pack works together like a well-oiled machine.

For a split second, I worry about Vash, but this is what they are born and bred to do: fight against demons. He leads his pack to the next demon. They take him down. Cali is easy to spot with her snowy coat. She's learned so much since our time on the Silico program. She seems at ease with her new form. Maybe it was always a part of her.

Sidelle is snapped out of her surprise. "Oh ... my ... Zoe!" she exclaims. "Do not ever do that to us again. Do you hear me?"

It's strange to see these sworn enemies finally working together for a common cause. King Oberon leads the charge against some Marquises demons, Queen Mab at his side. I can easily distinguish between the two groups of fairies; they all wear battle gear, but Summer holds wooden spears and shields. Winter only holds ice daggers. They don't need other armor because they throw up ice to block any attacks.

"I'm not planning on dying again any time soon, Sidelle," I say with a small smile, looking over Shay's shoulder since he is still hugging me. "Okay, Shay, help me up. Let's do this. It's time to end Sam's reign ... and I know what to do." Turning my head toward Aiden's retreating back. "You and I are not done. Not even close," I yell.

48
Zoe

I can see everything down to the base elements. Dust motes clear. Tree leaves shows every vein. Each blade of grass stretches toward the sky as they grow. Sweat beads sparkle all across the Void. I used to think there were seven standard colors of a rainbow, but I know now that there are many more than the human eye can see.

Everything is covered in a red haze.

My eyes lock onto Aiden's. He drops his Protective Shield. His head nods slightly, and then he flies away. He doesn't stay long enough for me to even thank, or throttle, him. I think he knew what he was doing the whole time. At least that's my hope.

"Come on," I tell my friends again.

They rejoin the melee and before long, each us has an

evil opponent before us.

A white shimmer catches my eye. It's a round, floating orb and waves like a flag. In the very center of it, a gold line is drawn, and something black is making its way out.

My stomach falls as I get a feeling that I know who has arrived at the fight.

I must stop him at all costs.

All my friends are fighting off a demon.

"Hey, guys," I shout over the clang of metal clashing. "Look." I point, and Kieran and Shay look where I point. "I think that's him. He's coming. We have to stop him. Now."

"Yeah, I think you're right, Zoe," Shay agrees. He disposes of his demon quickly with a swipe of his sword across the neck. He steps to my side, and we run to the orb as quickly as possible.

But there are still quite a few demons blocking our path. We punch, push, kick, and when that all fails, we cut through the crowd with our swords blazing.

It's still taking too long.

The line opens farther. Two hands appear, trying to rip the opening more.

I turn my head to look for Kieran and Vash. They are still battling a couple of steps behind us. They must get there in time. We all must.

That hesitation costs me.

A group of Marqs barrel into me, causing me to land on

the ground with a hard thump. Two pin my arms down while the other is ready to stab me through my heart. Right as the tip nears my chest, Shay's form knocks the demon away, and Vash is right there to end his existence. I breathe a sigh of relief. The demons holding my arms loosen their grip. I clutch my sword and swing, decapitating one of their heads, barely missing Shay in the process.

"Sorry, Shay."

"It's okay. I'm fine. You missed me. Remember to keep your focus." He extends his hand and helps me stand.

"Yeah, I lost it for a second." I place my palm over my heart. It's still racing as I though I was about to die—again. "Okay, let's get moving."

Vash nods and sprints after us. Cali isn't far behind.

"We have to make a circle around the Veil." I direct Shay to stand on my right and Vash on the other side of him. Shay lays a palm on Vash's massive shoulder. I don't need to tell Cali where to stand. She knows her place is next to her mate. She touches Vash with her front paw. Kieran joins us shortly after killing off two Knights, linking hands with me. I need my two boys close to me. "Kieran, I need you to contact Sidelle and Finn and get them up here. I'm going to need all the power I can get."

"What exactly are you going to do?" Shay asks.

"I'm going to borrow all of your Light and the fairies' glamour to close the rip before Sammael can come through."

"All right, Sidelle and Finn are on their way," Kieran says.

As I turn my head, searching for the fairies, ten Archangels surround us. They block any demons trying to get through our circle.

"We're here, Buttercup." Sidelle winks at me as she joins hands with Kieran. She turns back to Finn who has not taken her other hand. "What are you doing?" she demands. "You need to join me and take my hand."

"Not until you say it."

"Finnegan, we are not having this convo right now. Get up here." She points to the ground next to her. "If you don't get your wings up here right now, I'll tell my father to keep the scepter longer and your reign over Autumn will be less."

Her eyes flash bright green and Finn complies.

When did he come? Must have been with Mab. I feel bad for him because I know Sidelle will lay into him about this transgression, too. All the same, I'm glad he's here with us.

The circle is now closed.

I shut my eyes and pull my Light from within.

Blinding purple light pours out from my body and wings. All of the angels and Nephilims who had their wings hidden, have them out and extended.

"Hurry, Zoe." Shay squeezes my hand. "Sam's upper

body is pushing through."

I dig deep into the recesses of my mind, calling forth everything I have. The Ribbon Light swirls around me and extends past Shay and Kieran. My eyes open, and I see that all the angels in the circle have similar Ribbons. They, too, are giving everything they have.

Past them, everyone still battling the demons also have Ribbon Light around them. Suddenly, a shock wave hits my body. I'm propelled forward but not enough to break the circle. My wrist where the Heaven's Mark is heats to a blazing temperature, and white light shoots out, projecting a symbol into the air.

The Enlightens surrounding me emit the same power of light.

The orb containing Sam wavers and seals a fraction. His upper body has stopped moving forward, and one of his hands releases the side of the tear. A sucking sound rings in the air like a vortex is upon us.

But all the Light isn't enough. I'm tiring and notice that everyone else in straining, too. We aren't going to close the Veil if we don't find more Light.

49
Zoe

Something behind me draws my attention. My soul instantly aches. Aiden's eyes focus on me. A dagger is sticking out from his chest. I feel his pain course through my body. It's probably our bond. Since the time he held me captive, it's changed from that first moment. I know he's not really my soul mate. His connection to me is different than Shay's. It could be my wishing, but I don't love Aiden. With Shay, I gave him my heart, my love and was rewarded with a bond so deep that nothing will shatter it. Not even death.

"No," I scream until my voice is hoarse. "No, Aiden, what did you do?" I drop Shay's hand and run to him. My knees hit the ground as I kneel next to his body. I tug his torso in my lap.

"It's okay, Zoe. Go back to the circle and send him back to Hell," Aiden pants. "I guess it's my time."

"It can't be. Why did you do this?" I haven't moved, even though my people need me.

"You know why."

"No, I don't." Tears stream down my cheeks. "You didn't have to—"

"You know I did. You needed to have more Light, and this is the only way."

"But you'll never come back from this." I look at the royal fairies' dagger he used, still jutting out from his soul. Old glamour. He knew the consequences; he would actually die.

"That is my choice. Now, go." He coughs as red Light pours out from his dying soul. "Zoe, it's okay. You can't save everyone." It runs down the side of his body and pools on the grass next to me.

"Yes, I can." I try pulling the dagger out.

"Zoe," Shay urges. "Come on. We have to finish this. Aiden made his choice. It's time to make yours."

I turn my head back and gaze into Shay's aqua eyes, then into all my friends' solemn faces. They're right. Aiden did make his choice, and we need to send the King of Hell back.

It's like the world is frozen in time. I see the Archangels struggling to keep up with the sheer number of Marqs they are attempting to kill. Swords are motionless, stalled midstrike. I have no idea hcw many angels are no longer in existence, but I suspect there lots.

The area is spotted with wolves still attacking and some lifeless on the ground.

Both Summer and Winter fairies are petrified in their positions, ready to strike down Knights. Wings of every shade cast a rainbow of color on the field, the only bright spots in this dark battle.

Blackness surrounds the Void with the black cloaks of the Marquises demons, all the spilled blood from them, and the icky feeling of dread that lingers.

I know what I must do, but I'm still in shock that Aiden sacrificed himself and helped us. Me. He wasn't entirely evil, after all. It reminds me of the prophecy:

Glory.
First and last.
Heaven and unto Earth.
Receives the highest in jubilation.
Enlightens will unite; they shall band.
Triumph be if darkness is driven back.
Help found who love; the world will stand.

I always thought that last line was about my love for Shay, that we would prevail and stop the darkness. But now I know it isn't about me at all.

It's about Aiden. This whole thing is about him.

Nowhere in the prophesy is there a mention that the babe would be a girl. That was pure speculation. Aiden was still, and always has been, an angel, a fallen angel, but still an angel. And he's of the highest Order. He's a seraph angel like me.

Yes, I joined the Enlightens, but it was Aiden who had to stab me for my full Light to come. If I hadn't asked the Orders, we wouldn't be here for him to kill me.

And ultimately, it's him who found love—to make the ultimate act of love—to die for all of us, so we can live.

The world snaps back to life.

"Zoe." Aiden nudges my leg. "End this. Don't make my death for nothing."

"I'm sorry, Aiden."

"Don't be." He removes the dagger, letting the Light discharge out faster. "Let me do this—for you. Step back and let me give you my Light. It'll be enough."

"Are you sure?"

"Yes. It'll be more than you need. We are the only seraph angels on earth. I am the first, and you are the last. You cannot let Sammael through the Veil. He's also a seraph angel and once he's through, you alone will not have enough Light to stop him. Now, go." He coughs. "Please."

"I will see you again, Aiden—my brother."

"Until we meet again, Zoe—my sister." He sucks in a breath. *Tell my son that I'm sorry.*

The last of Aiden's Light pours out of his chest and seeps

into me. Aiden draws his last breath and his eyes close. I stand, rejoining my friends in the circle.

I can feel Aiden's essence inside of me, his red Light. It merges with mine and we become one. I feel kinda strange about that, but I can't dwell on it. We don't have any more time.

My attention goes back on the orb and notice that it's smaller. It's still wavering and shimmering. Sam's hand is still holding on for all it's worth.

A blast of Light shoots out of me; it's a mauve color, mixing my power and Aiden's. It's powerful, and I tighten my grip on Shay's and Kieran's hands, so I don't break the connection.

Everyone's tattoo burns brighter to the point it's all I can see and feel. I direct all the Light to encompass the orb, forcing it to close. The rip opens a bit more and an arm extends outward. A ball of black Fire Light is on the ready to be launched at me. I have no idea if Sammael can aim without seeing, or maybe he can see us.

I can't take that chance. He cannot come through. I think about everything I've done these past months. About everything I've had to learn to prepare myself for this very moment, of the people who supported me. The friends I've made. And of those who have lost their lives.

Anger courses through my body, making me see red. I'm about to lose control when there is a slight pressure on my soul. It brings me back to the present, and I hone in on that feeling. I can't be sure it's Aiden, but I like to think it is. He's still with me.

My anger converts to love. The swirling Light compresses around the orb, and I wish the Light would extinguish the slice in the Veil forever.

With an explosion of power, the Veil leading to this world closes, trapping Sammael behind it.

The battle is over. We won.

I have mixed feelings about all of this, though. A little more than three months ago, my whole existence turned upside down. I met the love of my life in a warehouse. Found out my best friend has watched over me since I was born and has been by my side ever since. Fairies and wolves befriended me. Demons roam the earth, creating havoc in their wake.

And all is never what it appears to be.

Aiden taught me that. It's his memory that makes me sad.

Yes, we managed to send Sammael back to Hell to stew in his anger, regroup, and plan for a later attack, probably wondering how an eighteen-year-old girl defeated him.

The Void is now clear of all demons. Either they have been sent back to Hell or they are dead. The ground is still speckled with black blood, but the Archangels are cleaning that up. It's easy for them. With Light protruding from their palms, they wipe it away as if it never happened — a life altering battle.

The fairies claim their own wounded and take them back to Fairyland. King Oberon and Queen Mab managed to survive after all. Green and blue glamour shoots like lightening all over the field, as fairies disappear.

Guardian angels assist the wolves, who have turned back into their human form, to gather their dead. They lay in a central location near their leaders.

I watch as Vash kneels by one of his own, saying a prayer for his brethren. Cali watches him for a brief moment and does the same on the other side. With a hand on the fallen's shoulder, each leader takes their free hand and holds it over the wolf's chest. I don't want to intrude on their sorrow. It seems very personal. Tears stream down both of their faces. They move on down the line until the final one has had its last rites.

The last body is familiar. They linger a bit longer over him.

Is that—?

"I'm sorry, Vash." I run to him for an embrace. "You, too, Cali. If there is anything I can do to help, ask." I look down at the face. The blank eyes of Jackson stare back at me. "No."

"He didn't suffer," Vash says. "I watched him fight bravely, and he died for all of us to live. Thank you, Zoe. It's because of you that earth has survived. As a pack, we'll mourn our loss, especially for my brother. It'll take time, but we are strong. We will survive."

Shay must have heard my cry. His arm drapes around my shoulders. "I'm sorry, Vash," he says.

"Thank you, Shay."

Kieran and Sidelle join us.

"Oh," Sidelle gasps. "I have no words."

Through my tears, Sidelle and Finn are holding hands. I'll have to ask about that later. Everyone needs comforting now.

"Both of you are amazing." I step out of Shay's protection and squeeze Cali's shoulders. "Take care of him."

"You know I will," Cali says. "Don't be a stranger. Minnetonka isn't that far away. You need to visit us, or we will come visit you."

"Love you both." I reach out to take Vash's and Cali's hands and squeeze, pouring all the love and sympathy I can offer them.

I watch them as they load Jackson's body into the bed of a truck and head to their home. They will continue to be a great couple and lead the Spiritus Pack.

"I guess that's our cue to leave, for now." Sidelle looks over the field. "I'll be back as soon as I can."

"Why?" I ask. "I don't need protection anymore."

"No, I guess you don't." Her wings droop. "I've been on earth for so long I don't know what to do with myself. You kinda have grown on me, Buttercup."

"Thanks, Sid. I love you, too. I hope you can come visit

me once in a while. I'll miss you."

"I'll miss you, too. Adventure is my middle name. And the walls of Aestas Castle cannot hold me in. Not anymore."

"Plus, you need a co-conspirator," Finn says.

"No, I don't." Sidelle glares at him.

"As I recall, I you said that you'd discuss that with me later. It's later."

"I think you heard wrong." Sidelle lightly punches him in the shoulder. "I would never say anything like that to you."

"I'll have to keep reminding you every sundown for all eternity."

"Um, Sidelle?" I ask.

"And how do you think you're going to do that?" She ignores my question.

"With this." Finn takes her face between his hands and kisses her. It wasn't just any kiss. Both of their wings glow with bright glamour. They rise off the ground as their bodies also light up.

Someone clears their throat, but they still are lip-locked.

Finally, they descend and Finn steps back. "I plan to do that to you and much, much more. You'll be swept off your wings in no time."

"Mmm." Sidelle touches her lips. Her eyes are a bit glossy.

"I love you, Delle. I always have. I can't tell you how

sorry I am. All I can ask is that you find a way to accept me as I am now. Before you, I wasn't anything but a Winter Prince. You made me yours the day you saved my soul on the beach. We will always be a part of each other, and I don't want to have a single sundown go by where I can't gaze at your beautiful face. Every day will be my mission to make you the happiest Queen of Spring in all of Fairyland. This is my solemn vow to you."

"Finn," Sidelle says. "I've never stopped loving you, too. You broke my heart, but I guess I'll have to find a way to forgive you because we will have to work together, along with your Queen and my Father. He told me that we now have our own lands. Castles are being constructed for each of us."

"Sidelle." I nudge her. "You must to forgive him after that declaration."

"We have responsibilities now, Zoe," Sidelle say calmly. "Sometimes, we can't always get what we want. As rulers—"

"Rulers?" I ask.

"I am the Queen of Spring, and Finn is the King of Autumn. When I saved him from death, I merged some of my magic with his and since then neither one of us are one hundred percent Summer or Winter."

"You can run, Delle, but you can't hide from me ever again," Finn chuckles. "Castle, Queen, and everything in-between will not stop me from finding you. If I recall, I have a death wish. I'll have to chance it by crossing the Mist for you." He looks behind him. Many of the Winter Fairies have disappeared. "It's time for us to part, Zoe. It's been a pleasure meeting you." He bows to me, extending his hand to Sidelle. With his free hand, he conjures a pale blue light. It widens into an archway. "Ready?"

"Yes," Sidelle say. "Wait." She rushes back to me and wraps her arms around my shoulders. "Until we meet again."

"It's not good-bye forever," I say.

We watch Sidelle and Finn step through the porta and return to Fairyland.

That leaves Kieran and Shay.

"Come on." I take each of their hands and walk away, leading us out of the Void.

I don't have to say good-bye to Kieran. He'll be hanging around since he still lives down the street. We have all summer to goof off before I start my senior year.

I stop.

He doesn't need to protect me anymore. He won't be my guardian angel.

"Are you leaving, too?" I ask him.

"I was wondering when you'd make that leap," Kieran says. "Yes, I can't stay here." He shakes his head. "I don't have another assignment yet; it might be a couple of days or years before I get one."

"Is there any way you can stay with me and not have an

assignment?"

"Not likely."

"What am I going to do without you?" My eyes start to blur. "I've known you since I was born. You can't leave me."

"You have Shay," he reminds me.

"But I need you, too. Will I have an assignment?"

"No. You're not a guardian angel."

"That's it? We save the world and you move on? And I go back to my life as if nothing happened?"

"Yes, basically."

"Well, that bites and is not acceptable."

"I have a feeling that you'll find a way to keep me here with you," Kieran says.

"You know I will." I hug my best friend.

Shay squeezes my hand.

Shay and me.

Us.

Epilogue

Shay has asked me to marry him. It isn't a huge ordeal because I know that we would be married someday, and his proposal was still romantic.

We flew to Minnehaha Creek in St. Paul, near where he grew up. There was a waterfall in the city park that many locals knew about that's surrounded by trails. It's always busy on warm, summer evenings, so we had to go after the park closed. Tiki torches lit an area next to the falls. When we came upon it, my mind immediately went back to my second date with him. That was five months ago already.

Twinkling lights sparkle in the trees, but after closer inspection, the flickering spheres were lightening bugs. They danced around us as we landed. The water glowed with angelic Light. Soft instrumental music played.

I hadn't expected a proposal that night. Shay took my hands in his, gave me his trademark smirk, and bent down on one knee. My heart leapt from my chest, beating rapidly.

He produced a small, blue box and lifted it toward me. The box itself also lit when he opened it. Inside sat the most beautiful three-stone diamond ring I could ever dreamed up. Smaller purple stones surrounded the center ones.

"Each diamond represents the past, present, and our future," Shay said. "And I know you must have purple. I promise to love you until my dying breath." For a split second, the moment made me sad. I knew he wasn't going to live forever like me. Someday, my soul mate would die, and I'd be the one to carry his soul to the heavens. I dismissed those unhappy thoughts, hoping that his death would be years away.

Of course, I said yes, but only after I graduate college. We have a huge list of places I want to see before I settle down.

I am still raw about finding out about being a seraph angel, having Light, and that my friends have stopped Sammael from destroying the world. I still grieve for everyone who died during the battle, over all the evil in the world, and how I couldn't save all of them.

Apparently, Quinn had died sometime when she was

taken to the hospital. The Archangels covered it up before Aiden's first visit. The angels knew something wasn't as it appeared to be with him, so they kept a watch over her. By Aiden's third visit, they were convinced that he was up to something and decided to have Gabriel disguise himself as Quinn. Which was the reason why Shay never had any contact with his father in person.

Now that I knew the truth about Quinn, Morgan, and Aiden, my heart flitters from all my grief. Kieran finds me curled into a ball on my bed since I stopped taking texts from him and Shay. Both try to understand what I am upset about. I think they know, but they also give me space to sort everything in my head and heart.

After the battle, there had been days when I locked myself in my room, refusing to see anyone.

My sister consoled me as much as she could. Sometimes, she would sit on my bed and touch my shoulder, not saying anything. Other times, she'd tell me about her day, how soccer practice went, how camp was, and on rare occasions, how it isn't healthy to be so withdrawn. She'd never had a single vision since Sammael has been locked back in Hell.

After a couple more weeks of that behavior, Kieran couldn't take it any longer. He relented and told me about an accident that happened when I was a toddler. A vehicle had broad-sided the minivan my parents drove on our way to the cabin. My real parents died right in front of Coffee Grind. Both were dead upon impact. Since I had been born, I had shown great potential at being more than an Ordinary. It was because of that budding possibility, Kieran decided to take drastic measures. He summoned help from Finn, who owed Kieran a favor.

They performed a spell and replaced my parents with changelings. Finn warned Kieran that it was a risk to use changelings for adults. Their odd behavior started to surface when I became a teenager. They didn't know how to deal with all my raging hormones. Neither one of them ever could have guessed or prepared for their child being kidnapped. There wasn't a script for them to follow. But their love for their child was true.

Looking back at all the times my mom and dad said strange things, I always thought they were weird and out of touch. They have always been a bit odd in their thinking. And now I know why. So what about Stella? If my parents were swapped out and changelings were in their place … the answer is fairies. Stella's a Vate because of them. She's half-fairy and half-human.

My real parents' deaths add to my mound of grief.

No more secrets between us. Everything is laid out on the table between Kieran and me.

My "parents" are throwing Shay and I a small engagement party. Today is a supposed to be a joyous moment, so I can't dwell on sadness too long.

I'll finally meet Shay's mom, Lindy. I had hoped to meet her sooner, but things didn't work out. I was too busy stopping Armageddon. And she was grieving from her own loss—Shay's father.

Shay asked that she meet us early in my backyard for introductions and for some privacy before she meets my folks. We sit on the patio chairs in my backyard; it's still an hour before the guests will arrive to our engagement party.

"Stop bouncing." Shay places a hand on my knee. "She's going to love you."

"I hope so," I say. "What if she doesn't, though?"

"She will. I've never brought a girl home to meet her, so she knows you're already special in my heart."

I fidget with my hair until Shay entwines his fingers through mine. It instantly calms me.

The creak of the back gate opens and in walks a petite woman with light brown hair. Her eyes sparkle, and her smile is infectious.

We stand when she approaches.

"Hi, Mom," Shay says and gives her a squeeze. "Did you find the house okay?"

"Yes, I did. Thank you, Shay, for asking." She addresses me. "You must be Zoe. Shay has told me a lot about you."

"Hello, Mrs. Curator." I extend my hand, but instead of shaking it, she pulls me into an embrace.

"No daughter-in-law of mine is going to call me Mrs. Curator. Please, call me Lindy." She steps back. "Now, let me look at you to see why my son can't stop talking about you."

Her blue eyes glow with Light as she scans me from head to toe. Something passes behind her eyes, and she frowns for a split second. She places her hand on my cheek.

That's unusual.

Her palm also lights up, and my face warms a bit.

She nods, as if finding resolution for something.

"I'm glad Shay has found his soul mate in such a sweet girl." Lindy hugs me again. "I know everything that you've gone through to get where you are now. Shay told me of the battle you fought and the friends you lost. I'm sorry."

"I'm working through it."

"Mom?" Shay asks. "What's wrong?"

"Nothing is wrong. Everything is right. Or ... it will be." She frowns again. "Would it be okay if I give the happy couple your engagement and wedding gift now?"

"Mom, you don't need to get us anything."

"That's right," I say. "Knowing that you'll be there on our special day is enough."

"That's the thing, though, kids. I won't be here for your wedding day."

"What? Why?" Shay exclaims.

"Son, I think you know why. Please let me do this for

you."

"Shay?" I turn to him. "What is she talking about?"

"Are you sure, Mom?"

Tears swell in her eyes as she nods.

I still don't understand. What does she want to give us that makes her cry? I look at Shay with pleading eyes. I recall that first night Shay took me flying. He told me how his mom had met Shay's dad. Shay told me his father picked her because he knew she would be able to make a sacrifice one day.

That day has arrived.

"You don't have to do this," I plead. "We can find another way."

"Hush now, kids. It's my choice. I've lived a long life, and the only thing any parent wants to see is their child happy. Now, I can go knowing that Shay has found his partner in you." Lindy holds up her hands even before either of us can speak. "I've taken the liberty of praying to your father. He should be on his way. So while we wait for him to arrive, I'd love to get to know you more. Tell me about your hopes and dreams."

"Um, wow, you don't beat around the bush, do you?" I ask.

"I always have done the direct approach."

"Well, I'll be a senior next year and after I graduate, I'm planning to attend the University of Minnesota. It's where my parents also attended."

"And so did I," Shay reminds me.

"Yes, you, too," I agree.

"What do you plan to study?" Lindy asks.

"I want to be a veterinarian. I love animals. Always have ever since I could remember. And the Spiritus Pack isn't too far away; maybe I could be their Pack vet."

"That's a great idea. I know everything will work out."

"It will be how it's supposed to be." An intense light flashes and Gabriel appears in his angelic form. "Good evening."

"Dad?" Shay asks. Tears form in his eyes. He hasn't seen in dad in months and never got to say goodbye. "How can you be here now?"

"Hello, Son." He drapes an arm around his shoulders. It doesn't really touch since he's ghost-like. "Hi, Love." He kisses Lindy on her cheek. "Are you sure?" he asks her.

"Yes." She looks at me, nodding. "Positive."

"Mom—"

"Shay, please don't talk me out of it. My mind is set. I'll be with your father soon. He's come to shepherd my soul."

My eyes burn as I feel the tears coming. I must be strong, though.

"Maybe I can come visit you?" Shay asks.

"Can I bring him?" I ask Gabriel.

"I don't know if you can. It's worth trying. But you

should say your goodbyes now in case."

"Shay, I'll let you have some time alone with your family." I take a few steps toward the house.

"No." Shay latches onto my hands. "You are my family, too. I need you here with me."

"Okay." I smile. "I'll stay." I squeeze his hands. We turn back to his parents.

"I love you, Mom," Shay says. "Thank you for —"

"I know, Shay, I love you, too. Be safe, be smart, and I wish you both a long and happy life."

He lets go of me to hold his mom.

I remain silent.

Eventually, Shay steps back. His aqua eyes water like a storm. I wish I could take his pain away.

"I love you, too, Dad." Shay hugs the only father he's known. He steps back.

"Son, before I go, I think I should tell you something, too. You know that I'll always love you. You are the son I never had. I watched you grow into a wonderful young man. I'd like to think you thought of me as your father."

"I did and still do."

"I met your mom after she was pregnant. I am not your biological dad. Another angel is."

He knows. Has he always known?

"Who is it?" Shay asks.

"The thing about angels is that we pass on some of our

angelic Light to others, offspring if you will." Shay nods. "Yours came from Aiden. It's why you share the aqua eyes. I should have told you sooner. For that, I'm sorry and you someday can forgive me."

"I'm … I think somehow I've always known that he and I were similar. While he may be the one who gave me my Light, you, Gabe, will always remain as my dad. There is nothing to forgive. You can leave here knowing that your son still loves you."

Shay and Gabriel embrace as well as a ghost form can. I see sparks of Light flutter about all around them. They step away from each other and stare, then to Lindy.

I know that Shay will need to work through what Gabriel has told him. And I'll be there every step of the way. I can tell Shay about the good I saw in Aiden, especially the sacrifice he made for all of us.

Aiden and I will meet again. That I'm sure of.

"I'm ready." Lindy nods to Gabriel.

"Press your hand to Shay's chest," he says. "Call for your Light, all of it. Think about it. Let it surround you. Pour it from your soul into Shay's. Let it flow." The backyard lights up with swirling indigo, cobalt, and cyan. Gabriel nods his approval. "Yes, that's it."

Sapphire blue Light once again illuminates beneath Lindy's skin and seeps outward as if it's an outer shell. It darkens as she continues to pull it from within her body. It becomes faint and changes to white. The Light creates a funnel as it makes its way into Shay's chest.

His silver Light brightens with Lindy's.

Gabriel is at the ready. He gently lays her body to the ground as her spirit is stripped. Her hand loses contact from Shay. He stumbles back. I'm ready to catch him if he falls but he doesn't.

Shay kneels on the cement next to his mother. His head is bowed. "Be at peace, Mom."

A tiny piece of Lindy's blue Light remains outside her body. It lengthens to match the same height as Lindy. Her form materializes like a ghost. She smiles that infectious smile at us. Her gaze is intense, and I feel it in my soul.

I look at Shay and Gabriel. They both are staring at Lindy's floating soul.

As if the wind knows it's supposed to carry her to another place, Lindy's spirit fades. She's shaking her head, not wanting to leave quite yet.

Gabriel's extends his wings appear. He takes Lindy's hand and carries them both to the skies.

Shay and I are left with Lindy's human body on the ground but not for long. It, too, disappears.

I wasn't surprised that I loved Lindy instantly; she is one of those people who radiate kindness. I know why Gabriel chose her and her love for Shay shows.

Which is why when she found out who I was and what

I had done to save the world, she knew it was her time; her time to guide and watch over Shay was completed. She gave up her life, the part which made her have a longer than normal life, to Shay. She made the ultimate sacrifice for her son.

Now, Shay would be by my side for all eternity.

The End

ACKNOWLEDGMENTS

I have so many people to thank.

First, to all the fans of the Enlighten Series. Thank you for sticking with me to the very end. Your many emails telling me about which character you love the most, when is the next book coming, to you inspire myself to write a book. I took all of those to heart, and ask that you keep sending them my way. I know it's been a long time between *Swords & Stilettos* to *Daggers & Dresses*, but you all hung in there and coaxed me to finally write this last book. So thank you for the continued encouragement.

To my wonderful editor Rebecca Jaycox. Yes, I know I like to use the words: smirk, grin, just, and what was that last one? Oh yes, slowly. Thank you for developing my characters and taking them to a deep more meaningful level. Without you, I don't think I'd have cried at the ending of the series.

To Angela for another fantastic cover. We didn't have to do many rounds of edits, as I think you just 'got it' for what I was going for on the look and feel. You rock!!

To my beta readers: Genevieve, Jena, and Tiea. You've been with me since the very beginning and have read how my writing has grown over the years.

To the Six Queens: Rhonda, Sarah, and Hilary. Thank

you for allowing me to be part of the great collaborative marketing effort. I know that we'll smash it out of the park!

To the Indie Writing Community. Thank you for the words of wisdom, thoughts, suggestions, and everything in between.

To all my family and friends who have stood by me. For letting me indulge in sharing my stories with the world. It's time away from you and the sacrifices made that allows me to do this.

And lastly, as the Enlighten Series draws to a close, I wouldn't be where I am today, without my loving husband. I love you, Babe.

Call to Action

I hope you've enjoyed Zoe's final adventure in
Wars & Wings. If you've read any of my books, please
leave a review!

Enlighten Series:
Swords & Stilettos, Book One
Daggers & Dresses, Book Two
Wars & Wings, Book Three

Novellas:
Fires & Fairies, Sidelle's Story
Arrows & Angels, Kieran's Story

Short Stories:
Poisons & Princes, Finn's Story
Ninjas & Nephilims, Shay's Story

Slayers & Protectors Series:
Dragon Magic, Prequel
Dragon Slayers, Book One
Dragon Wars, Book Two
Dragon Protectors, Book Three

Follow me online
Website | Instagram | Twitter | Facebook | Pinterest

USA TODAY bestseller, Amazon bestselling, and award-winning young adult author, Kristin D. Van Risseghem grew up in a small town along the Mississippi River with her parents and older sister. Currently, she lives in Minnesota with her husband and a Calico cat, named Daizy. Kristin also loves attending book clubs, going shopping, and hanging out with friends. She has come to realize that she absolutely has an addiction to purses and shoes. They are her weakness and probably has way too many of both.

In the summer months, Kristin can usually be found lounging on her boat, drinking an ice cold something. Being an avid reader of YA and Women's Literature stories, she still finds time to read a ton of books in-between writing. And in the winter months, her main goal is to stay warm from the Minnesota cold!

Kristin's books are published by Kasian Publishing LLC.

www.ingramcontent.com/pod-product-compliance
Lightning Source LLC
Chambersburg PA
CBHW050901250626
47155CB00001B/52